A Spring in the Desert

A novel

by

Joan Koblas

Briar Patch Press

Copyright © 2014 Joan Koblas

For author appearances, inquiries, or interviews, contact by email or regular mail:
joan.koblas@gmail.com

ISBN-13: 978-0-692-24257-5

Cover art by Lia Littlewood
Cover design by Lia Littlewood and Joan Koblas

Briar Patch Press

For my beloved Paul -

You have inspired a lifetime of forevers. Thank you for giving me all the passion and love that I have imparted to Jake and Carrie in this love story.

Acknowledgments

A writer could not have a better editor than Isaac Russell. Thank you for all your knowledgeable and careful attention to detail in working with my story.

The gorgeous cover art was done by the incredibly talented artist and muralist, Lia Littlewood. Her ability to perfectly capture the setting of *A Spring in the Desert* is uncanny.

I am forever grateful for my family whose unfailing support and encouragement for my writing has kept me at it for so many years.

Chapter One

Carrie Turner stood staring out the window of her office at the cold, gray city below. It was April Fool's Day, and she felt more the fool for feeling so alone in this life she had so carefully built for herself. Not that she didn't love the work she did as a wilderness photographer for Mediaphoto, Inc. A brass nameplate on her office door proclaimed to all that passed her portal that Caroline M. Turner was the holder of this space. One wall of her office was filled with books about photography, exotic places, and copies of her large coffee table books filled with her own beautiful photographs. So far, she had had two books of her photo essays published. One book was on Alaska and one was on Glacier National Park. A securely locked cabinet held much of her equipment. Its shelves were filled with cameras, lenses, tripods, equipment bags, and cases of various kinds of film.

She loved the fieldwork part of her job; the travel to places of some of the country's most gorgeous scenery. She had carte blanche freedom and funding for her work due to her growing reputation as a world-class outdoor photographer. Her photos of wilderness scenery were in high demand by magazines and book publishers, as well as other print media producers. Some of her most famous photos were used as backgrounds by advertising agencies. She had more than enough money and an investment portfolio to hold her for life. Through hard work and an extraordinary talent, she had made a name for herself in a highly competitive filed dominated mostly by male photographers.

Her work took her to some of the most empty, rugged places in the country. She was adept at backpacking her way through wilderness areas and up steep mountains. She carried her own photographic equipment into areas most people would hesitate to go, even without carrying fifty pounds of gear. She was athletic and strong and persevered to get the kind of photos that had made her famous. She had an artist's eye for detail and composition. She had every right to feel proud of her accomplishments.

Today, however, the cold darkness of the view from her window seemed to mock her. She knew that the promise of spring was locked inside this gray day, but nothing seemed to promise a future where she wasn't alone. Friends told her she had it all, and she believed she had almost everything she needed except for the one thing she longed for most in her life. Love. From her office window she gazed upward to the ninety-story building that held the office of Clayton Jordan III, Esq. A third generation attorney in his father's law firm, Jordan & Steel, his devotion to his law career turned out to completely eclipse his devotion to the life she thought they had been planning together.

Carrie had met Clayton at a showing of some of her photographs which were on public display in the lobby of his office building. They seemed to hit it off together and Clayton began asking her out. They fell into what could only be described as a comfortable relationship. Clayton was happy to have Carrie on his arm for the kind of entertaining that was required by his law firm. She was beautiful, talented and people always appeared to genuinely like her. Carrie and Clayton enjoyed a lot of the same things like operas, symphonies, plays, and fine dining together. Clayton never seemed interested in hearing about her wilderness adventures from her photo projects, but Carrie chalked that up to Clayton being a dyed-in-the-wool city man.

When their relationship progressed to a sexual one, it turned out to be passionless and perfunctory. Carrie was a virgin when Clayton finally took her so she knew little about how people were supposed to feel in a sexual relationship. They both drifted along together, each mainly concentrating on building their own careers. Carrie believed much was missing from their relationship but assumed it must be the same for everyone else, as well. Romance stories were just that. Stories. She prided herself on being a pragmatist. Real life was seldom as rich or glamorous or passionate as stories led people to believe.

She spent three years in the relationship before Clayton presented her with a pre-nuptial agreement and an engagement ring. It was during a dinner together at Clayton's private club one evening last October. She was excited and surprised and it was only when she closely read the pre-nuptial agreement that her surprise turned to shock and dismay.

Carrie had assumed at first that the pre-nuptial agreement would be a "money thing" and she had no desire or need for Clayton's money. Many professional couples with separate careers had pre-nuptials. She almost signed it without closely reading it, but in thumbing through it quickly, one particular section caught her eye. It regarded something about children. She quickly paged back to find that section and read it carefully. The clause stated that she would be agreeing that there would be no children conceived or adopted during their marriage. She looked up at Clayton as he absently fumbled with his wineglass and napkin while pointedly refusing to meet her questioning gaze. She continued staring at him, waiting for an explanation. She could tell by his evasive body language that he knew exactly which section she was looking at.

Clayton was one of those people who had trouble making or keeping eye contact with the people he was talking to. He was very tall and lanky, with ape-like arms that looked like they belonged to someone much taller than he was. They hung down way below his hips, halfway to his knees. He was awkward in his physical movements from a lack of physical exercise. He was balding with only a small ring of hair left around his ears and the back of his head. His skin had the perpetual pasty look of someone who spent all his time in an office building under artificial lighting.

Carrie hadn't picked him as her companion for his looks. But it was the shiftiness of his eyes that always bothered her the most. She was instinctively wary of people who couldn't make eye contact with others, but attributed this characteristic of Clayton's to his awkward social skills. The law he practiced was corporate in scope and he didn't have to interact with clients very often. He mainly stayed in his office dealing with corporate papers and accounts. His father was the gregarious member of the law firm and Clayton was the bookworm. It was those shifty eye movements that were setting off the alarm bells in Carrie at the moment.

"Clayton, what does this mean exactly? I always assumed you wanted a family with me. You never seemed to dislike kids. I don't understand. What's going on here?"

"Carrie, Darling, you know how much I love you, but having kids can't be part of the equation in our life together. It's true that I don't dislike kids, as long as they are someone else's." Clayton gave a small laugh at is own joke and continued. "I have my career, and you know that I will be taking my father's place in the firm someday. That's a big responsibility. You're gone a lot on your little picture-taking adventures. I don't have the time or energy to raise a family. I always assumed you had figured that out for yourself long ago, and I don't understand why you are so surprised. I simply wish to formalize our arrangement before we marry so there will be no misunderstandings between us. I'm a lawyer, after all and these details should be settled up front."

"Arrangement? Equation? Little picture taking adventures? I thought we were building a life-long relationship, not an equation or and arrangement! And my career travels are not little picture taking adventures, I'll have you know." She hated the fact that she knew she sounded petulant.

Carrie looked down at the sparkling 5-carat diamond solitaire in the tiny velvet-lined box. How could she have been so blind? She never should have assumed that Clayton wanted to have a family with her. They had never discussed the subject of children; of course, it seemed like something so natural to Carrie that there wouldn't be any need to discuss it.

As an only child, Carrie knew the pain of growing up without siblings. As a child, she longed for a brother or sister to share growing up together. Now with both her parents dead, she was an orphan and felt alone in the world. She always pictured herself having two, or perhaps, three children. She never wanted a child of her own to go through the same kind of loneliness she suffered as a child and was suffering now at being alone in the world. She wanted her future grandchildren to grow up with aunts, uncles, and cousins in the world. She looked forward to having children in her life with a husband to share this special joy between a man and a woman.

Trembling with a sudden loathing for this man, she shuddered and removed her napkin from her lap, placing it back on the table. She struggled to maintain her composure and to mask her hurt and anger. Reeling from the crashing realization of how worlds apart she and Clayton were, she stood up from her chair, set the velvet box on Clayton's dinner plate and in one fluid motion, ripped the pre-nuptial agreement in half. Ignoring the curious stares from the other diners, she threw the torn pages of the rules for their "arrangement" onto the table and stormed from the dining room. Clayton stared after her in clueless disbelief. She took the elevator to the lobby, had the doorman hail a cab for her, and returned to her own apartment.

Now, nearly six months later, looking out on the dreary April day at the dirty left-over winter's snow melting in the streets below, Carrie felt more lonely than ever. She hadn't seen Clayton again since that disastrous October night. She refused to take or return his calls. She sent back his flowers and unopened letters. After a while he stopped calling or trying to contact her, which was fine with her. Other men had asked her out and showed an appreciative interest in her. She had dinners with a few of them, but never accepted a repeat date.

At twenty-nine, she was what most people would call a "knock-out." She was the proverbial five-foot-two, eyes-of-blue blonde. She had a trim and muscular, athletic build, both strong and graceful. A thick head of hair framed her fine-featured face, reaching to the middle of her back. It had a natural wave to it, which her stylist kept trimmed, so it always hung perfectly with a minimum of upkeep. She'd sometimes sweep it up into a French twist. By wearing a simple black dress and nothing more than a pair of earrings, she looked like an elegant model off the cover of a glamour magazine. It only added to her charm that she was utterly guileless regarding her stunning beauty. When she thought at all about her looks, she thought of herself as merely ordinary.

Right now, she desperately needed a new assignment, in a place far away from the shadow of Clayton's imposing office building. She needed to get away to someplace where spring had already arrived, in order to revive her sagging spirits. As if on cue, her office phone rang, startling her from her gloomy thoughts.

"Carrie, Sweet. I have a spectacular project we need for you to shoot. It's in a place called Big Bend National Park, somewhere in Texas. Have you heard of it? Well, of course you have, Dear. I should know that. You've heard of all these kind of places." It was Diana, the president of Mediaphoto. Diana was a dyed-in-the-wool city girl. She couldn't understand how anyone would want to go to a place with no hot tubs, health clubs, or room service.

Carrie smiled to herself. "Yes, Diana, of course, I've heard of Big Bend. You'd hate it. Its full of all kinds of creepy-crawlies and most of the people down there don't even speak English - not New York English, that is. There isn't a five-star restaurant for 500 miles. There are real cowboys and Indians out there, too," she teased.

"Well, it's a travel magazine client and they specifically asked for you. I'm sure you've heard of their magazine, Outdoor Adventure Travel. They'll settle for nothing less than the best, and you're the best, as they see it. They've seen your other work and they want you to do their photos. I've already made all the arrangements for you.

You'll leave tomorrow morning. They want lots of everything. Color and black and white. They want mostly backcountry photos, not just more of the same ones you see in most travel magazines. No blue-hair tour bus stuff. They want to publish a book that will appeal to the eco-tourist crowd, the kind of people who travel with a Lonely Planet Guide in their backpacks instead of a Michelin's in their Gucci."

"Oh, gross, Diana, can you imagine anyone traveling like that?" Carrie teased with a laugh. "With a backpack, yet? Don't worry, I'm very familiar with their magazine and I know what kinds of material they would want. I can handle it," she assured. "I welcome the challenge, and roughing it is just what I need to be doing right now. I've done lots of this kind of photography before, but not in a desert. I'm going to need a guide while I'm down there. I can't just rent an SUV and go tooling off through the wilderness on my own, especially in the desert." Carrie stood staring at the Big Bend area on her large wall map of the United States as she talked with Diana. "I'm looking at my wall map right now, Diana. I see that there are only a couple of paved roads in the entire area, and the rest of what look like roads, are probably little more than dirt trails. I've seen places that look like this before on a map, like in Alaska. Actually, it looks very intriguing to me."

Diana had already anticipated Carrie's request for a guide. Carrie always used guide services on her shoots. Professional guides knew their territories better than any outsider did. They knew where the most unusual parts of an area were and how to get there quickly, and hopefully, safely.

"I'm way ahead of you on that, Baby. I've found the best. He occasionally agrees to take on a client and he's agreed to do this assignment. He's a guy named Jake Stockton. He was highly recommended by all my sources. He was raised in that country and has roamed every square inch of the place since childhood."

"He'll meet you at the motel I've booked for you as soon as you get in. He'll be expecting you to arrive sometime in the afternoon of the day after tomorrow. I'm sending your tickets and reservations to your office as we speak. Spend as much time as you need there to get all the shots we'll need. Keep in touch with me with your cell phone, Sweetie. If you need anything, just sing out. And Carrie, I understand what you've been going through these past few months. Please try to have some fun and forget about that jerk, Clayton Jordan, snob extraordinaire. He doesn't deserve you in this lifetime or any other, Baby."

"Thanks, Diana. You've been there for me through all this. I don't know how I could have made it without you. I'll be sure to check in with you whenever I can, but I'm not sure about the cell phone capability down there. It's a lot of nowhere to cover by cell towers and probably not many cell phone users, I would guess. I'm sure they still have the old-fashioned land line phones, though. I'll call whenever I can. Please don't worry about me. I'll be fine."

Carrie hung up the phone and felt euphoria flood her spirits. It was the same feeling she got with each new assignment. The great lifting of her spirits by the promise of an extraordinary adventure about to unfold, and it couldn't have come at a better time. Diana was right, that self-centered, self-absorbed jerk, Clayton, didn't deserve her at all. But why did she feel so lonely and incomplete? Surely there was a man who would be just right for her somewhere in this world. She wasn't looking for some handsome prince to come and rescue her. She was an independent, self-sufficient woman who was happy with who she was and with her career, but she still longed for someone to share life with her. She wanted a husband and a family at this stage of her life.

She was pretty sure she wouldn't be meeting him in Big Bend National Park, though. But she was exceptionally excited and thrilled about this particular wilderness photo shoot for some reason that she couldn't quite put her finger on.

Jake Stockton swung his long, lean six-foot four inch frame easily over the side of the back of his pick-up truck. It was only seven thirty in the morning but the blazing sun already beat down mercilessly from a dry, blue sky. He had begun work at five o'clock when it was barely dawn, in order to finish the morning's task before the searing sun made working in the desert a dangerous proposition. He had another four hours left before he wanted to be indoors during the heat of the day. The rest of his chores could be completed after three o'clock in the afternoon, when the sun wouldn't be so high and fierce in the empty sky.

He was unloading bales of alfalfa for some of his cattle. His arm and shoulder muscles swelled, filling out his western style shirt rolled up to his elbows. Rippling beneath the colorful cotton, his powerful bulk was proof of the strength of a man who wasn't afraid of hard, physical labor. The past winter had been unusually dry and the grazing had been lean pickings, even for his range-suited Santa Gertrudis and Brangus cattle. The desert range on his ranch had produced far less cattle feed than was usually available during the winter months in West Texas. Santa Gertrudis and Brangus cattle could graze desert lands, putting on pounds of prime beef by eating range plants most other animals ignored. But when it was exceptionally dry, there weren't many plants for grazing. Jake hauled the alfalfa out to the range once a week and the cattle would run toward Jake's truck, bawling and shoving each other in an attempt to be first at the feed pile.

Sometimes, Jake and his men would use giant blowtorches to burn the thorns off some of the plentiful prickly pear cactus plants for the cattle to eat. The ranchers called these torches "pear burners". The cattle would hear them fire up the torches and come running for miles around. They had learned to associate the sound of the pear burners with food. The cattle loved the juicy, nutritious prickly pear cactus plants, but even their range-toughened mouths couldn't handle the two-inch sharp, spiny thorns. Prickly pear cactus grew everywhere in this part of the desert. It was a prolific plant that spread like wildfire and came back heartier than ever after a singeing. But pear burning was a labor intensive, expensive way to feed cattle. It was only used in emergencies to carry cattle through a rough winter when little else was available. No rancher would stand by and watch his cattle starve.

Jake reached for his water jug and poured most of an entire quart down his throat in a few quick gulps. The front of his sweat-dampened, dark brown hair grazed the tops of full, masculine eyebrows. His hair had a natural curl to it and hug in ringlets around the edge of the collar of his shirt. He was deeply tanned from working in the sun most of his life. He dried his wet face on the sleeve of his shirt while his jade green eyes searched the sky for any sign of rain clouds moving in. He was looking for the high, wispy clouds called "horse tails" that signaled the possible approach of a storm. Although he knew that the sightings of horsetails could often fool a person, they sometimes they indicated rain would move in within a day or two. He had grown up in this country and had learned to read all its subtle signs.

He had left his beloved ranch several years ago, only long enough to get a college education. Starting off in engineering, he later switched to agriculture so he'd be better able to manage the ranch's many resources. Jake was gone from the Big Bend area for six years, until he finished his Master's degree. He then returned for good. His parents turned the ranch over to him, retired, and moved to Palm Springs, California to enjoy their elder years. His father never loved the land like Jake did. Jake's paternal grandfather had wanted the land to pass to directly to Jake, as he saw from early on that Jake was the person who would love it and care for it much as he did.

But at thirty-one years old, Jacob Morgan Stockton still carried the scars of the tragic loss of his first and only love and their baby when he was only nineteen years old. After twelve years, he still couldn't completely shake the guilt and pain. He sometimes thought he'd never love again and couldn't see how he'd ever meet the right woman for him - living out here in the middle of nowhere. She wasn't likely to just drop out of the sky, was she?

He occasionally dated one of the local girls but he never found anyone who moved him in the special way he was searching for. He seldom called back for a second date. His brutally handsome good looks generally caused women to fawn over him shamelessly. He never understood why they made such a fuss. He was unaware of the raw sexuality that seemed to ooze from every pour of his gorgeous body. He longed for someone to share his life, someone who would love this land as much as he did. He wanted a family and all the joys that would come from raising his children in this beautiful country.

So Jake buried himself in the work of his ranching business and made use of his intimate knowledge of the land by occasionally hiring out as a guide for rich city people looking for an adventure. It gave him some greatly needed contact with the outside world and he loved showing off this vast desert land he loved so dearly. He thought about the new client he had taken on who was due to arrive the day after tomorrow. It was the first time he'd taken on a female client. Most of his clients were rich businessmen looking for a safe adventure that they could go back to their homes and brag about. This new client coming down was a city girl, working for a big media agency in New York. She was a famous photographer and wanted to take lots of pictures of the backcountry wilderness. Tonight, he'd plan out all the secret places where he knew she could take pictures of places out of the ordinary. He wondered if she would be up to the rugged, backcountry travel that would be required to get to the places he wanted to show her. He'd find out soon enough.

"Come on, Bart, load up!" He opened the passenger door of the truck and Bart leaped in. Jake climbed in the driver's seat and received an affectionate face licking from his best ranching dog. He told everyone that Bart was part coyote and he could herd and control cattle like he was one of them. Bart was his shadow and went everywhere with Jake. When it was hot, he'd wait patiently in the shade under the truck, sometimes for hours at a time, until Jake was ready to go. Jake poured some fresh water into a bowl he carried in the truck for Bart and set it on the front floorboards. Bart drained the cool liquid, slurping water all over the floor. He jumped back up onto the seat, licking his lips and panting from the heat. Jake always thought Bart looked like he was smiling when he did this, and he liked to think that he really was.

"Let's go find some lunch and have us a siesta, Bart. We've got to get ready for a New York lady coming to visit soon."

Chapter Two

Carrie spent the entire next day traveling from New York to the small town of Alpine, Texas. Alpine was still eighty miles shy of her final destination of Terlingua, Texas. That was where she was supposed to meet up with her guide. She first flew from New York to Dallas, then from Dallas to Midland, Texas, where she boarded a shuttle flight from Midland to Alpine. These multiple flights consumed an entire day, and she had yet to reach her final destination, the closest town to Big Bend National Park. Carrie marveled at the vast distances in the state of Texas. Somehow, she had absently figured that once she got to Dallas, she'd be almost there. She had forgotten that Texas was more than eight hundred miles across and eight hundred miles from top to bottom, and that Terlingua was still a heck of a long way from Dallas.

By the time she arrived in Alpine after bumping along on the tiny propeller driven shuttle flight for several hours, her body was cramped and exhausted. Arriving at the Alpine airport at 6:00 in the evening, she went directly to the Aerflite Auto Rental desk to pick up the rental car reserved for her by Diana. She loaded her bags into the new Jeep Cherokee and got directions to her hotel. She was scheduled to drive down to Terlingua the next day.

The cute little hotel she was booked in was a welcome surprise. Diana, God bless her, had reserved Carrie a room at the Corner House Bed and Breakfast. It was known as the Best Little Guest

House in Texas, and from the looks of it, this assessment was correct. There were only five guest rooms, each with private baths. Diana had reserved the room called the Tree House Room for Carrie. She was welcomed warmly by name and escorted to her spacious room, decorated in a rustic, Texas-Spanish style motif. After a casual dinner, she was ready for a good night's sleep before starting out for Terlingua, the place she considered would be the true beginning of her next big adventure.

As she lay in bed that night, waiting for sleep to claim her, she thought about her boss and best friend, Diana. What ever would she have done these past few years without her? Diana was her mother-substitute, both nurturing and protective of her, demanding of her professionally, but in a constructive kind of way. Diana had recognized Carrie's talent as a photographer and guided her in maturing her craft. The gruff, no-nonsense, crusty, typical New York demeanor Diana presented to the rest of the world, wasn't something she ever turned on Carrie. Diana was responsible for a tough competitive business in a tough competitive field, and she needed to be tough in order for her firm to be one of the survivors. She could do whatever it took to get the best clients and keep them in a fast-changing media world. Carrie's artful photography was her firm's best drawing card and she treated Carrie with the respect, professionalism, and friendship she deserved. Carrie knew how lucky she was to have such a wonderful boss and friend. She had heard enough horror stories from other female professional friends to realize how lucky she was to have Diana in her life.

The next morning, the Corner House B&B staff loaded Carrie's luggage into her Jeep while she enjoyed a huge Texas-style breakfast of eggs, ham, hash brown potatoes, thick slices of homemade sourdough toast, orange juice and mugs of fresh-brewed coffee. Used to only a bagel and black coffee in the morning, Carrie felt like she would burst at the seams. The food was home cooked and so wonderfully flavorful that she couldn't stop herself from eating far more than she was used to eating. The waitress told her she'd need all the energy she could get if she was off to adventure in Big Bend. This comment left Carrie tingling with anticipation about what would lay ahead for her on this photo shoot in the desert.

After looking over a Texas road map, she climbed into her Jeep and set off down Texas Highway 118 for Terlingua. Alpine, Texas sits at an elevation of forty-four hundred feet so the early morning air was hovering around a comfortable sixty-five degrees. Carrie had checked weather reports for the average temperatures in West Texas in April and packed clothing accordingly. She expected the daytime high temperatures this time of year to be in the low 80s. After driving about ten miles in the rising sun, her Jeep heated up quickly and she kicked on the air conditioner. She tried to tune in something on the Jeep's radio and got a faint NPR station, and only a couple of music stations. One was in Spanish, with Mexican-style music, and the other was a Country Western station. She switched off the radio and opted for the quiet hum of the Jeep and her own thoughts as she sped along the narrow, two-lane highway.

The scenery became more and more spectacular as she descended in altitude from the little town of Alpine into the lower desert regions of the Big Bend area. In all her travels, Carrie had never been in a desert in the springtime. She was awed by the colorful desert wildflowers carpeting the area. The shoulders of the road were covered by bright blue Texas Bluebonnets, the Texas state flower. Bright gold patches of wildly blooming Tickseed were interspersed with patches of purple Verbena punctuated by the deep pinks of Texas Thistles. Farther back from the road shoulders, the vegetation became more typically desert-like. Many different kinds of cacti and succulents grew in abundance and they all seem to be blooming at once, competing with each other with their own showy flowers. Lots of Prickly Pear cactus showed off pretty purple blooms and many other cacti she couldn't name blossomed in yellows, creams, pinks, purples, reds, and blues.

As she descended from the higher altitude of the Alpine area, deeper into the desert, Green Eyed Yellow daisies lined the road.

Giant Ocotillos became more prominent, with their fifteen-foot long thorny tendrils tipped with bright scarlet blooms, visible in the lower altitude areas.   There were Yuccas, and Desert Candles, and the occasional Century Plants, which sent up twenty-foot tall spikes bearing whole bouquets of creamy, orchid-like blossoms.   She was amazed by the riot of color bursting forth from a place she had pictured as empty, dry and lifeless.

Driving down the road past this dramatic, ever-changing landscape, she thought again that this was exactly what she needed right now. Memories of Clayton intruded unexpectedly through her shifting thoughts but she quickly pushed them away as fast as they came.   She was determined to erase him from her consciousness for good, and this looked like just the place to accomplish that.   She came to a tiny abandoned mining town with a few dilapidated and falling down buildings.   A road sign proclaimed this to be the town of Study Butte. A small sign informed newcomers that the town's name was pronounced "Stoody Boot."   According to the sign, there were supposedly one hundred and twenty people who lived here, but for the life of her, she couldn't see where the one hundred and twenty people were living. She noticed a Quicksilver Branch of the First National Bank and was reassured to see a twenty-four hour ATM machine sitting out front.   A doll-house-sized post office completed the picture.   "Interesting place," Carrie mused out loud to herself.

She turned off the main highway at a sign pointing to the town of Terlingua, hoping it was bigger than Study Butte.   When she came Terlingua's city limit sign, it indicated that its population was twenty-five.   "Oh no," she said to herself with alarm.   This was not looking good.   She pulled in and stopped in front of the Big Bend Motor Inn, the motel she knew was her next stop.   It looked better than what she was expecting after passing through Study Butte.   She didn't need to worry about finding it, as it was the only one in town, right on the main road.

There was a gas station and a small general store nearby, a tiny post office, and what looked like very little else, just the same kinds of falling apart adobe buildings like the ones she saw in Study Butte. She saw several signs propped against the walls of some of the abandoned-looking buildings advertising guide services, river rafting trips, mountain bike rentals, Big Bend Stables for horseback riding, the Big Bend Touring Society, and off-road vehicle rental and tour operations. Artists, craftspeople and antique dealers had claimed some of these ancient adobe buildings. She noticed that there appeared to be no electricity or phone lines to many of these places and saw another sign referring to Terlingua as a famous ghost town.

She pulled up in front of the office of the motor inn and shut off the Jeep. When she opened the driver's door, she was greeted by an unexpected blast of hot air. It had to be at least ninety-five degrees. She was more than a little surprised to find it so hot, considering it was still morning. The weather reports had indicated that this area would be in the low eighties. She went into the small office and was greeted by a broad smile worn by a deeply tanned, leather-skinned woman whom she guessed to be in her mid-seventies. She found it shocking to see what the hot desert sun could do to a person's skin. She made a mental note not to venture outside without plenty of sunscreen and a broad-brimmed hat.

The old woman spoke up first. "Why you must be Miss Turner, Honey," the clerk drawled with a warm smile that embraced Carrie like a big warm bear hug. "We've been expecting you. Why, you're a right pretty girl, being a Yankee from New York, and all."

"Yes, well, thank you, I think. I believe I'm supposed to have a room reserved for me here. I don't know how long I'll be staying, yet. Will that be a problem, me not knowing how long I need the room for, that is?" Carrie wasn't used to feeling so off-balance with people, but the warm intimacy exuded by this old woman threw her a curve. It was so different from the New York style she had grown accustomed to.

"Why not at all, Sugar. You just go on and stay as long as your little heart desires. The local guys sure won't mind seeing the likes of you around this place, and that's a fact." Carrie guessed the woman was the owner of the motel and she seemed to be genuinely happy that Carrie was going to be a guest there.

"I'm supposed to be meeting my guide here. His name is Jake Stockton. Have you heard of him?" Carrie inquired, hopefully.

"Heard of him? Why not a person around here hasn't heard of Jake Stockton! He's almost as pretty as you are!" The woman giggled at her own teasing comment, like a little kid. "Every girl from here to El Paso would like to get a handle on Jake Stockton. You'll have all the local girls hating you on the spot, when they catch you with Jake. You two will create quite a stir around these parts, and that's for sure the truth, Darlin'," she chortled.

"He's only going to be my guide while I'm here, and I'm not figuring on creating any kind of stir with him while I'm here. This will be a strictly professional association," Carrie insisted. To listen to this woman, a person would think she already had them married off to each other, and they hadn't even met. Carrie didn't come to Big Bend to get married to a cowboy.

"Well, not if Jake has anything to do with it, but whatever you say, Honey. I didn't mean you no insult, mind you. I was just reckoning how well suited the two of you would be for each other. There's nothing the likes of you come through here in a coon's age, and with poor old Jake being all alone out on that ranch, well, I couldn't help but think you'd be a breath of fresh air for him. That's all. 'You single? I don't see no weddin' ring on your little bitty hand," she asked while staring intently at Carrie's left hand.

Carrie skillfully avoided answering what she considered too personal of a question, but found she was hoping that the old woman's comment about "poor old Jake" didn't mean Jake was old. It rattled her that she should even care how old he was.

"Do I need to register or sign in or anything? I need to get the key to my room and unload my Jeep and unpack. I need to call Mr. Stockton to let him know I'm finally in town. He's supposed to be meeting me here sometime later today, and I'd like to be settled before then."

"You're all set, Sweetie. Your woman, Diana, called ahead and made all the arrangements. You don't need to do a thing except enjoy your stay with us. I put you in Room 18, a nice big room. One of our best. 'Even has an extra large bathroom and a coffee maker and one of those tiny refrigerators with real ice. There's a phone, too, with free local calls. If you need anything at all, just ring the front desk. My name's Pearl, and you just ask for me if you got any needs or concerns." Pearl beamed broadly at Carrie again.

"Thank you very much. It was nice meeting you, Pearl, but I need to hurry now and let Mr. Stockton know I'm in town. It seems to have gotten late really fast." Carrie turned to leave the office and just made it to the door when Pearl spoke up again.

"Oh, Honey, you don't need to worry about that none. He'll already know." Carrie stopped with her hand on the doorknob, turned, and with raised eyebrows, sent Pearl a questioning glance.

Pearl explained, "Word travels faster than greased lightening around here and he will have already heard from somebody who saw you drive into town and stop here, I guarantee you." Pearl, noting the surprised look on Carrie's face and added, with a mischievous twinkle in her eye, "Everybody here has been waiting for the famous picture taking lady from New York to arrive."

Carrie was caught completely off-guard that she could show up in a tiny town in the middle of nowhere and already be such an instant celebrity. She had never thought of herself as famous and was always much more comfortable just blending in. Now she found herself glancing outside nervously, peering through the office window for the spies who would be reporting her every move to this Jake Stockton guy. Who was this man? And why did he seem to be such an icon in this place? She surely had a lot more questions now than when she agreed to take this assignment, but she had always approached assignments with a certain sense of adventure, didn't she? This shoot would be no different from any other, she was fairly sure. But was she really?

Carrie left the office and got back into her solar heated Jeep. It was hotter than an oven. She'd have to remember to leave the windows down next time she got out of it. The temperature inside her Jeep felt like it had climbed to at least one hundred degrees in the short time she was inside the motel office. She mused about Pearl and the fact that she had always thought she hated people who called perfect strangers "Sweetie" and "Honey" and "Darlin'." But with Pearl, it was different, somehow. It didn't come across as insulting or insincere. It was just who Pearl was, and here in this wild, otherworldly place, it seemed perfectly normal and acceptable. "Strange," she muttered to herself with a smile.

She was hoping to be able to park the Jeep in some shade, but looking around, there wasn't a shady spot to be found anywhere. Oh well, thank God it was a rental car and not her own vehicle. She supposed people around here got used to their vehicles melting in this desert sun. She parked in front of room 18. She lowered all the windows hoping the desert breeze would keep the Jeep from baking to a crisp. When she opened the door to her room, she found it wonderfully fresh and cool inside, with the air conditioner humming away. It wasn't fancy and Diana would hate it, she thought to herself with a chuckle. But Carrie thought it was clean and inviting and knew it would be perfectly adequate for her needs. She guessed she'd be spending most of her time getting the photos she came here to take, and not sitting around in her motel room.

Carrie had barely finished loading the last of her bags and camera gear into her room, when the bedside phone rang. She figured it was Pearl, her newfound best friend. A strong, masculine voice asked, "Is this Miss Turner?" The word "miss" was spoken in a slow, drawn out Texas drawl, as if the word Miss ended with two 'z's instead two of 's's.

"Yes, this is Miss Turner." Carrie replied formally. Her accent was more Mid-Western than New York. She spent a lot of time traveling all over the country so she hadn't developed the typical New York accent most New Yorkers were noted for. It seemed that she spoke in a manner not easily pegged as being from one particular region or another. The only thing that could be said for sure was that she was not from anywhere in the south.

"My name is Jake Stockton, Miss Turner, and I'm the man your secretary hired to be your guide while you're down here. I was wondering if you had any plans for dinner tonight, and if not, I'd like to come over and take you out to eat. It'll give us a chance to meet and get to know each other a little before we head out tomorrow morning. Your secretary said you'd want to get started right away." Jake held his breath waiting expectantly for her reply, hoping she'd accept his dinner invitation. He was curiously excited about meeting her after Pearl's breathless phone call to him a few minutes ago.

"This is rich," Carrie laughed to herself. She couldn't wait to tell Diana that Jake Stockton thought Diana was Carrie's secretary. And Pearl had referred to Diana as "your woman." If they only knew she was Carrie's boss, not her secretary, or her woman, and that Diana ran one of the biggest media companies in New York! She and Diana would die laughing together over this one.

"I haven't even thought about dinner, yet, and yes, that would be nice to meet with you and tell you more about what I have in mind for the photos I hope to get. That way, you'll know better about where to take me to find the places with unusual scenery." Carrie remembered that she hadn't noticed any restaurants anywhere in town as she drove in. She couldn't imagine where they'd go for dinner and was glad she didn't have to worry about how to find a place. She wondered if they'd have to drive the eighty miles back to Alpine to get something to eat.

"We have a place in town called the Starlight Theater that's awfully good. We've also got the La Kiva and the Desert Opry. What kind of food do you like? You need to let me know if there's anything you really hate. I'm sorry I can't offer you anything like what I'm sure you're used to eating in New York, like sushi and gourmet food, but most of the food served around here is pretty good." Jake sounded apologetic about the limited choices available in the area.

Carrie thought his manner of speech was charmingly quaint, but she could tell Jake was trying to be very considerate of her and she appreciated this aspect of his nature. His ideas about what people in New York ate were laughable, though. She had imagined that Texas cattle ranchers were rough and crude in the manners department, and Jake didn't seem to be like that at all. She found herself noticeably relaxing as she talked with him.

"I eat almost anything, really. Why don't you just pick the place, since I know nothing about this area?"

"Good enough. I'll surprise you. I'll be by to collect you about seven o'clock. Will that be all right with you?"

"That will be just fine. Do I need to dress up?" she inquired.

A hearty laugh came over the line as Jake processed this question. If she really knew what any of these places were like, she'd probably die. It would be interesting to see how Miss New York would react to the Starlight Theater in Terlingua, Texas. He'd learn a lot about her by just watching her reaction to that place.

"No, not at all. People mostly wear jeans, boots and shirts, if they are dressed up at all. Shorts and T-shirts are OK, too. You can wear whatever you're comfortable in, Miss Turner. Believe me, no one will care one lick."

"Fine, then. I'll be ready at seven o'clock. I'm in room 18. I'll see you then." Carrie added and hung up the phone.

She wondered even more what Jake would be like after hearing his voice. He sounded strong, sure of himself and very polite. She wondered if he knew anything more about her. What was he expecting? From what Pearl said, he was good looking and women threw themselves at him. She would find out for herself soon enough as it was already almost six o'clock.

Jake replaced his phone on its charger. Miss Turner had sounded younger than he thought she would be when he first accepted the job. Her secretary had never said anything about her age, but he had just assumed since she was so famous, that she'd be an older woman. He had no way of knowing that Diana was her boss. Come to think of it, Diana had never volunteered that information during their conversation when she hired him and it had never occurred to him to ask.

Jake had one of Carrie's books of photos in his personal library, a work she had done about the Alaskan wilderness. Pearl had called him the minute Carrie left her office and told him she was a real "looker" and she didn't think she was married because she wore no rings on her hands. Leave it to Pearl. She was always on the lookout for someone for him. She worried after him like a mother hen and he loved her dearly. In fact, everyone in Terlingua loved Pearl.

Jake went into his library and found his copy of Carrie's Alaska photo book. He looked through it hoping to find a picture of Miss Caroline Turner amongst the credits. No luck. He looked at the gorgeous photos and he knew she could do the Big Bend area proud. He looked forward to her showing the world what a beautiful place it was by using her wonderful talent with a camera. He couldn't suppress the excitement growing in his gut when he thought about meeting Miss Turner in only an hour.

"Well, Bart, old pal, maybe Pearl really has found me a winner this time? Let's clean up the truck and get ourselves on into Terlingua."

Carrie stood at the bathroom mirror experimenting with her hair. Should she wear it up or down? She finally decided to wear it in a French twist since she had no idea where they would be going for dinner and what might be appropriate. She checked her make-up. She used very little, just a small amount of blush and some lipstick. Her natural beauty and beautiful skin tones left little need for improvement.

She was dressed in a pair of designer jeans and a watered silk blouse of various shades of blue, which enhanced the deep blue of her eyes. The jeans hugged her beautiful legs like a second skin and the dropped waistline emphasized her lean torso. Satisfied with her appearance, she switched off the bathroom light and sat down on the edge of her bed so she could watch for Jake Stockton from her motel room window. She felt an excitement building inside her and butterflies threatened her composure.

She couldn't remember when she had felt this excited about meeting someone. Friends were forever trying to set her up with blind dates. When she began refusing their blind date offers they would invite her to dinners where some single male candidate just also happened to be there. She appreciated their well-meaning efforts but these evenings often turned out to be disasters. She had given up on meeting anyone in that manner. She believed deep in her heart that there was someone waiting for her out there somewhere, who would be perfect for her. She just couldn't imagine how she'd ever find him. In the meantime, she had her exciting work to fill her life and right now she was determined to concentrate on this current project.

A bright red pick-up truck swung into the parking lot and angled toward her room. It looked shiny and clean as opposed to all of the other dust-encrusted trucks she had seen all over these West Texas roads. In the desert, it was impossible to tell if vehicles were old or new under the heavy layers of grit coating them. Down here in the southwest, there was no need for salting the roads in the mild winters, thus older vehicles didn't carry the rusty body cancer of vehicles driven on salty northern winter roads which made them appear years older than they were. She noticed a large, friendly-looking mixed-breed dog in the front passenger seat. Sure enough, the pretty red truck pulled up right in front of her room.

She could see a large male form filling the driver's side. The sun glared off of his windshield making it impossible to see any of his features. He said something to the dog and both of them climbed out of the truck. The dog sat down obediently on the shady side of the truck and Jake ambled toward her door. Saying to herself out loud, "Well, Carrie, this is the big moment," she jumped off her bed, grabbed her purse, and opened the door before he had a chance to knock. She had no intention of inviting a perfect stranger into her motel room, even for a minute. Not with the way news apparently traveled in this town, that was for sure!

Jake stopped dead in his tracks, staring spellbound at the heavenly vision of womanhood standing in the doorway. His eyes quickly traveled down her form - from her head, appreciatively to her beautifully manicured toes encased in a pair of leather sandals. He then openly stared into her clear blue eyes. Carrie blushed endearingly. "Oh my, Lordy, I can see trouble comin' here," he thought to himself. Pearl had told him she was a real looker, but you never knew with Pearl. Someone Pearl considered a looker could end up being anything, as long as it was a female under the age of 40. He removed his hat almost reverently and asked, "Are you Miss Turner?"

Carrie found herself speechless, openly staring, mesmerized, into the greenest eyes of one of the most gorgeous men she'd ever laid eyes on. His face could have been chiseled from warm Italian marble, a Texas version of Michelangelo's David. High cheekbones, lush, full lips, and a brilliant smile full of white, perfect teeth added to the picture. His thick, rich brown hair curled attractively at the edge of his shirt collar. He wore tight blue jeans and she didn't miss that his legs were lean, long, and strong beneath the denim fabric. He looked seven feet tall, in his classic western pointed toe boots, standing with a cowboy hat clutched nervously in his hands. He wore a jade green striped western shirt, that perfectly matched his unusual jade eyes, the kind of shirt with snaps down the front and on the cuffs and pockets. The bright cotton did nothing to hide his strong, well-developed chest, shoulder and arm muscles underneath, which spoke of regular use and powerful strength. She was shocked by her brazen thoughts of what he might look like without his shirt and jeans. God! When was the last time she found herself with thoughts like that popping into her head about any man? Never.

She found her voice and replied "Yes, I'm Miss Turner but please call me Carrie, Mr. Stockton." Remembering her manners, she offered her hand to shake in introduction. He fumbled with his hat, transferred it to his left hand and reached to grasp the small hand she offered to him. He clasped it in his own huge muscular hand, which completely enveloped hers. He squeezed it gently.

"Please call me Jake, Mamm, I mean, Carrie." At the touch of their hands, in a simple social handshake, a jolt went through both of them, as if they had been hit by lightening. Her tiny fingers were long and her well-kept nails were tipped with the same subtle coral shade of nail polish he had noticed on her small toenails. Her hand displayed an unusual strength for its size and her grasp was strong, not the timid, limp-wristed handshake of most of the females he had known. Hers radiated confidence and security, even though she felt like her insides were melting into a puddle in the doorway of her room.

Each of them suddenly realized they were still shaking hands, they both blushed and quickly disengaged their hands. As they shifted nervously from foot to foot, embarrassed by their unexpected mutual reaction to each other, Carrie found her voice first. "Well, I'm ready to go and I'm starving." She gave a small nervous laugh and still had difficulty looking away from his captivating eyes.

"Let me help you into my truck." Jake politely offered. Carrie locked her motel room door and strode toward the passenger door. Bart jumped up and hurried around to the side of the truck, his tail wagging excitedly and nuzzled at her hand, begging her for attention.

Jake spoke gently to his dog. "Bart, now you be polite to Miss Carrie here. She's a lady and our guest, so you go on and leave her alone."

"No, it's alright. I love dogs." Carrie dropped to one knee and scratched Bart's neck and flanks, speaking to him affectionately and accepting his wet kisses. Bart was acting like a puppy, eagerly begging for more and more of her attention. Carrie didn't seem to mind that he was dusty from laying in the sandy parking lot under the truck waiting for Jake. "I can't have a dog in the city. I live in a high rise apartment and I'm gone a lot on photo shoots. It wouldn't be fair to a dog. I grew up with dogs and I'd love to have another someday when I'm in a place where a dog can run freely and play outside."

Jake watched Carrie openly embrace his best friend, Bart, and his heart melted. She wasn't turning out to be the stereotypically cold New York career woman he had expected. In fact, nothing about her was anything like he expected. Watching the small patch of porcelain skin peek out just above the waistband of her jeans as Carrie squatted down to caress of Bart, caused him to begin feeling noticeably uncomfortable as his body involuntarily began swelling in private places in an involuntary reaction to her. The heat of the late evening sun, still shining high in the southwest Texas sky, heated her skin sending the womanly scent of her body radiating in his direction. It wasn't the sickeningly sweet, overly-perfumed smell of most women he knew, but a clean, light floral scent that made him think of all the spring desert flowers blending together in a wonderful bouquet in the evening desert air.

Jake shifted and hoped his bulging male physical reaction wasn't too visible. Carrie stood up and reached for the door handle. Jake beat her to it and opened the passenger door.   Bart immediately started to jump in the front seat and Jake told him to get in the back of the truck. Bart instantly obeyed with an impressive, agile leap up and over the side into the truck bed. Carrie stretched a shapely leg up onto the running board and as Jake held the door, he watched her beautiful womanly form pass inches in front of his face as she hoisted herself into the high seat.   Inhaling her floral scent, he thought he might come undone.

It had been so long since he had been with a woman, he could barely remember. The physical release was welcomed but it always turned out to be a disappointment for him. He would rise and leave before dawn in the morning, having no desire to stay and provoke an ugly scene the next morning. He'd leave feeling bereft, guilty, and emotionally depressed.   Women always wanted him to stay and become more seriously involved with them but his own vacant feelings just made him want to get away as fast as he could. He used to have hopes of finding someone he wanted to share his life with, but the right woman never seem to come along. Pearl always accused him of not looking hard enough and being too picky.

Carrie fastened her seatbelt and Jake closed her door. He walked around the back of the truck to the driver's side, using the opportunity of going around the back to readjust the crotch of his jeans outside of Carrie's view, in hopes of not embarrassing himself in front of her. He spoke to Bart as he rounded the back of the truck, sympathizing with Bart's disappointment at being relegated to riding in the back, away from the nice lady he had taken a real shine to. Jake had never seen Bart react to anyone like he had to Carrie. He was a friendly enough dog by nature, but he could pretty much take or leave everyone but Jake. He remembered that dogs could sense a person's true character far better that people ever could. He felt elated that Carrie had met Bart's enthusiastic approval.

Carrie sat in Jake's truck with a million thoughts and emotions flashing through her mind. She had never reacted to a man in such a primal, unexpected way in her life. When he stepped closer to her to open the door or assist her into his truck, she felt her body flame from the heat radiating from his body. He smelled soapy clean with an underlying hormonal male musk smell that had and instant physical affect on her body. She never remembered Clayton smelling like anything except the expensive men's cologne he always wore. There was never this underlying, high male hormone aroma to Clayton like there was to Jake. Maybe that's why the little sex she and Clayton shared was robotic and unimaginative. With Clayton, she never felt passion would ever blaze into a raging fire, consuming them both. She had the disturbing but exciting feeling that Jake was a man who could cause her body to, literally, burst into flames.

This physical reaction to Jake Stockton shocked and disconcerted her. Just being next to him caused her mind to involuntarily imagine all kinds of erotic scenes. She'd read lots of romance novels as both an antidote to her sterile love life, and to pass long hours on a plane or in hotel rooms when she traveled. She enjoyed the excitement and the adventures in the stories and she envied the rich, erotic sex life of the characters. But she sadly believed none of these experiences would ever happen to her. She couldn't imagine recreating some of the passion-filled scenes she read about with Clayton. The chemistry just wasn't there. He was comfortable and safe but their sex was mechanical and ended quickly, leaving her frustrated and empty. She had never experienced the kind of physical reactions to a man like she had read described in her romance novels. Until now.

Jake slid into the driver's seat in one fluid motion as he had a thousand times before. He started the engine, rolled up the windows and switched the air conditioner onto high. They drove out of the parking lot of the motel and both waved to Pearl, who was watching them from her motel office window. A huge grin split her wrinkled face and she gave a thumbs up as they drove away. Jake was sure Pearl would grab up her phone the minute they were out of sight, giving a detailed report of his meeting with Carrie to everyone in town, keeping the phone lines buzzing for hours.

Jake told Carrie they were going to the Starlight Theater for dinner. She hadn't noticed any restaurants when she drove into town. He explained that it was only a few blocks away. She was more puzzled than ever. Almost immediately, he turned into a parking lot outside a large, old adobe building. It looked abandoned, but there were a lot of vehicles out front. She saw the hand-painted sign identifying it as the "Starlight Theater" on an old movie marquee over the front door. This must be a joke. He parked the truck and came around to open the door for her, like a true Texas gentleman.

"Sorry, New York. No valet service here," he teased warmly. "Its Saturday night and the parking lot is always full like this, but don't worry, I made reservations for us." Carrie stared at the sandstone-colored adobe façade of the building. It appeared to be an old adobe movie theater. As they got closer to the entrance, she could hear live Mariachi music filtering outside as if it were coming out through the roof. She was increasingly intrigued.

They entered the door and Carrie stopped in her tracks, staring upwards. There was absolutely no roof on the building! It was packed with people. There were couples and large extended families with old grandparents, parents, giggling children and babies in high chairs. Large groups of laughing friends crowded around wooden tables, seated in old chairs and on wooden benches. Mariachis were strolling amongst the tables full of people, stopping here and there to play their lively music at people's requests. Appreciative listeners stuffed dollar bills into a large sombrero they carried with them. Waitresses circulated amongst the crowd delivering frosty Marguerites and cold bottles of beer and pop on skillfully balanced trays suspended precariously above the patrons' heads. Everyone seemed to be enjoying the festive evening tremendously.

"Here comes Angie. She owns this place. I'll introduce you and she'll show us to our table," Jake pointed in the direction of a friendly, smiling woman, carefully picking her way across the room toward them through the crowd of customers. "Angie, I'd like you to meet Carrie Turner. She's down from New York to take some serious pictures of our gorgeous scenery."

Angie grabbed Carrie's hand, "I heard all about you from Pearl. Why, you're even prettier in person than she described! You never know with Pearl," and then she let out a bubbling laugh that filled the air. "I'm so happy to meet you, Carrie, Darlin'. Follow me, and I'll take you and Jake to the best table in the house." Angie continued to hold Carrie's hand as she led them single-file through the crowded room. Carrie couldn't help but notice people turning and staring, whispering as she passed with Jake following possessively behind her. He looked like the cat that had swallowed the canary.

"Here you go, you two. If you need anything, just tell your waitress Angie said to get it for you. I hope you enjoy your dinner, and please come back and take some pictures of my place, Carrie. I've never had a famous photographer come here before, at least not that I knew about. Maybe you could put a picture of my establishment in one of your fancy magazines so people could see what we've got down here."

"Thank you, Angie. I'd love to come back and take some pictures. One of them might end up in a magazine, as no one would ever believe a place like this existed if they didn't see a picture." Carrie wasn't kidding. She couldn't imagine convincing her New York friends she ate in a restaurant with no roof or that such a place even existed. They'd think she was pulling their legs.   She couldn't stop staring at the décor in disbelief. There was still the old movie screen at one end of the building but someone had painted a gaily-colored Spanish-style mural across it. There was a large mirror ball hanging in front of the painted-over screen, spinning slowly and casting brightly colored lights gaily around the room. The old ceiling beams were still in place and from these were suspended old cow skulls, Mexican plaster parrots and Mexican pinatas. Large ceiling fans whirled from some of the beams, drawing in the cool evening air and wafting the marvelous aromas of pungent Mexican food all around the restaurant.

"I hope you like Mexican food, because that's mostly what we eat down here," Jake asked cautiously.

"I love Mexican food, but it's never very good in the northern United States. It certainly never smells like this, and I can only imagine how good it must taste here." She looked around at some of the plates of food sitting on the nearby tables and her mouth watered.

A waitress appeared and handed them menus.   "Why, Jake Stockton, who have we got here?" she quipped, speaking only to Jake while never taking her eyes off of Carrie. She hovered too closely to Jake as far as Carrie was concerned, but she caught herself wondering why that should bother her.

"Penny, this is Carrie Turner, a client of mine. Carrie, this is Penny." Turning to Carrie, he asked "would you like one of Angie's famous Cuervo Margheritas?" Carrie nodded affirmatively trying to ignore the hostile, green-eyed glare she was receiving from their waitress. Jake seemed embarrassed and placed their drink order with a dismissive tone of voice.   "We'll take two of Angie's jumbo Margheritas, and I'll have a shot of Cuervo Gold on the side. Be sure to bring plenty of extra lime wedges and a saucer of rock salt. We'll order dinner later, after you bring our drinks." He turned his attention immediately back to Carrie, pointedly ending his conversation with Penny.

The waitress sulked away with a pouty look. Pearl had warned
Carrie that the other girls would hate her when they saw her with
Jake. Carrie was used to dining out in places where no one hardly
knew anyone else and could care less about who was with who. She
had never lived in a place where people knew absolutely everyone and
everyone's business. It made her uneasy but she refused to let it spoil
this fascinating evening. She couldn't help finding herself wondering
if there had ever been anything between Jake and Penny. Not that
she cared, of course, but she found herself strangely curious about
his past. Why was such an incredible specimen of a man still single?
She could tell he appreciated women by the way she caught his
positive appraisal of her from the corner of her eye when she
thought he wasn't looking. The way he looked at her heated her
blood in a way she found impossible to ignore.

They both became engrossed in reading their menus. At least
Carrie was engrossed in reading hers. Jake was mostly engrossed in
staring at Carrie. He already knew the menu by heart after eating
here nearly every Saturday night for years. Carrie had a hard time
deciding what to order. Everything sounded fabulous, and she was
starving. Then she realized she hadn't eaten any lunch. Their
waitress arrived with their drinks, roughly set them on the table in
front of them, and asked if they were ready to order dinner.

Jake nodded to Carrie to order first. Carrie met Penny's hostile
gaze and replied in her sweetest voice, "I'll have the Cheese Enchilada
plate and a bowl of the Tortilla Soup, please."

Penny then turned to Jake, her pencil poised. "Bring me the Pork
Chop Chipotle and Tortilla Soup, as well. Also, please bring us a
large bowl of guacamole and some warm tortilla chips to have with
our drinks. We'll think about dessert later, if we have any room left
after dinner." Without another word, Penny turned and disappeared
into the crowd in the direction of the kitchen.

Jake was clearly embarrassed by Penny's treatment of Carrie. "I'm
sorry about our waitress. She's just like that. Everyone around here
knows how she is and just tolerates her. I'm sorry she's been so

openly rude to you."

"You don't need to apologize, Jake. Her behavior isn't your responsibility. I run into people like her all the time in New York. My strategy is to give back politeness in return for coldness. I refuse to stoop to their level and become as pitiful as they are." Carrie cautiously lifted her huge Margherita glass and sipped it cautiously. It must have held 20 ounces of the citrus-y beverage. It was fantastic! She had never tasted a Margherita to equal it. "What do they put in these to make them so wonderful?" she exclaimed. "I've never tasted one anywhere close to as good as this one!"

"The secret is in the Jose Cuervo brand tequila and the tiny key limes. The key limes are only about one inch in diameter and a pale greenish-yellow color. They are very different in flavor from the egg-size dark green limes you usually see. But don't let their little package fool you. They are loaded with juice and flavor. Most places use cheap tequila and frozen, watered-down, reconstituted lime juice, and way too much sugar to cover the bad ingredients. In this part of the country, they use good tequila and only freshly squeezed lime juice. It makes all the difference in the world, don't you think?"

Carrie continued to sip at the delicious concoction. It caused a pleasant warm burn all the way down to her stomach, instantly entered her bloodstream in a rush, and began relaxing her from head to toe. Jake watched her over his drink, his own blood warming, but not from his Margherita. They both glanced around at the other diners, the décor, and the Mariachis, but again and again their gazes returned to stare into each other's eyes. Neither one seemed to be able to control it. Each time their eyes met the stares would last longer and longer, each one capturing the other's eyes in a magical kind of magnetic hold.

Penny brought their guacamole. Jake picked up a warm chip, scooped up some of the green dip and offered it to Carrie. She was feeling dizzy, hazy, and relaxed after drinking down half of her Margherita on an empty stomach. She thought he was handing it to her but he gently brushed her hand aside and fed it to her himself.

She blushed and giggled then playfully picked up a chip herself and offered a scoop full to Jake. When she placed it in his open mouth, he bit down lightly and teasingly, slowly sucking on the ends of her fingers holding the chip. "Oh my God! What is happening to me?" Carrie thought.

Carrie blushed furiously and pulled her hand back. She felt like an electric current had passed through her body. Jake continued to hold her eyes captive and watched the play of emotions wash over her beautiful face. In an instant he glimpsed ragged desire, fear, hesitation, and longing. He recognized them all so well as he was experiencing those identical feelings himself. They both had to get a hold of themselves. Everything seemed to be moving way too fast, and at the same time, not fast enough. They'd be spending the next week or more together, much of it in the wilderness, alone. God help them both if this brushfire blazed out of control.

"Tell me about the kinds of photos you'd like to take for your project," Jake asked, returning to a safe subject. He could see Carrie was grateful for his perceptive evaluation of their situation.

"I want some unusual shots of the kinds of places that most tourists will never get to see. I've noticed from maps that there aren't many roads in Big Bend, but most of the pictures you see in books and magazines are only of features you can see from one of the established roads. I'd like to capture the wild and out-of-the-way places that shows people what's out there beyond the roads." Jake thrilled at how Carrie's eyes lit up when she talked about wanting to capture the scenery of a place from a different perspective. He had always loved the backcountry spots where he could feel one with the land.

"I've seen your photo essay of the Alaskan wilderness. In fact I own a copy. I fell in love with it when I saw it in a bookstore in Alpine about a year ago. It was only recently that I realized it was your work." Genuine admiration for her work showed in Jake's eyes and warmed her heart. She couldn't remember Clayton ever asking to see any of her photographs and he certainly showed no interest in owning any of her books. He never wanted to visit anyplace outside of a big city like New York and had no intention of going to what he considered an aboriginal place like Alaska. He tolerated her job as one would tolerate someone else's eccentric hobby. It was always clear to her that Clayton placed no value on her work, whatsoever, so she never discussed it with him at all.

Their dinners arrived and they spent the next half-hour eating and chatting about their upcoming visit to the backcountry. The Mariachis wandered over to their table and Jake made some requests of them in fluent Spanish. They handed Carrie a long-stemmed red rose and began serenading her and Jake with Mexican love songs. Even in Spanish, which Carrie couldn't understand, she could understand they were love songs. She was thrilled and felt shy and very feminine and treasured in a way she'd never felt before with anyone. She watched Jake's warm smile as he watched her reaction to the Mariachis. When they finished, he tucked a wad of bills into their sombrero and warmly bid them good night, again in their native Spanish. Penny cleared their table and they told her they were too full for dessert.

"Jake, you need to take me back to my room now. I'll never be ready for tomorrow if I don't get some sorting and planning done in advance, not to mention, some sleep." After the potent Margherita, the huge dinner, and the excitement of the day, she suddenly felt extremely tired.

Jake reluctantly stood up and helped her out of her chair. "I know you're right. If I may suggest, we should start early, about six o'clock, and work before it gets too hot. We can stop in the middle of the day, and continue when the sun isn't so blazing hot later in the afternoon. It's dangerous to stay out in the mid-day sun. I can bring some sandwiches from home for our lunch and I always carry plenty of water," he offered.

"That sounds great. I never even thought about those details." Carrie wryly mused to herself that she wasn't considering many details at all after that giant, potent Margherita and a huge carbohydrate laden dinner. In fact, she was having trouble thinking at all.

Jake paid the bill and said good-byes all around. They picked their way through the parking lot full of vehicles back to where they had left Jake's truck. Bart was going crazy in the back; he was so excited to see them. Carrie stopped at the side of the truck, rubbed Bart's head and spoke softly to him. He nearly jumped over the side but Jake told him to stay. They drove the short distance back to her motel and he walked her to her door to see her safely inside. After she opened the door with her room key, she turned, and sincerely thanked Jake for the most enjoyable evening she'd spent in ten years. She stood blocking the doorway, knowing she couldn't trust herself if she let him in, even for a minute. He smiled warmly at her and took her hand in his and brought it to his lips for a gentle kiss.

"I had a wonderful time tonight, too. In fact I can't tell you the last time I enjoyed an evening so much. I'll be back first thing in the morning. There's not any place to get breakfast early in the morning around here, so I'll bring a couple Chorizo and Egg burritos and a jug of fresh orange juice that we can eat on the road." She could sense his reluctance to leave.

Jake willed his body to turn and quickly open the door to the truck before he changed his mind and did something he might regret. He couldn't trust himself to stay at her door another minute with the provocative view of her framed in the soft porch light with the huge queen-size bed invitingly behind her. But he wanted to take things slowly and not scare her off before he even got a chance.

Bart whined and yelped in the truck bed. Jake spoke to him. "Quiet Bart, it's late and people are trying to sleep around here. OK, you can ride home up front with me. Come on and get in."

Carrie watched Jake and Bart drive away in a cloud of West Texas dust. She couldn't wait for dawn when she'd be with him again and wondered what in the world was happening to her heart.

Chapter Three

Carrie set her bedside alarm clock for 5 o'clock in the morning. She jumped up at the first ringing and headed for the shower. Excitement made her whole body tingle. She dressed quickly in a cotton tank top and a pair of khaki hiking pants, the kind with cargo pockets and zip-off legs to make them into shorts if it got too hot out. She fished her daypack out of her suitcase and filled her CamelBack water system with cool water from the bathroom. She inserted the CamelBack bladder into the daypack's pocket designed to hold it, carefully threading the water tube out through the top opening. She clipped the drinking end to the top of the shoulder strap. She figured it wouldn't hurt to have an extra two liters of water along considering how much hotter it was in this area than she expected. She rubbed a layer of sunscreen into her exposed skin before adding the rest of the tube to her daypack.

Next went in a wrinkle-proof cotton cover-up shirt if she began getting too much sun, her cell phone, a hairbrush, and a couple of granola bars. She tossed in a tiny, paper-wrapped bar of soap from the motel bathroom in case she needed to wash her hands before lunch. She then removed her driver's license, medical insurance card, credit cards and cash from her purse and tucked it into a zippered pocket of her daypack. She'd leave the rest of her purse contents in the motel room so she wouldn't have anything extra to put in the truck. She could see her pile of belongings growing on the edge of the bed. She knew how some guys could be about women taking too much stuff with them everywhere they went.

Next she packed her camera bag with two 35-mm SLR camera bodies and a selection of lenses and filters. She wanted to have one camera loaded with black and white film and one loaded with color. She also packed a new digital camera she hadn't had the chance to use much yet, and a small, fold-up tripod that could be positioned on any kind of uneven surface. She removed her cold pack from the motel room refrigerator and then packed her film supplies and some spare batteries. She got her photography vest out of the closet and added this to the pile. She would need the vest, with all it's convenient pockets, to easily carry her equipment if they needed to walk a distance from the truck to get a good shot. She also checked to be sure that she had her hat and sunglasses.

She opened the curtains to her room and sat on the edge of her bed, watching for Jake. Her stomach was beginning to growl anticipating the breakfast burritos Jake promised to have with him. She felt an ever-mounting excitement growing within her as she thought of the adventure that the coming day promised, but more than just the adventure, she realized her excitement was over the prospect of spending the day with Jake. She put on her comfortable hiking socks and laced up her sturdy hiking boots. She had worn them many years doing photo shoots in the Alaska wilds and many other wilderness areas. They should be perfectly suitable for desert work, as well.

She couldn't help recalling the incredibly wonderful time she had shared with Jake the night before. It was just a simple dinner in the most unusual restaurant she had ever dined in. Even in the Alaskan wilderness, she hadn't experienced such a primitive place. The whole evening could have happened in a dream. She was surprised she was able to relax so completely with Jake and let the flow of the experience carry her along. The powerful Margherita, the incredible flavors and spiciness of the food, the music and laughter filling the place, and intoxicating presence of Jake Stockton, all combined to lend a hazy, dream-like quality to the evening's memories. He seemed so intelligent, genuine, caring, and full of life. She hadn't experienced this combination in a man before. All of the New York men she had dated had turned out to be self-absorbed and shallow, in her opinion. Jake was a refreshing exception and renewed her dream that someone existed who could steal her heart.

She took the opportunity before Jake arrived to place a quick call to Diana. She called her home number, as it would be nearly seven o'clock on Sunday morning in New York. Diana answered, sleepy sounding, on the fourth ring.

"Hey, this is Carrie, way out in Texas country. Wake up Sleepy Head." Carrie's voice sounded so different to Diana, she almost thought it was a prank call and hung up.

"Well, don't you sound like Little Miss Sunshine! What in the world's going on out there? I haven't heard that brightness in your voice in years." Diana was now fully awake and wondering what could have possibly transformed Carrie into this happy-sounding, excited creature, seemingly overnight.

"I'm off in a few minutes for a day of wilderness photography and I wanted to check in with you before Jake arrives to pick me up," Carrie rushed on in a near-breathless voice, as if she were in some kind of terrible hurry.

"It sounds like you're on a first-name basis with this Jake guy already. That's record time for you, and what accounts for this unusual excitement, Babe? It sounds to me like that big Texas cowboy has your motor running," Diana teased.

"Don't be silly, Diana. He's just very nice and we get along well. I can't wait to tell you all about our dinner last night, and you just aren't going to believe it when I do! I'm going back later to take some photos of the restaurant, because no one will ever believe it exists if I don't have proof. Oh, my God! I've got to go. I see Jake's truck pulling in. I'll call you again in a few days. Don't worry about me." Carrie hung up immediately and rushed to open the door to her room like an excited little kid.

Diana replaced the phone in its bedside cradle. She had never heard such excitement and life in Carrie's voice, ever. Carrie always seemed to hold her responses to life 'close to her vest,' so to speak. It was as if she was afraid to let her feelings get too far ahead of her control in order to protect herself.   "Damn that Clayton, son of a biscuit! He caused Carrie to lock herself up so tightly, she wouldn't allow any man to ever get close to her," she cursed out loud to herself.   But this morning she could sense that something very dramatic had changed. She could hear it in Carrie's voice. She hoped so much that she had heard right, for Carrie's sake. She deserved to be loved and treasured for the remarkable woman she was.

Jake couldn't get to town fast enough. The bag of warm burritos sat on the seat between him and Bart, with Bart occasionally sniffing hopefully at the bag. Jake wished the truck could fly; he was so excited about the coming day. He could hardly sleep last night, replaying his and Carrie's every conversation the evening before. Her lilting laugh, gorgeous body, and penetrating eyes haunted his thoughts. He had never reacted to a woman like that before. He went over and over in his mind why she should be so different from any of the other women he had ever known.

As he lay awake tossing in his bed, praying for sleep to claim him, his thoughts raced back in time to his beloved Rachel, only 18 years old, and his first and only love. That was 13 years ago, for Heaven's sake! Why did the memories continue to haunt him so? What happened wasn't his fault, it was no one's fault, so why did he feel so guilty and responsible for it all? And why did the overwhelming sadness and loss still hang over him like a big black cloud? His family and friends had tried so hard to help him move on and find someone else to fill his life but their efforts were useless.

Up until yesterday, he had thought he was a hopeless case. Then he met Miss Carrie Turner and his whole world suddenly turned upside down.   A large crack appeared in the carefully constructed shell he'd built around his heart. For the first time since Rachel's and the baby's death, he felt like he might be ready to risk giving a part of himself he might lose again, to someone else. If he and Carrie became close, he'd have to tell her what happened in his past, it was only fair. He'd carefully never let anyone get close enough to him that he'd have to relive the terrible pain by telling him or her what happened that fateful night. He was more than a little frightened by the idea of this, but for the first time, his excitement and hope were winning the war with his reserve and fear.

As he pulled up in front of Carrie's room, her door burst open and she stood there looking excited and ready to go. Her beautiful smile sent his spirits soaring to new heights. He opened his door and Bart all but pushed him out in a rush to get to his beautiful new friend. Bart ran up to Carrie, his tail wagging furiously, whining for her attention.

"Hey, Bart. How are you this morning?" Carrie cooed to him, scratching his neck and back. Bart curled his furry body around her legs as if he were giving her a big hug. Jake was secretly wishing he had more of Bart's puppy-like attention from Carrie. Oh well, he would have to be satisfied with living vicariously through Bart, for now. He had hopes of getting that same reaction to himself from Carrie someday.

"I'm all ready to go, Jake. I'll just get my stuff. Do you think we could put some of it in the back so that Bart could ride up front with us?" She rushed back inside and grabbed her daypack, and camera bag off the bed. Jake peeked into the room and could see that she only had her photographer's vest left to bring out.

"Is the vest the only thing you have left to bring? If so, I think there's plenty of room behind the front seat for your little bit of stuff. That way, it can stay inside the truck with us where it will be cooler. I've got a carryall box built into the back, but it will get awfully hot inside it in the desert sun. I don't think that would do your camera equipment any good." Jake then added, "Are you sure about wanting this mangy mutt of mine riding up front with you? He'll probably drive you crazy, nagging you for attention. I've never seen him act like such puppy for anyone before." Carrie stood looking pleadingly at him with Bart leaning against her trying to be a close as possible to her. Bart had the same pleading look in his big, soft brown eyes. He watched Jake's face, searching for a sign that Jake would let him ride up front. "Crazy, dog," Jake muttered while shaking his head. "He acts like he knows exactly what we're talking about!"

"Of course he does, don't you, Bart?" Carrie flashed a devilish grin at Jake and opened the passenger door to Jake's truck. "Go on, Big Guy, get in. You can sit with me any day." She began putting her camera bag and daypack behind the seat.

"Bart, get your butt off the burritos! You're squishing them all to heck!" Jake grabbed for the paper sack of food out from under Bart and moved it to the hood of the truck until they got settled. He laughed out loud. "I hope you don't mind eating mashed burritos, Carrie, 'cause it looks like that's what we're having for breakfast this morning, thanks to Bart."

Carrie flashed a brilliant smile and climbed in next to Bart and fastened her seatbelt. Then she realized that she hadn't even closed her motel room door. She unhooked her seatbelt and hopped back out of the truck and ran up to the door, which immediately set Bart to whining plaintively at her sudden departure. She took one last look around her room to make sure she hadn't forgotten anything, then locked the door with her room key. She climbed back into the passenger seat and refastened her seatbelt. She curled her left arm around Bart and settled him on the seat, pulling him close to her body.

Jake grabbed the sack of burritos off the hood and got into the driver's seat. He passed the bag to Carrie to hold. He started the truck, backed out, and, spinning the wheels a little for effect, drove out of the lot and back down the main highway in the direction of Study Butte. "We'll be taking Highway 118 at Study Butte, the road you took to get down from Alpine, only we'll be heading south from Study Butte toward the boundary of Big Bend National Park. The road is called Maverick Drive from Study Butte to Panther Junction, where the Park Headquarters and Visitor's Center are located. We'll stop at the Visitor's Center so you can look around at all the interesting information they have there. We can eat our burritos at a picnic table just outside the center, then wash up and be ready to head for the backcountry. How does that sound to you?"

"That sounds perfect. I'd like to see some of their historical information on the area. I can only imagine that it's probably wild and fascinating. I'm also interested in getting a feel for the geology of Big Bend so I can understand what kind of scenery to expect. The geology of an area determines some of the more interesting features in the landscape. These features often result in the most dramatic photos." Carrie found herself thinking that pictures of Jake would make the best photos she could imagine right now. She was determined to get more than a few pictures of him in this rugged environment that he called home. "Wildlife in its natural setting," she silently mused to herself. He seemed to be as tough as this desert was tough, but as gentle as one of the many delicate flowers which flourished within it. She found this combination of ruggedness and gentleness in Jake, a potent, heady mixture, which moved her deepest feminine instincts.

As they drove along Maverick Drive, she was amazed at the alien beauty visible out every window. There were rocky buttes that looked like they had been thrust up whole from the desert floor by unimaginable ancient forces. There were house-sized boulders and all kinds of other size and colors of boulders and rocks everywhere. More kinds of cacti grew amongst the rocks and all were blooming brightly around here also, as she had seen on her way down from Alpine. There were more yuccas around here and a plant Jake called a Sotol, which looked like a yucca at the bottom, but sent up a perfectly straight, two-inch thick stalk with flowers, closely clinging to the top foot or so of the stalk. There was an abundance of the Prickly Pear cactus growing everywhere in the rocks and the sand. There weren't any trees at their elevation, but she could see what looked like pines and cedar-like trees higher up near the tops of some of the mountains they passed.

They soon arrived at the Visitor's Center and Jake parked the truck in front of a picnic table, which sat under a cluster of Mesquite bushes. Their brushy bottoms had been trimmed to resemble small trees and offer a modicum of shade for the picnic table. It was the closest thing to a tree she had seen. They opened their truck doors and Bart jumped out, and ambled over to the bottom of a distant mesquite bush to pee. Jake grabbed the jug of orange juice and some cups from behind his seat when he noticed Carrie's death-grip on the sack of burritos.

"You wouldn't be hungry now, would you?" he teased her.

"I'm starving! I thought I might have to get into these several miles back. They smell absolutely delicious. Where in the world did you come up with these, Jake?" Carrie sat down at the picnic table and began unloading the burritos while Jake poured them each a large cup of cold juice.

"Out at the ranch, I have a caretaker couple who have been with us forever. Carlos and Maria are like family to me. Maria takes care of the house and does all my cooking. She is incredible and I love her to death. I don't know how I'd survive without them. Maria was excited to put these together for our breakfast. She made them earlier this morning than you'd care to think about. She gets up every morning at 4:30 without fail. She goes to bed early at night, though. Carlos can do about everything else that needs doing around the ranch. He supervises the other hands, which turn out to include many of his own sons. They were born and raised on the ranch and Carlos can actually run the place completely on his own when I'm not there, when necessary."

Carrie began eating her burrito with gusto. "What is inside this thing? It's wonderful," she exclaimed with her mouth full.

"It's scrambled eggs with Chorizo sausage and some homemade refried beans. Chorizo is a spicy Mexican pork sausage; a bright red color from the chili peppers used in seasoning it. Maria makes her own. There are also some pickled Jalapeño peppers, carrots and onions in there." Jake had his first one eaten, and was starting on his second. Carrie was close behind.

"I believe this is one of the best things I've ever tasted! What a fantastic breakfast food item. It sure makes a bowl of instant oatmeal dull in comparison." She unwrapped her second burrito and looked sadly at the now-empty paper bag. "Boy, these sure disappeared fast," she commented, almost to herself.

"Don't worry, they are more filling than they look. Give them a few minutes to settle and you'll be surprised at how long they'll hold you. I have a good lunch packed, too. We should be fine until we get back to town for dinner later this evening." Jake drained his cup of juice and poured himself another. "You need to drink as much liquid as you can hold, Carrie. This desert heat and dryness can evaporate the water right out of your body before you know it. You can dehydrate and find yourself in real trouble. The closest medical care around here in clear back in Alpine."

Carrie finished her burrito, then drained her cup of juice. Jake refilled her cup. Carrie groaned. "I can't hold anymore, Jake. Besides, if I drink this much juice, I'll need to stop like old Bart here, every ten minutes. Besides, I haven't seen any rest areas around here, either."

"There are lots of rest areas around here," he said with a grin. "They are behind every big rock and bush or cactus plant." He laughed at his own clever joke, watching Carrie's pained expression. "I'll stop whenever you want to stop. Just sing out."

Carrie shot him an embarrassed but amused glance, finished her second cup of juice and began putting their breakfast trash into the empty burrito sack. Bart had been nosing around the ground around the picnic table while they ate, hoping to find a stray crumb or two left over from some other picnic. Jake told him to stay, and he obediently sat down in the shade of the Mesquite bushes to wait for them. The parking lot was virtually empty; just a few RVs full of retired people out to visit the park in the spring, before it got too hot and crowded. It was still too early to get lots of families, since school was still in session. Big Bend was too far of a drive from any big cities for a casual weekend visit. She dropped their trash into a can by the door to the Visitor's Center.

The Visitor's Center looked fairly new. It was made of native stones and was build low and into the hillside. It pleasingly blended into the landscape instead of intruding on the natural scenery like the proverbial sore thumb. It was cool inside and had a wonderful selection of displays. They both made an immediate trip to the bathrooms. Jake took Carrie down a set of wide stares to a giant relief map laid out on a ten-foot square table. It depicted a three dimensional map of the entire park. On this map, he pointed out where they'd be going that day so Carrie could get a feel for the kind of topography they'd encounter. He showed her a place called Elephant Tusk, and another called the Mariscal Mine, which hugged the shoulder of Mariscal Mountain. Walking back and forth around the huge map, he pointed out to her that from those places they'd be able to look down the Mariscal Canyon all the way to the Rio Grande River.

Carrie noticed dotted lines on the map indicating primitive roads going to these sites he pointed out, and some backcountry campgrounds lying along the roads. It looked like it would be fascinating scenery and she couldn't wait to get started. Jake seemed to read her mind.

"Why don't we come back here later, and spend some extended time looking at all the displays and information when it gets too hot to be outside?" he suggested. "They have a great video about the park that runs about a half hour. If we see all there is to see here now, we'll lose the whole morning while its reasonably cool."

Carrie agreed with him and headed back up the stairs to the front door. Jake stayed behind her, savoring the view of her beautiful backside as her hips swayed seductively as she climbed each stair step. He caught himself thinking it would be one heck of a long day if he was going to have those kinds of sexy thoughts every time he watched her move. He figured it was well worth the price, though, as it was a pretty pleasurable kind of suffering.

They hurried back to the truck, loaded up Bart and got back on the road. The view was spectacular as Maverick Drive began descending steeply towards the desert floor. About ten miles down the road, Jake turned off to the right onto a dirt two-track road marked only by a small square post stuck in the sand. Carrie looked at him with worry and alarm in her eyes. "Are you sure this is the road we saw on the map? Somehow, it seemed more substantial, looking at it on the big map in the Visitor's Center." Before she could barely finish her question, she saw a small wooden sign indicating that it was 20 miles to Elephant Tusk and 30 miles to the Mariscal Mine.

Jake could hear the concern in her voice. "Hey, this is considered a really good road compared to most of the roads out here." He smiled encouragingly at her while delivering this piece of information. "It'll probably get worse, but don't worry about a thing, this is a four wheel drive truck and I've got a monster winch that'll attach to anything that could pull us out of the bottom of a canyon, if necessary."

"That's exactly what I'm worried about," she commented half-heartedly. "I don't want to have to get hauled out of the bottom of some canyon. I suppose I'll just have to trust you, though, as this is your neighborhood."

"You bet, New York! Don't worry about a thing. We'll be back safe and sound tonight in time for dinner, and boy, do I have a place to take you to eat tonight! If you thought the Starlight Theater was a shock, well you aren't ever going to believe this next place." He was grinning from ear to ear as he watched the surprise turn to excitement on Carrie's lovely, expressive face. He could tell she was game for about anything really, and this thought pleased him enormously.

Carrie was about to say something when the truck lurched violently through a deep hole and bounced over a rock in the road, throwing Bart into her lap. She grabbed onto the handholds just in time to keep her head from hitting the window and Bart from falling onto the floor. She looked out at the deteriorating road, now little more than a trail, as she wrestled Bart back off her lap and onto the seat next to her. She just managed to accomplish this fete when she spotted another huge rock and hole in the road. This time she grabbed the handholds right away and held on for dear life, riding the bouncing truck like one of those mechanical bulls she had seen in country western bars in magazines. She couldn't imagine 30 miles of this kind of road until they got to today's destination.

"Great job, Carrie! You're getting the hang of this really fast. Pretty soon you'll be able to anticipate what's coming up and your body will relax and you'll just ride through it naturally."

She shot him a skeptical glance, not daring to take her eyes off the road ahead to be able to anticipate what might be coming up next. The truck climbed up some shale over a small ridge and bumped down the rocky other side, sending Carrie completely up into the air off her seat. She couldn't believe this was even a road anymore. She'd never experienced anything like it in her life. Jake laughed and howled with excitement while bumping his truck over this unbelievable terrain. Carrie figured it must be some kind of primitive 'guy thing' and wondered if she'd ever survive this day intact.

She was worried about Bart, but when she stole a momentary glance at him to make sure he was all right, he looked like he was smiling, nearly as much as Jake! He had relaxed his body and rode with the flow, so to speak. Carrie figured if Bart could do it, for Pete's sake, she should be able to do it, too. After a few more miles of this off-road experience, she found herself actually enjoying the excitement of the ride, more than she ever believed possible. It was better than a roller coaster ride at the fair! Diana had no idea of what this place was like when she sent her on this shoot, and probably wouldn't believe half of what she'd tell her happened to her when she got back. The momentary thought of going back sent an unexpected instant pang of loss through her that she wasn't at all prepared for. She had never had a thought like that pop into her thoughts in any other place that she had been on assignment. What in the world was going on with her?

Jake didn't fail to notice this change in her demeanor and it pleased him enormously. It seemed she never failed to surprise him by turning out to be different from anything he had ever expected of a big city girl. He found himself wanting to bump down this road forever, as long as it meant that Carrie would be by his side, laughing along with him. How he loved introducing her to all the silly, fun things there were to experience in his beloved land. His spirit felt light as a feather with her and he wanted the feeling to never end.

Jake turned off of the primitive trail at a post marked with a small hand-carved sign with names of places with arrows pointing in various directions. They came to another wooden sign designating this wide spot in the road as the Glenn Springs Campground. Jake stopped the truck and Carrie almost collapsed when her legs hit the ground, feeling like they weren't going to support her. She imagined it was the way seafarers felt when walking on dry land after months at sea. She hung onto the truck a few extra seconds waiting to get her balance. She looked around hopefully for a bathroom.

Jake read her thoughts. "You go over behind those rocks over there," pointing off to her side of the truck, "and Bart and I will head over off our side. And watch for rattlesnakes. They hide in the shade of the rocks. Don't squat anyplace you haven't thoroughly looked over." He whistled for Bart and turned to go over behind his pile of boulders.

"Hey, wait a minute," she cried with alarm. "Nobody said anything to me about rattlesnakes being out here. You can't just expect me to know where they might be lurking. I've never done any desert shoots, and where I usually go, you need to look for bears, not rattlesnakes!" He could hear the mild panic in her voice as she began visually inspecting every rock on the ground around her, without moving an inch away from the safety of the truck.

"Well, we have bears out here, too, New York, but they mostly run as fast as they can away from people. A person almost never sees them, except in campgrounds if people don't dispose of their garbage properly." He watched Carrie scan around the campground area, looking for any sign of improperly disposed of trash. She saw none; it was clean as a whistle.

"Stop calling me New York. I'm not a scairdy cat. It's just that I'm not used to poisonous snakes. They don't exactly hang out in Central Park, you know." She began to step cautiously toward the boulders he had pointed out for her use.

"From what I understand, there are lots of poisonous snakes in Central Park, the two-legged kind that'll kill you deader than any rattlesnake, and twice as fast. If you see anything that worries you, just call out for me and I'll come running." He continued on over behind his rocks.

"Oh, right," Carrie mumbled to herself. "Like I'm going to call him over while I'm squatting over a rattlesnake taking a piss," she thought. She walked only as far behind her rocks as she thought would shield her from Jake's view, and squatted as quickly as possible. She wiped herself with a piece of Kleenex out of her jean pocket and shoved it under a small piece of shale. She figured it would completely disintegrate within a short period of time in this climate, leaving no trace. She got herself back together and was reassured to see Bart standing next to her. She walked back toward the truck, and for the first time, noticed the gorgeous view. There were rugged, rocky mountain peaks all around them. She opened her door and got out a camera from her bag behind her seat.

Jake watched the expert way she handled her equipment and admired her natural ability to see what was most dramatic in the vistas. She snapped several shots from different perspectives and in several directions. She smilingly turned and snapped some shots of Bart. Then she turned her lens on him. He colored and blushed and told her he didn't take a good picture. She quickly realized that in the future, she'd have to catch him when he was unaware of her training her camera on him. She knew from experience that self-conscious, posed shots were most often disappointments. She was experienced enough in getting superb shots of difficult subjects enough to patiently wait for another time.

"We'll go another ten miles to the Elephant Tusk campground and have lunch. We can pass the heat of the day there, as there's a little shade from some Mesquite brush around the campground. You'll have a great view of Elephant Tusk Mountain from the campground. We'll rest for a while, then continue a few miles further to the old Mariscal Mine. Its on the side of Mariscal Mountain, and from there, you'll feel like you can see forever. You can see down a long canyon, clear to the Rio Grande River and across and for a long way into Mexico. Its spectacular, and you won't find those kinds of pictures in the average travel magazine." He insisted she take a long drink of cool water from his trail bottle, then waited for her to put her camera away, and climb back up into the truck. Silly Bart jumped right up into her lap and over her to settle down in the middle seat. She giggled at his antics and fastened her seatbelt snugly. She had always thought a person would need a seatbelt in case of a crash. Today, she found out she needed a seatbelt just to keep from being thrown out of her seat! Jake closed her door, walked around the truck and got inside. He fastened his own seatbelt and tousled Bart's head in a loving caress. He started the engine and they were off, back on their way down the rock and sand-strewn desert road.

Chapter Four

They bumped along the road, which seemed to deteriorate even more as they got deeper into the backcountry, on the ten miles to Elephant Tusk Campground. It was already one o'clock in the afternoon and the heat was stifling. Carrie thought that calling this place a campground was really stretching it. There were no restrooms, picnic tables, water spigots, or trash barrels. There were a couple of fire rings made out of stones that had obviously been used by prior visitors. A few scraggly Mesquite bushes provided the only covered shade for miles around in any direction, but there were some large boulders nearby, offering some respite from the blazing hot sun.

"All the weather reports I saw showed high temperatures in West Texas were in the low eighties this time of year. This place is like a blast furnace. Isn't this heat unusual for here?" Carrie helped Jake carry their water and the jug of left over orange juice over to a shady spot next to some large boulders where the ground was clear.

Jake was unfolding a large piece of canvas tarp over the soft, shady sand. "Those reports mostly show the temperature at the higher altitudes north of here. The Big Bend area is always about twenty degrees hotter than what you see on weather maps because it's several thousand feet lower in altitude than Alpine, where the weather reporting station is located. It's even hotter than it is here, down at the river level." He unloaded the lunch Maria had packed for them out of a small cooler and placed it on the tarp. He then poured a bowl full of water and set it on the ground for Bart. Bart lapped up every drop. Paper plates and napkins appeared from another bag. The sandwiches he removed from the cooler smelled delicious.

Carrie sank down on the welcoming tarp, grabbed a paper plate and unwrapped a sandwich. It was made with lots of thin slices of beef and lettuce and fresh onions and a delicious smelling spread. The thick slabs of bread looked and smelled like homemade sourdough. She took a large bite and couldn't believe the marvelous flavors flooding her taste buds. "What is in this? The meat is so tender and flavorful. I've never had a beef sandwich this delicious!" she exclaimed between bites.

"It's slow roasted, mesquite-smoked bar-b-q brisket. We do our own at the ranch using the meat we raise ourselves. It's slow cooked in a deep pit for about twelve hours. Maria bastes it every hour or so with what we call a "mop" sauce. Then she thin slices it to have around for hearty sandwiches for all of us. Sometimes we eat it slathered with bar-b-q sauce on a bun with onion slices and Jalapeño peppers. That would be too messy for a picnic like this. Someday, we'll have some like I just described, though. I know you'll love it."

Jake was shocked when he realized what he had just said to Carrie, in his off-hand comment about the bar-b-q. He had implied that she'd be around long enough for such a meal with him at his ranch. He had never taken any woman to his ranch before. It was his private place where his heart and emotions were safe. He'd never before shared it with anyone he'd dated. He'd never wanted to. Now, here he was talking about taking Carrie there. But it just seemed so natural and right.

Puzzled with himself, he unwrapped his sandwich and began eating. Carrie drank some of the orange juice left over from their breakfast and poured a cup for him. She watched his handsome face as he ate. God! He was so gorgeous! He was also the nicest, most fun-loving man she'd ever spent time with. Her heart did funny flip-flops in her chest. Bart nudged her in the side as if to encourage her to get up and play with him. She stroked his muzzle and spoke to him softly, as if he could understand exactly what she was saying.

Noticing that Jake had finished eating and relaxed back on one elbow across the tarp, Carrie grabbed an apple and got up and strolled over to the truck to get her camera. Bart followed her like a shadow. She dug her hat out of her daypack and put on her sunglasses. The sun felt merciless. No wonder people out here always talked about staying out of the heat during the mid-day. She decided to zip off her pant legs and turn her hiking pants into shorts. She was glad she had worn the tank top and didn't have on a bra. She finished her apple and gave the core to Bart. Jake surrepticiously watched her change her pants into shorts, sloe-eyed and longingly, with all kinds of erotic images flashing through his mind.

Carrie wandered around the campground area, taking pictures of the distant scenery and some close-ups of the pretty wildflowers dotting the area. Bart followed her every step, panting in the noon heat. She knew she shouldn't stay out in the sun too long, so she wandered back over to the tarp where Jake lay stretched out invitingly. She plopped down next to him cross-legged in the shade. Bart did the same. She was feeling a little sleepy after getting up so early and eating the huge lunch.

"How long will we stay here before we go to the mine?" Carrie was hoping they'd be there long enough for her to take a quick 'power nap,' as she called them.

"Oh, I thought we'd lounge here for about an hour, then drive the rest of the way to the mine. By then, it should be safe enough to spend some time out in the sun. You'll want to get some photos around that area as there are some spectacular views there."

Carrie set her camera down on the edge of the tarp in the shade and let out a long sigh. Jake reached for her and gently pulled her back where she could rest against his body.

"Just use me like a big, old pillow, and see if you can doze off a while. You look as sleepy-eyed as Bart." She looked over at Bart who was already stretched out, sound asleep. She relaxed her body and let Jake pull her back until her head was resting comfortably across his stomach. She uncrossed her legs, stretching them out next to Bart. Within minutes, she was asleep.

Jake couldn't sleep for staring at Carrie. She was so incredibly beautiful. She had pulled out her hair clip when she leaned back and now her gorgeous, natural blond hair flowed across his mid-section. He reached out tentatively and fingered a few of its silky strands, being careful not to wake her. He let his gaze slowly wander down her beautiful female form, lingering first on her full breasts, rising and falling with each breath she took. He could see her nipples outlined by the soft cotton fabric. He longed to caress their peaks as he had done with her hair. He continued down her slim midriff and then involuntarily lingered on the triangle juncture of her thighs. He found himself wondering if her pretty feminine curls would be as blond below as she was above. He grew harder thinking about this particular thought.

He continued looking his fill down her strong, muscular legs. She obviously got plenty of exercise, as her legs held the shapely curves of someone who took good care of herself. He imagined it was from climbing steep hiking trails to get the beautiful nature photographs she was noted for taking. No need for a StairMaster machine in a pricey New York health club for this woman. Her small feet were encased in sturdy hiking boots, which only fueled his image of her scaling a steep trail to the top of a gorgeous mountain somewhere.

He was growing increasingly less comfortable in his tight jeans, his erection swelling by the moment. He shifted his position slightly and Carrie roused a little, shifted from her back to her left side, and curled up her legs. He thought he would burst as he found her face mere inches away from the source of his extreme discomfort. He didn't dare move a muscle. This was pure torture. He didn't know how much longer he could stand it. He needed to think of something else, anything but Carrie's gorgeous mouth next to his burgeoning erection, separated by only some cloth.

Jake wondered about her past love life. It was hard to imagine guys didn't trip all over each other for her. He wondered if she had ever been married, or had a steady boyfriend? She wore no wedding ring and there was no telltale, pale indentation on her finger that a wedding ring inevitably leaves. She seemed so innocent, hardly the type to be running around on someone she had made a commitment to. No, he was absolutely sure that wasn't the case. Carrie wasn't that type of woman. He wondered if someone had hurt her deeply? What kind of idiot would hurt a woman like her? He found himself feeling angry at whoever might have done such a thing, and feelings of protectiveness for her welled up inside him. He hoped she would eventually share some of her past with him. He planned to ask a few discreet questions to try to draw her out. He just had to know as much about her as she would share.

He surprised himself by dozing off for a while. Carrie woke, and blushed furiously with embarrassment when she realized where her face had ended up in her sleep. She lifted herself quickly off of Jake, which woke him instantly.

"We've got to get going, Jake. I have no idea how long we slept, but I'm sure it is time we moved on to the Mariscal Mine." She jumped up and began gathering the remains of their lunch. She put everything back into the cooler. They could throw out the trash when they got back to Terlingua. There was clearly no place to dispose of it here, in spite of the place being called a campground.

Jake shook out the tarp and folded it back up. He carried the empty orange juice jug and Bart's water bowl back to the truck. He put everything in his carryall in the back now that the food was gone out of the cooler. Carrie took the opportunity to slip behind a boulder to relieve herself before they headed out again. Jake did the same.

Back on the trail again - Carrie refused to call it a road anymore - they were on their way to their next and last stop for the day. The truck bucked and rolled across the un-maintained track as it had been doing all day, ever since they turned off the paved road earlier in the morning. Carrie was getting used to it now and had learned to roll with it instead of fighting it.   She found this was much more comfortable and caused far less tension in her muscles.

As they approached the old, abandoned Mariscal Mine, the truck struck an exposed ridge of shale with exceptional force.   There was an immediate, explosive sound from under the hood and steam began furiously pouring out from the front grill and around the wheel wells.

"Oh, my God!" Carrie yelled with alarm.   "Are we on fire?"

Jake immediately shut off the engine.   "No, no, Carrie.   It's just steam from the radiator coolant.   Everything's fine.   I'll fix it.   Don't worry."   Jake's voice held an involuntary note of alarm.   He carried extra coolant in the carryall, but if something was broken beyond his ability to fix it out here, they'd be in real trouble.

Jake pulled the hood release and jumped out of the truck.   He opened the hood and more steam boiled out in a rush.   He stepped back to allow it to clear so he wouldn't get burned.   The steam evaporated into the hot desert air.   Carrie opened her door and stepped out.

"Jake!   Look!   There's water pouring out from under the truck!" He could hear the panic in her voice.   She came around the front to stand next to Jake.   He climbed up on the front bumper and peered into the engine compartment, then got down and crawled partly underneath the side to view it from the bottom.   "Shit!"   He exclaimed to himself.

A large ten-inch slit was clearly visible in the radiator hose underneath.   It wasn't something he could even wrap duct tape around in order to limp back to town.   "Damn!"   He swore.   He struggled to compose his worried features before he got back out from beneath the truck to explain what had happened to Carrie.   He could see the worried look on her pretty face.   He better come up with something fast, or he'd have one freaked out woman on his hands.   He stood up and brushed the sand off his jeans and hands. He put on his most confident face and faced Carrie.

"I'll tell it to you straight, Carrie.   The radiator hose is ruined.   I can't fix it without a new hose." He watched her features relax and she went back to her side of the truck and produced her cell phone out of her pack. With a confident smile, she came back over to him and dropped it into his hand.

"See, even a city girl can come up with something valuable out here," she crowed, grinning smugly at him. She reached over and pushed the power button on the phone. It came to life but the signal strength icon registered nothing. Carrie looked at it with alarm.

"I don't know what's wrong. It has a brand new battery and is fully charged but the display shows no cell tower within range." Carrie tapped the case of the phone lightly, hoping to see the familiar cell strength symbols appear.

"Carrie, I don't know how to tell you this, but a cell phone is useless out here. There isn't a cell phone tower within three hundred miles." He watched her demeanor instantly change from confidence to fear.

"Well then what are we going to do?" Her voice rose in pitch, indicating her growing panic. She looked around into the distance and saw absolutely nothing manmade for as far as she could see. She remembered how long they had been driving to get this far and they hadn't seen another soul along the way. She was at a loss as to how they'd get any help out here and she didn't think anyone knew where they were going or when to expect them back. She had told Diana not to worry about her and she'd call her in a few days. They could both be dead out here in a few days in this unforgiving desert area!

Jake grabbed hold of both Carrie's arms turning her to face him. "Look, Carrie. Trust me. I can get us out of here safe and sound. Remember that I was raised here, and I've been up and down these mountains and canyons many times. We need to keep our wits about us and think and make a plan. You've got to listen to me, and trust me, but we need to do this together. Carrie, can you trust me to pull us through this?"

Carrie's eyes searched Jake's face. She wanted, no needed, to believe him, and above all, trust him. "Jake, I'm so frightened. This desert can be deadly; I've come to realize that.   I do trust you, really, Jake, but I'm afraid.   I don't see how we'll get out of here alive, on foot."

"Carrie, I already have a plan.   I know this area and have done this before with Carlos.   It'll be a trek, about ten miles, but you're strong and I'm strong, and I know how to find what we need to keep us alive in this country.   You've just got to believe in me.   We need to get started, though, and get to the first good stop before dark.   Come with me, and I'll point out to you exactly where we're headed."   He took her hand firmly and led her over to where there was an unobstructed view down the mountain to the Rio Grande River in the far distance below.

He pointed down a long canyon to the river, which looked a hundred miles away to Carrie.   "You see that faint trail heading down into the canyon?   Well, it continues along down the bottom of Mariscal Canyon, all the way to the river, and it's downhill all the way. I know where there's a natural spring about half way down where we can overnight and get more water.   We'll make it the rest of the way to the river late tomorrow afternoon.   There are boats going up and down the river and we can hitch a ride on one of them downstream to where there is a paved road out and a park ranger's headquarters. Its called Rio Grande Village."   He kept talking reassuringly, with a death grip on her hand, before she could bolt in panic.   He continued explaining his plan.

"There's a tiny camper's store there with food and gasoline and telephones.   There's a large campground, not like the ones we've seen all day, but a campground full of other campers, electricity, and running water.   There are tiny Mexican villages along the river with people and food and water.   Any one of them would provide us with a boat ride to the ranger station.   I've known those people for years and they all know me very well.   When we get to a phone, I'll call Carlos and he'll come get us.   Some of my other guys will bring parts and come fix the truck and drive it back to the ranch."

Carrie stared down the long trail and got a hold of herself.

Listening to Jake's confident solution to their predicament gave her courage that they'd survive just fine. She was more determined than ever to show Jake she wasn't some sniveling little Barbie doll who couldn't deal with unexpected adversity. And who could tell? This might turn out to be the greatest adventure of her lifetime. She turned to Jake and gave him her most confident smile.

"Well, then Mr. Jake Stockton, let's go back to the truck, get some of our stuff, and get started." She whirled around and began to stride purposefully back to the disabled truck, with Bart tagging closely behind her. Jake stood, dumbfounded, staring after her.

He let out a slow breath. He wasn't sure how she was going to react to his plan. It was really their only hope. It was much too far to walk back out the way they came in. That was close to thirty hot, dry, dusty miles, and there was no water at all in that direction. They wouldn't last a day in this heat. It was only about ten miles downhill to the river. Once they got there, they'd have it made. He sucked in a ragged breath when he thought of them spending the night together, in the wilderness, alone, at Mariscal springs. He reluctantly shook off that thrilling thought and hurried after Carrie.

She pulled her daypack out from behind the seat, watched Jake climb into the bed of the truck, and open the carryall box. He pulled out what looked like a full backpack with a sleeping bag strapped to the bottom. He explained to her as he got organized, "I always carry a pack and a bedroll in the back of the truck, in case I get stuck way out on the ranch tending cattle. Sometimes I need to sleep out and go home the next day. I've got a couple sealed packets of dog food for Bart, some energy bars, a big hunting knife, a smaller Swiss Army knife full of miscellaneous useful tools, some matches, a small first aid kit, a couple extra trail bottles full of water, and a backpacking water filter. That way, I can refill the trail bottles using the filter to make sure we only drink pure water. Otherwise a person is likely to get sick as a dog drinking water from just anywhere. I've got some other miscellaneous useful stuff in here, too.

"What do you have with you in your daypack, Carrie?" She dug through her pack, pulling out two granola bars, her tiny bar of soap, her hairbrush, her cover-up shirt, her sunscreen, and her useless cell phone. Jake disguised his disappointment at the lack of much useful there. Carrie dropped these things back into her pack and added the bottoms of her pants she had zipped off earlier, and one of her cameras and several extra rolls of film. This photo equipment she believed to be absolute necessities, since the whole reason she came to Texas was to get some unusual photos. She had a strong feeling she was about to get the most unusual photos of her life, if she lived through the next two days, that was.

She noticed him curiously eyeing the plastic tube attached to her daypack strap with a small piece of Velcro. "I've got a CamelBack in here, too. It has two liters of water in it. I filled it right before we left the motel. I can suck water out of it by biting on this little valve on the end of the tube, just like a straw. It makes it easy to drink enough water without having to stop to dig out and unscrew a trail bottle."

He looked intrigued and thought to himself that was probably one of the most valuable things Carrie had along with her. A person needed to drink a gallon of water a day to safely survive in this country. Between them, they should have enough to get to the springs where they could refill for the next day's hike to the river. He was figuring in water for Bart, too, of course.

Carrie shot him an inquiring look. "I suppose it's safe to leave the rest of my equipment here in the truck? It'll be too much to comfortably carry with me. This doesn't exactly look like a parking lot in Harlem, where it would be picked clean the minute we are out of sight."

Jake openly chuckled and replied, "You don't have to worry about a thing getting stolen out of here. I'm not even going to lock it, so when I send the guys back from the ranch to repair it and drive it out, it'll be easy for them." He shouldered his backpack and adjusted the strap around his lean waist. Carrie did the same with hers.

"You lead the way, Jake. This is all your show now," she laughed.

They set off down the rocky trail, beginning what would become, unknown to either of them, an adventure that would change both of their lives forever.

After walking a few hundred yards down the rough trail, Jake stopped and slipped his large knife from its sheath on the side of his pack. He stepped a little ways off the trail and cut off two of the long, dried out woody stalks from two Sotol yucca plants. He brought them back to where Carrie waited, watching him curiously. He trimmed off both ends and scraped the pale yellow wooden stalks with the edge of his knife blade. He made sure they were perfectly smooth and free of splinters and thorns. He handed one of the smooth, straight sticks to Carrie, and she marveled at its light weight and seeming strength.

"Use this as a hiking stick. It'll help take the stress off your knees when the trail gets steeper as we make our way downhill. It'll also help you keep your balance so you don't stumble and fall." Jake turned and continued on down the trail. Carrie believed this was the prettiest hiking stick she'd ever seen. She thought to herself that she'd keep it forever, as a memento of this incredible trip, and Jake.

They walked down the rugged, rocky trail for what seemed like hours. Carrie drank from her water tube from time to time as the heat increased as they descended deeper into the canyon. She was sweating profusely from the vigorous exercise in the heat and her hair clip was slipping, allowing trailing tendrils of her beautiful hair to hang down and stick to her sweaty skin. She could feel her body losing precious liquid. The only saving grace was the stiff wind blowing up the canyon from below. Although it was a hot, dry wind, it felt better than no wind at all.

Jake looked back and saw that Carrie was struggling, in spite of her efforts to put up a good front and not be a complainer. He admired her courage and resolve, but she wasn't used to hiking in desert heat. He stopped next to some large, house-sized boulders where there was some early shade, and told Carrie they were taking a break. The sun was beginning to slip down the west side of Mariscal Mountain, which would mean an increasing amount of shade across the trail as they made their way to the springs. This would bring a slow but steady decrease in temperature.

"Carrie, sit down for a few minutes. Drink some more water and rest while we stop here for a few minutes." He helped her slip her daypack off her sweat-soaked shoulders. He removed his own pack and dug out one of the energy bars. He opened it and cut it in half, giving Carrie the larger piece. He then pulled out a canvas, fold-up water bowl from his pack and poured it full of water from his own trail bottle, setting it on the ground for Bart. Bart drained it and nuzzled Jake, whining softly. Jake broke off a piece of his energy bar and fed it to a grateful Bart.

"When we stop for the night, Bart, I'll give you some real food. Until then, you'll have to get by on this, Big Guy, just like we're doing. You're such a good boy, Bart," he said affectionately while ruffling Bart's hot fur in a caress.

Speaking of food, Carrie was wondering what they were going to eat tonight. She was famished and the only other things they had along were one more power bar and her two granola bars. She thought she could probably eat Bart's dog food, she was so hungry, and they still had a ways to go, she guessed.

"How much farther is it to the springs, Jake," she asked and her weariness was evident in her shaky voice, in spite of her best efforts to sound upbeat.

"Only about another couple hours, maybe less as we'll make better time now that the heat is decreasing." Jake tried to not let his own weariness show. He knew he needed to get them up and moving before total lethargy set in, making it almost impossible for their tired muscles to go on. He stood and reached for Carrie's hands to pull her to her feet.

When he pulled her up, it seemed only natural to fold her into his arms and kiss her, if only for encouragement. It was such a spontaneous act, and it caught them both off-guard and by surprise. Then Carrie began to lean heavily into his body and parted her lips, fully returning his kiss. Jake was lost. His tongue reached out tentatively outlining the most sensitive areas of her lips. In response, she opened her mouth further, allowing his exploring tongue to delve deeply inside and taste her deeply. A strangled moan escaped from her throat and Jake thought he would completely lose his self-control. He could feel his body instantly harden against her stomach as they swayed together in their mutual embrace.

Jake groaned and broke off the kiss. They stood staring into each other's eyes shocked by the intensity of their kiss. They could both feel that something had drastically changed in their relationship and they were moving rapidly into dangerous and uncharted territory. Would they each be ready to risk the ultimate danger of falling in love again? Could either of them stop it now, even if they wanted to? Jake was the first to speak.

"Carrie, we've got to keep going. We need to get to the springs where there's water and shelter for the night before it gets dark. We don't have much water left."

Carrie nodded her head in agreement in a daze. Jake turned and began hiking down the trail towards the springs. Carrie mechanically followed along after Jake, with Bart trailing protectively after her. She was glad to have the rugged trail to concentrate on, but she couldn't stop her cascading emotions.

"My God," she thought to herself. "I'm falling in love with a man I've only known for two days!" But it felt like they had known each other a lifetime. She had dreamed about, and waited her whole life to find a man like him. No, not a man like him, but the real him, Jake Stockton. She didn't like to think she had left the course of her life up to fate, but fate had clearly brought her to this unbelievable place and into the same sphere of the universe as Jake Stockton, right at this particular moment in time.

Jake was also struggling to pay attention to the trail in front of him. He was reeling with the intensity of his feelings for Carrie. The more he thought about their brief relationship, the more it didn't make logical sense to him. But often, the best things to come along in life didn't always make logical sense. He never thought love could find him again, but here was Carrie, warm and real, rapidly becoming critical to the very beating of his heart. True love followed no timetables and often defied logical thinking. It felt like she was surely meant for him and it had to be a benevolent God, indeed, who sent her into his lonely life at just this space in time. He was determined to not reject this precious gift out of sheer emotional cowardice. He'd claim her for his own, if it was the last thing he did.

Chapter Five

As the afternoon sun set further down the West Side of Mariscal Mountain, the trail became more and more shaded. It became steeper as they descended into the canyon and Carrie found herself grateful for her hiking stick to help absorb some of the shock to her knees from the steeply, twisting downhill trail. As tired as she was, she couldn't help noticing the beauty of the desert along the trail and in the canyon. Everything seemed to be blooming at once and she could hear the hum of bees in the dry air as they visited the colorful blossoms.

She recognized a lot of the flowers but many of the others were new to her. Bright yellow Black-eyed Susan, delicate, burgandy Winecups, and Indian Paintbrush flowers in different colors than she'd ever seen before surrounded her. Some were the usual shades of scarlet and orange, but she also saw yellows and purples. Golden Huisache Daisies perfumed the air with their freshly-mown hay fragrance as they carpeted the ground beneath the desert chaparral growing along the sides of the canyon. Feathery pink Basket Flowers emerged from rock crevices. She noticed small lizards darting for cover as they passed by. Jake told her the lizards were called Whiptails, and some of them were almost a foot long. She recognized desert Horned Toads with their spiny-frilled necks and she noticed more kinds of cactus in the canyon than she had seen just speeding down the roads in vehicles.

There were clusters of Hedgehog cactus, small barrel-shaped cactus with a circle of yellow flowers blooming around their tops, looking like little lids. There were flat Beaver Tail cactus with bright rose-colored blossoms erupting from the ends of each flat "tail." Carrie noticed desert mice and rock squirrels scampering among the rocks and saw her very first Roadrunner bird. She knew at once what it was, having watched the Roadrunner cartoons on television as a child. It was a bigger bird than she had thought it would be, looking almost the size of a skinny chicken. More and more birds were visible as the desert shrubbery became more abundant, deeper in the canyon. There was clearly more water available to the plants here, and they had more shelter from the broiling sun. She noticed wrens and ravens, and saw giant turkey vultures, with their bright red heads and necks, circling overhead. She smiled to herself thinking wryly, that she wasn't totally sure that seeing circling vultures was such a great omen.

She was surprised that the time passed so quickly when she concentrated on the beauty surrounding her, instead of whining to herself about the heat and ruggedness of their trek. But the heat, dust, and challenge of the hike held its own charm, she mused. She was grateful for this unexpected opportunity to fully experience the desert up close, and her more positive nature took over. She decided to make the best of their situation. She noticed the vegetation around the trail noticeably begin to change and become more dense as they approached an area beneath a sheer rock wall along the side of the canyon. The trail grew even steeper and narrower and the canyon walls became closer together. Then the trail suddenly leveled out and got sandier with a lot fewer large rocks. Jake detoured down what looked like a side trail, heading over closer to the face of the rock cliff.

He stopped next to a clear, sandy-bottomed pool of water being fed by a spring running right out of the side of the cliff, as if someone had left a faucet turned on by mistake. Carrie stared in disbelief at this incredible oasis that appeared out of nowhere! Bart lapped greedily at the clear water. Jake unbuckled his pack from around his waist and slipped it off his shoulders. He helped Carrie do the same with hers.

"Well, what do you think of our stop for the night? Not too bad, if I do say so myself." He shot her a huge grin. "Just up above us a little ways is the stone shell of a building, built by an old prospector roaming this area fifty years ago. There's no door, roof, or glass in the window frames, but it'll make a great little motel room for us for the night." Jake kneeled down next to the edge of the pool and splashed cool water over his face and head. Bart was still lapping at the water, standing in it up to his chest. Carrie continued staring at the pool in disbelief. She wanted to jump right in, clothes and all, it looked so inviting. Stories of desert mirages flashed through her mind and she thought this is what must be happening to her - imagining a mirage! Never, did she expect to run across a place like this out here.

"This is unbelievable, Jake! It looks like paradise right now." Carrie stepped to the edge of the pool and stooped down towards the inviting water.

"Don't drink any of it, Carrie. As good as it looks, it isn't safe to drink. You see old Bart here, standing in it, well; every other animal around here gets into this pool. I'll use my water filter and fill our trail bottles and your CamelBack and we'll drink from those. Later, you can take a bath in it, if you'd like. It's plenty clean enough for bathing. I know I'm sure going to. You don't have to worry about privacy, either, as there's not another soul around here for miles and miles."

Jake stood up and began climbing up some small stone steps, barely visible in the bushes behind the pool area. Carrie grabbed her camera and followed him. About fifteen feet up the stone steps, they came to the small building he had told her about earlier. It was really just one room. He whacked off a piece of rabbit brush with his knife and began using it to sweep some of the dust off the floor in an area she assumed he'd be putting their one sleeping bag. The thought of them sharing that single bedroll caused her heart to skip several beats and her breath to catch in her chest. Jake stepped over near the door and tossed the rabbit brush broom aside.

Carrie moved around the small stone building viewing it from the perspective of an accomplished photographer. It was a photographic gold mine! She began snapping pictures with her camera. It was clearly built of the same rocks she saw everywhere around the immediate area. This collection of various size building stones were held together by a cement-like substance, and the builder had smeared what looked like a plaster coating over the one wall which contained a fireplace. There were windows and a doorframe made of deeply grooved, weathered wood that had aged to a brownish gray color. There was no evidence that the wood had ever been painted in the first place. Any window glass that might have once been present was now long gone, as was the missing door. There was no roof anymore, but Carrie could see that around the top of the walls, some pieces of corrugated iron remained along the edges. She guessed that the whole roof once consisted of this same material.

Jake stood silently watching her work with her camera and admired her artist's eye for detail. She noticed there was a beautiful view of the opposite side of their canyon out what was once the front window next to the missing door. It overlooked the tops of the shrubbery growing around the spring. She stood back and took photos of the view as seen looking through the empty weathered window frame. When she was satisfied with her photographs, they both walked back down the stone steps to the pool area.

"I'll build a fire soon and get dinner started. You can take a bath and relax and unwind before we eat. First, I'll go get you some shampoo. You have your tiny bar of soap from your motel room with you, I noticed." Jake made this statement as if they were in a luxury hotel somewhere. She had no idea what he was talking about. He spoke a command to Bart. "Bart, hunt rabbit." Bart immediately whirled and disappeared into the brush. She continued to stare at him in disbelief!

Jake walked a ways across the trail to a yucca plant. He dug at its base with his large hunting knife, pulling out some of its tuber-like pieces of root. He brought them back over to the pool and washed them off, scrubbing them with a piece of coarse brush. He found a flat, bowl-shaped piece of shale and picked up a small round rock. He placed some of the root pieces into the stone bowl, added some water from the pool and ground it all together into a thick pulpy paste.

"Here's your shampoo, Princess. You'll never use anything nicer in your life." He set the bowl down next to the sandy pool where she could easily reach it. "I'm going to disappear for about fifteen minutes to give you some privacy. Take your bath while I'm gone and I guarantee you'll feel like a new woman. I need to gather a few more things for our dinner. I'll whistle when I'm coming back."

Carrie stared at him in disbelief. "You keep talking about dinner as if you had just invited me over to your apartment in the city, and you were just going to whip something up. You must be nuts! All we have is one energy bar and two granola bars!" She was starving and all this talk about cooking a dinner made her crazy with hunger.

"We'll save the granola bars for breakfast and we'll share the last energy bar for lunch tomorrow. 'Sorry it'll be such meager fare for the rest of the hike, but we'll be at the river and a Mexican village by late tomorrow afternoon, so my good friends in the village will take care of dinner tomorrow night. You just wait and see, Carrie. You'll be feasting on Wild Gourmet a la 'Desert tonight." His laughing eyes held the promise of some kind of ace up his sleeve. She couldn't begin to imagine how he was going to produce such a meal out of nothing, but she had learned pretty quickly not to discount anything Jake Stockton said.

Jake took his hunting knife and disappeared through the thick brush that grew around the spring pool area. She recognized some of the bushes as mesquite and small desert willows. When she looked closely, she noticed beautiful ruby-throated hummingbirds visiting some of the blossoms on the shrubbery along with the bees.

She was amazed that such a delicate creature as a hummingbird could be living in the desert!

It was beginning to cool off. She guessed she'd have to zip the legs back onto her cargo pants if it continued to drop in temperature as it got dark. She'd heard that desert nights could get quite cold in spite of the terribly high temperatures during the day. She began removing her sweaty boots and clothing and her hair clip, shaking out her sweaty hair. She stepped carefully into the pool of water. She remembered that she had the small bar of motel soap in her daypack, but decided to try Jake's squished up yucca root concoction instead.

The water was refreshingly cool. She sat down and leaned back on her elbows across the sandy bottom of the pool, immersing her entire body. She dunked her head back to wet her long hair. She reached into the stone bowl and scooped up some of the strange yucca paste. It had a fresh herbal smell to it. She began rubbing it into her hair and was surprised at the shampoo-like lather it produced. She dipped her hair back under the water to rinse it. She took up another scoop of yucca and washed her hair a second time. This time she rinsed it thoroughly. Her hair felt squeaky-clean, and at the same time feeling soft and silky, as if she had used an expensive conditioner.

Next she stood and took another scoop of the paste and washed down her whole body. She reached over to her clothes pile and found her panties. She washed them out with the yucca soap, as well. Their thin silk would dry in the desert air before she would be finished with her bath. She squeezed them out and draped them over a nearby rock. She sank back down into the pool to rinse off her body. She felt wonderfully clean and her skin had the same soft, silky feel as her hair. This yucca stuff was amazing! She continued to lounge in the cool water, thoroughly enjoying this incredible experience. Diana would never believe her, for sure, when she told her this story. She laughed to herself imagining Diana's reaction to the roofless stone motel room and yucca root shampoo.

She heard Jake whistle and stood up in the water. "Just a minute,

Jake! I'm not dressed yet!" she yelled. She climbed out of the water and shook as much water off her body as she could. She noticed her skin was drying rapidly in the warm, dry air. She put on her almost-dry panties, then her tank top and hiking shorts. She stood in the soft sand barefooted.

"You can come back now, Jake, I'm decent." she declared. She watched him appear through the bushes gingerly carrying some pear-sized purple fruits, some small prickly pear cactus leaves, and some more larger yucca roots.

"I bet you were pretty darn decent even before you got dressed," he said to her, teasingly. Carrie blushed and shot him a shy, totally feminine glance from under seductively lowered lashes. Jake stood staring at her, mesmerized by the sight of her damp blond hair tumbling around her bare shoulders, which were exposed by the skimpy tank top straps. He couldn't help but notice her hard nipples poking out from the thin cotton fabric of her tank top. His eyes immediately darkened with desire to a deeper jade green, as he stared at her, momentarily unable to speak.

Finally finding his voice he asked, "What did you think of my soap and shampoo, all in one? I hope you saved a little for me." He glanced over at the stone bowl still sitting next to the edge of the pool. There was plenty left, he noted.

"Its fantastic! I never imagined you could come up with something like that from nothing more than some plant roots. But I don't know why I should be so surprised, though. The shampoo makers put Aloe Vera in shampoo all the time, and that's just a plant extract. But that seems like a long way from watching you smash up some roots that I watched you dig up, and turn them into soap on a piece of stone." She laughed out loud at seeing the irony of it.

"It's just an old Indian trick, Carrie. Native peoples learned to use the plants growing in their environment for many purposes. They didn't have Dove soap and Prell shampoo lying around. They had to figure out how to use what was available to them in their own environment. Many of them still do the same things as their ancestors. They like it better than a lot of what's available in the few stores around here, and it's a lot less expensive, besides. Most of the native peoples living around here, Indians and Mexicans, have little money for store-bought luxuries that they can make better at home, and for free, besides. This desert holds a bounty of useful materials, and healthy, delicious food items. Its possible to obtain every essential nutrient off what modern nutritionists call the food pyramid, from right here around us."

Bart slipped back through the shrubbery and dropped a large dead rabbit at Jake's feet. "Good dog, Bart," he praised, while vigorously rubbing Bart's neck and sides. Bart wagged his tail furiously and whined and wrapped his body around Jake's legs in one of his dog hugs. "You'll be getting your share of this rabbit after Carrie and I have eaten out fill, Old Boy. You're terrific, Bart, my best pal."

Carrie stared open-mouthed at Jake and Bart, as Jake picked up the rabbit and his hunting knife and walked down the trail a ways to clean it out of Carrie's sight. He figured a city girl wouldn't care to watch him clean a rabbit in front of her. He dug a foot-deep hole in the sand away from their camp and buried the innards and skin so it wouldn't attract wild animals in the night. He placed a huge rock over the hole after burying everything with sand. He gathered up some pieces of dead brushwood for a campfire, picked up the cleaned rabbit, and went back to the pool area.

Carrie was sitting on the sand petting Bart, who rushed back to camp ahead of Jake. She watched Jake make a fire ring out of stones and build a small oven-like structure out of flat pieces of shale beneath where the fire would be burning. He piled the sticks and pieces of wood around the inside of the ring, with the smallest sticks on the bottom. He lit the small sticks on fire with some matches out of his pack and Carrie watched as he blew on it and it blazed up, catching the larger wood on fire. Next he scrubbed off the larger yucca roots he had returned to camp with after her bath, and placed them inside the small oven-like structure he had designed into the fire ring. He placed a few larger pieces of wood onto the fire and stood back looking at his handiwork with pride.

"Perfect! In about thirty minutes, there will be enough coals to cook our rabbit, and by the time the rabbit is cooked, our baked yucca roots will be ready." He then carefully picked up the prickly pear cactus leaves and the small purple fruits he had brought back earlier. He placed them on the rocks around the edge of the fire ring. Using two sticks like a pair of tongs, he turned each of them over and over in the flames, singing them.

Carrie watched him curiously. "What are you doing with those cactus leaves and purple things?" she asked.

"I'm burning off the thorns, then I'll roast the cactus leaves. Native peoples eat the smaller, tenderer leaves of the prickly pear cactus all the time. The Mexican people call these Napalitos, and use them for vegetables, pickles, nachos, and salads, etc. They are loaded with vitamin A and calcium." He continued telling Carrie more facts about their unusual meal as he worked with the food items around the fire.

"The purple things, as you called them, are prickly pear cactus fruits. I stole them out of a rock squirrel's winter cache, out from under some large boulders across the other side of the canyon. I'm sure he won't miss a few, once he gets over his fury at my stealing them from him." Jake laughed to himself, clearly thinking about his encounter with the furiously chattering, complaining rock squirrel. "They are left over from last fall. All these pretty purple flowers you see on the prickly pears this time of year will turn into delicious, juicy fruits next fall. I'm burning off their tiny patches of stickers that protect the fruit from most animals, and humans hoping to eat them. They are deliciously sweet and full of Vitamin C."

He next propped the singed cactus leaves among the fire ring rocks so they would slowly roast without burning. He inspected the fruits to make sure all the stickers were burned off and set them on the sand beside the fire ring to cool a little. He later picked them up and thoroughly washed them off in the pool, setting them on a flat rock to dry.

"These will make a delicious dessert, he commented," wonderfully pleased by the amazed and impressed looks he read on her expressive face.

Jake next cut a long straight stick of green willow and scraped off the bark and leaves with his knife. He threaded the rabbit onto one end of the stick, and using another sturdy stick stuck in the sand next to the fire ring; he propped the rabbit over the heat radiating from the hot coals. From time to time he turned the rabbit so it would cook evenly. She had never eaten rabbit before, but it smelled absolutely wonderful to her. She was so hungry she could hardly think. Jake fished the baked yucca roots out of the makeshift oven using his knife. He set them on a flat piece of shale he had placed between them to use as a dinner plate, so the roots would cool down a little. When the rabbit was completely cooked, he placed it on the shale next to the roots and cut it into serving-size pieces. He then cut the roasted cactus leaves into long strips and the baked yucca roots into bite-sized chunks. From his backpack he pulled out a small plastic film canister containing a mixture of salt and pepper. He sprinkled some over their food.

"Dig in, Carrie. This is our dinner for tonight." He didn't have to tell her twice.

Carrie picked up a piece of rabbit meat and began nibbling the juicy meat off of the bone. "Hey, it tastes just like chicken!" Next, she tentatively tasted a piece of the baked yucca, then a strip of roasted prickly pear leaf.

"This is fantastic! How can you have something taste this good when just hours before, you were making soap out of it? I don't understand." Carrie took another piece of the yucca while she continued chewing the meat off of her rabbit bones. Jake was eating almost as fast as Carrie. Bart hovered patiently nearby, waiting for his turn at the food.

"Lots of native plants have more than one use. The natives make sandals and mats and bags out of the long stringy yucca leaves and soap and food from the roots." Jake reached into his pack again and this time pulled out one of the small, sealed packets of dog food. He peeled it apart and set it on the ground for Bart. Bart immediately devoured it and then resumed his hopeful vigil, hoping for his share of the rabbit. Jake and Carrie ate most of the rest of the rabbit and almost the entire yucca and roasted cactus. When Jake was sure that Carrie had eaten her fill, he slid their shale plate over to Bart, who proceeded to eat everything left and lick the shale clean, besides.

"Now its time for our dessert." He stood up and retrieved the prickly pear fruits from the rocks at the edge of the pool. He brought them back over on a clean piece of flat rock, cut them in half and then into manageable pieces. He offered her a piece saying, "Eat the juicy inner fruity parts, leaving the tough peel. You can spit the seeds out or swallow them whole, whichever you choose."

Carrie tentatively tasted the deep purple-colored pulp of the fruit Jake handed her. "This is wonderful!" she exclaimed excitedly. "It tastes like a cross between blackberries, raspberries and pears." Jake noted that the fruit juice sensuously stained her beautiful lips. When they had finished their fruit, they got up off the sand and went over to the edge of the pool where they washed their messy hands with some of the yucca soap. Jake tossed the fruit peels into the dying coals for disposal. These weren't something Bart would have eaten as he did with the rabbit bones and vegetables.

"Let's take the rest of our packs up to our little motel room and get set up for the night." It was rapidly getting dark and the temperature was falling fast. Carrie had begun to shiver in the evening air, something that had not escaped Jake's notice. They picked up their packs and Carrie followed Jake back up the stone stairs, hidden in the brush behind the spring. Stars were beginning to become visible in the sky overhead. They shimmered and twinkled in the heat of the dry air rising off of the warm rocks and earth.

Jake removed a rip-stop nylon ground tarp from his pack and placed it over the sandy floor of the room. Then he unrolled the sleeping bag on the tarp, shaking it out to fluff it up. They placed their packs next to their bed.

"You go ahead and crawl in the sleeping bag, Carrie. You look dead tired and I can see you starting to shiver in this cooling air. I'm going back down to the pool to fill all our water containers with my filter, then I'm going to take a quick bath in the pool. I also need to make sure the fire is completely out. I'll bring everything back up here so no animal will run off with our stuff in the night." What Jake didn't tell Carrie was that he was going back down to erase any traces that they were ever at the spring. He didn't want any two-legged animals to know they were anywhere around. There was no use in scaring Carrie with this information and having her worrying about it. If they got lucky, she'd never have to know that they might have had a problem on their hands.

Jake left the stone room, heading back down to the spring pool. Carrie found herself alone with her thoughts, staring at the single sleeping bag. She couldn't stop the thrilling feelings flutter her insides when she thought of sleeping close to Jake all night. She glanced down at her dusty shorts and figured she should take them off instead of getting into his clean bedding with dirty hiking clothes. She could sleep in her silk panties and her tank top, which wasn't too dirty. She'd be a lot more comfortable than having those cargo pockets biting into her skin all night. She folded her shorts and placed them next to her pack on the edge of the ground cloth and crawled inside the warm sleeping bag.

It was lined with soft flannel and felt wonderfully comfortable in spite of not having an air mattress underneath. It smelled like Jake. She suddenly felt exhausted. With her belly full, a nice clean bath, and a confident feeling of security, the thought of sleep overwhelmed her. She folded her hands underneath her face and fell asleep almost immediately while thinking about Jake.

Jake set about erasing their campfire ring. He scattered its stones haphazardly around the sandy site and piled sand over all the evidence of their fire. He looked around to make sure they hadn't left any of their stuff lying around. He then stripped, leaving his clothing in a pile next to the pool and got in the water. He lay down on the sandy bottom and scooped up some of the yucca soap, lathering his hair. He rinsed it out then grabbed for some more and lathered up again. He stood in the water and soaped down his whole body, scrubbing away at the grit with his fingernails. He sank back down letting the water cover his body, rinsing him clean. He swished more water through his hair and stood up again. He tossed the stone containing the yucca soap into the bushes at the back of the pool. He then stepped out of the water onto a flat rock and stood in the cool evening air, allowing natural evaporation to dry the moisture from his skin. He ran his fingers through his thick hair, slicking it back from his face and out of his eyes, using his fingers for a comb. He'd have to remember to borrow Carrie's hairbrush in the morning.

When he was mostly dry, he decided to run up the stairs naked and grab the extra pair of clean underwear he always carried in his pack. He had forgotten to bring it down with him earlier. He stood on the bottom stone step and took one final look around the area. Anyone coming along and stopping at the spring in the dark would never know anyone had been there tonight. He ran up the stairs and into the tiny stone enclosure. He stopped in his tracks and saw that Carrie was already asleep, curled up like a little girl in his sleeping bag. He didn't know how he would be able to get through the night, sleeping right next to her beautiful warm body, the two of them all alone out here in this magical wilderness. He steeled his mind not to think about things like that. Otherwise, he'd go totally crazy.

He dropped his clothes on the edge of the tarp along with Carrie's shorts, and made sure his hunting knife was within easy reach by his side of their bed. He quickly slipped on his pair of clean under shorts, crawled into the soft flannel, trying not to wake Carrie in the process. Bart stretched out on the tarp next to their sleeping bag. As Jake worked his way slowly further down into the bag, Carrie roused from sleep, sighed softly and snuggled against his body. He couldn't help himself. He wrapped his arms around her and pulled her even closer to his body in a loving embrace.

Carrie's body involuntarily responded to the feel of Jake's warm embrace and she began to rouse from sleep. She could feel her lips almost touching his and inhaled the clean aroma of the yucca soap mixed with Jake's own special smell, which created an immediate assault on all her senses at once. She became more and more aware of the feeling of the entire length of her body, molded to his from head to toe, in the small space of the sleeping bag. She found it impossible to ignore his hardening arousal and the intoxicating effect it was having on her. She opened her sleepy eyes and stared deeply into his, which reflected the starlight of the night sky forming the only roof over their heads.

Jake closed the short distance between their lips with a gentle kiss. Carrie's response was instantaneous as she kissed him back with growing intensity, which caused him to deepen his kisses with a passion barely under his control. His mouth became more demanding and insistent with Carrie's response to the mounting intensity and deepening of his kisses.

Jake reached behind him and unzipped his side of the sleeping bag allowing him more room to move his arms and hands. He lowered his head to taste the sides of her warm neck and throat, inhaling her clean, womanly smell. His hand moved around to the front of her body, pushed her tank top down over her breasts, and closed over one of them. His thumb stroked her already peaked nipple, which instantly hardened even more under his touch. Carrie moaned deeply and arched her body toward him in response. Jake slipped his other arm out from under her body, and raised his body over hers. He dipped his head lower; taking one of her peaked nipples into his mouth and sucked hungrily.

Carrie could barely breathe. Jake's sucking on the taunt bud of her nipple caused an immediate contracting of the nerves that ran down the inside of her belly, connecting her nipples to her womb and the womanly flesh between her legs. She could feel her juices beginning to flow, readying her body for Jake's. She had never experienced such an instant, fevered reaction to anyone before. When Jake switched his hungry mouth to her other nipple, while continuing to explore with his hand the one his mouth had just abandoned; she almost climaxed on the spot. A ragged groan escaped from her throat while she reached out her hands to run them over Jake's exposed flesh. She found she wanted to touch all of his body, reassuring herself that this wasn't just an incredible dream.

Jake responded to Carrie's body with reactions he'd never imagined could be so intense. When she groaned under the ministrations of his hands and mouth on her swelling breasts, he almost lost it completely. He ran his hand down her tight belly and fingered the small band at the top of her silk panties, slipping his fingers past it and into her soft curls underneath. Carrie grabbed the top of his head with both her hands and moaned into his hair, parting her legs to allow him access to her flaming womanly flesh. He slipped his fingers under the silk, deeper between her legs until his fingers found the swollen, erect bundle of nerves he sought. He stroked her gently, causing her to writhe and moan in his embrace. Her panties were soaking wet. He continued his exploration of her deeper between her legs until his fingers found her opening. He slid first one, then another finger inside of her, gently probing deeper and deeper, massaging the walls of her passage, until he could feel the very opening of her womb.

Carrie was clawing at him frantically, running her hands down his chest and belly until she reached the top of his underwear. She slipped her hand beneath the elastic and wrapped it tightly around his huge erection. She stroked and caressed his body like a fine-tuned instrument, causing him to nearly lose his mind. He withdrew his fingers from Carrie and tore off the thin silk panties that formed the last barrier between him and his goal. She quickly slipped her tank top over her head and then reached for Jake's underwear, clawing at them, indicating for him to quickly remove them. He slipped them down his hips and threw back the top part of the sleeping bag covering them. He feasted on the vision of her beautiful body in the starlight, open and ready and pleading for him.

He closed the distance between them and kissed her deeply,

murmuring words of love into her hungry mouth. She babbled love-speak back at him and again reached frantically for his swollen erection that was probing at her searchingly between her legs. She was wide open and ready for him. He allowed her to guide his rigid flesh to her opening, where he slowly began to enter her body. He maintained the most control he had ever mustered in his life, because he wanted to give Carrie the maximum pleasure possible before he succumbed to his own. He sank deeper and deeper until he was buried to the hilt, with the head of his erection gently teasing the opening of her cervix. Carrie writhed, crying out for completion, using primal thrusting, rhythmic movements of her body.

He began to move inside her, matching her body, thrust for thrust. He teasingly pulled almost out of her until she would clutch his hips, crying out, pleading and begging with him, not to leave her body. Then he'd sink back down inside her, gradually increasing the frequency of this pace until Carrie screamed out his name and he felt the violent contractions of her body's climax. Only then did he allow himself to slip over the edge along with her, flooding her with his musky male essence.

Jake collapsed over her body, covering her with tender kisses. Her eyes were hooded and damp with unshed tears of passion. He kissed each of her eyelids gently, savoring her salty taste.

"Carrie, my darling Carrie. I can't come up with words to describe what this experience has done to me. I've never felt anything to equal it in my life! It's like I've found the other half of my soul, the piece that has been keeping me from feeling complete, until now. I swear, these past few days with you have completely changed me forever."

"I can't even think straight, Jake. I've never responded to a man with all my heart and soul at once. I never knew making love could be like this and I've never had my body feel so hungry and out of control. I know we've only known each other for a few days, but love doesn't always follow a set timetable. When it's right, your heart knows its right." She sighed and kissed his face, nuzzling her body into to him, basking in the hazy afterglow of the greatest sex she had ever experienced.

Jake rolled off the top of her, pulling her along with him so they would remain joined. She draped her top leg over him, locking them together. He pulled the top of the sleeping bag over them to keep off the increasing chill of the night air. He wrapped her tightly in his arms, holding her as close to his body as he could get her.

Carrie murmured to him, "I'm feeling lethargic, sated and, oh, so sleepy now, Jake. It must be illegal to feel this heavenly." She was asleep almost before she finished her last sentence. Jake drifted off right behind her, wishing they could go on like this forever.

Chapter Six

Jake awoke with a start when he heard Bart emit a low, rumbling growl and felt him stand up on the tarp next to them.

"Bart, quiet! Sit down, Bart, and stay! No noise, Bart." Bart sat down as told, but Jake could see his ears still cocked forward, listening intently to sounds only he could hear. Jake held his breath and listened as intently as he could. He knew Bart could hear things much farther away than he could. Bart was staring intently out the door in the direction of the lower trail.

Soon, Jake could also hear noises and voices approaching, moving purposely up the trail. He heard the sound of the hoof beats of one donkey, maybe two. He could hear voices coming from two different men as they spoke Spanish back and forth to each other. He could understand enough of their conversation to know they were going to stop at the spring for water and a brief rest. His heart beat faster in a speeding rhythm. If he and Bart and Carrie could be absolutely silent, maybe the men would pass by without ever realizing they were there. He couldn't think of any reason why they would climb up to the stone house, unless, of course, they heard a noise coming from it.

Carrie stirred when the cool night air hit her body as Jake sat up in their bed, his body lifting the top of it off of her. He reached down and clamped his hand tightly over her mouth. Her eyes immediately flew open in alarm. He leaned close to her ear and whispered.

"Carrie, it's alright. I need you to be absolutely silent and don't make a single sound. Not even a move!" He could see the fear and questions in her eyes in the starlight.

"There are some men with donkeys down by the spring. They aren't nice people, Carrie. They are drug runners, called "mules". They have one or two donkeys with them, which I'm sure, are loaded down with drugs. If we're silent and don't make a single sound, they won't know we're here." He saw absolute terror wash over her expression. She shook her head up and down, indicating she understood what he was telling her.

He removed his hand from her mouth and continued whispering close to her ear. "I can understand their Spanish. They are stopping only briefly, just to get water for themselves and their donkeys. Then they'll move on. They only come through here in the dark, never in daylight when they would be seen by the border patrol or DEA agents." He placed a steadying hand on Bart, telling him with his body language to stay still. Bart was trembling with the effort to stay seated and not bark at the intruders he felt were threatening them in the night.

Jake heard the alarmed snorting and shuffling of the donkeys when they smelled Bart's scent on the air. One of the men swore at the donkeys, and he could hear the two men discussing what could have upset their donkeys. He listened to the men splashing in the water and heard the gurgle of water filling canteens. At that moment, some coyotes began to yelp and howl across the canyon from the spring. Jake heard the men laugh to their donkeys. "Aye, solamente coyotes, loco burros." Her eyes wide with terror, Carrie silently mouthed the words "What did they say?" to Jake.

"They said 'Its only coyotes, crazy donkeys.' Those coyotes probably just saved our lives. The men thought their donkeys were upset by smelling the coyotes instead of Bart." Jake could identify the noises made by the donkeys drinking from the spring pool.

He placed his index finger in front of his lips, indicating no more talking. He heard one of the men approach the bushes next to the stone steps to their room, and his heart momentarily stopped. He silently reached for his hunting knife and prepared himself for what might happen next. He tightened his grip on Bart's fur, which was standing up in alarm along the ridge of his spine.

Carrie heard the same sound of the approaching stranger, too. When Jake grabbed his hunting knife, she almost stopped breathing; she was so paralyzed with fear. They both listened to the sound of a zipper being unzipped, and then the sound of a stream of urine hitting the bushes and ground. When the man finished urinating, they heard him zip his pants back up then walk away from the stone steps. They could hear the men driving their donkeys away from the spring and back out onto the main trail. The men's voices became fainter as they spoke back and forth to each other, as they slowly began making their way on up the canyon trail.

Jake and Carrie didn't move a muscle until they could no longer hear the men or their donkeys at all. They remained still as stones for a good ten minutes after that. Jake knew sounds carried a long way in the desert air. They barely breathed and Bart continued to tremble the whole while. Jake kept his hand on Bart's back making sure he wouldn't suddenly bolt, and bound up the trail after the men he felt were a threat. Bart's protective instincts ran deep.

Jake finally let out a long breath and stood up, slowly uncoiling his cramped muscles. Bart jumped up, too. "Bart, you stay here, you hear me? No running off and attracting any attention. We dodged one, Bart, and I don't need you scaring up any extra trouble."

"Jake, why didn't you tell me that drug runners used this trail. You let me believe that we were all alone and perfectly safe out here. How could you do that to me? I feel like you tricked me!"

Jake stooped down close to Carrie's face and took hold of both of her arms. "Look, Carrie. They don't come along here every single night. If I had told you about them, it would have scared the living daylights out of you, probably for no reason. That wouldn't have done us any good. You were worried enough about our predicament without adding something that might not even happen to the mix. I knew I could handle anything that might come along. Me and Bart, together, that is." He smiled into her eyes reassuringly.

"Well, I still think you should have warned me," she pouted prettily, sitting naked on the sleeping bag with her beautiful breasts bathed in the starlight. Her eyes met Jake's and she instantly read the thoughts running through his mind. He tried to control his wandering mind, and eyes, and return to being sensible.

"Carrie, we should try to get some more sleep before daylight. We've got a long day tomorrow and its still a couple hours 'til dawn, yet." He watched hopelessly as Carrie boldly stared at his naked body, which was already beginning to betray his resolve. She provocatively stared at his manhood growing hard for her. He groaned and sank down on the sleeping bag next to her, gathering her in his arms and pulling her back down on the bed with him.

"Tell me you forgive me, Witch, or I'll torture you until you do," he teased her, while nibbling on her earlobe and fondling her exposed breasts.

She answered him in a smoky voice. "Well, if you put it like that, then maybe I won't tell you I forgive you, until you've done your worst with me, or should I say, you're best?"

"But, wait a minute, Jake. I'm worried about more of those drug runners coming along. Suppose they came along just when I was crying out with the intense pleasure you were giving me? Or heard us laughing and moaning together making love? My God! When I think what could have happened to us, it scares me to death! I'm still afraid, and I don't feel like we're so safe anymore out here."

"Carrie, its not a freeway out on that trail. Those guys are long gone. They need to be to their destination before dawn with their load of drugs. No one else would be coming along anymore, because they wouldn't have enough time left to make it to the top of the trail before daylight. Besides, Bart would warn us. He hears sounds long before humans can hear them. He was the one who woke me up when he heard those other guys coming."

Jake could sadly see that Carrie was too nervous to enjoy anymore lovemaking this night. She was wound tighter than a drum. He could see the raw hunger in her eyes, mixed with fear and uncertainty. He knew she would never be able to relax and enjoy the pleasure he longed to give her. He gave up any plans he had for that and decided they could enjoy each other tomorrow night, in the safety of the village of San Vicente. He settled back in their sleeping bag and pulled Carrie close to him under the warm bedding, cradling her head against his chest.

"Lets try to get another couple hours of sleep, Carrie. Like I said before, Bart will warn us of any approaching trouble. Please try not to worry, Honey." He was hoping she could relax enough to go back to sleep rather than lay there and worry the rest of the night. Bart had settled back down in his spot on the tarp next to their sleeping bag.

Carrie relaxed her head on Jake's shoulder and looked up at the bright stars overhead. She decided to try concentrating on something other than the horror of what might have happened to them if those men had heard or discovered them in their stone room. It was true that Jake had his hunting knife, and Bart offered some protection, but what if those men had been carrying guns? Neither Jake nor Bart would have had a chance. And then what might have happened to her? She thought that if she were lucky, they'd only have killed her but doubted she'd have gotten off that easily. They'd kill her afterwards. Ugh. It was too disturbing. She didn't want to think about it anymore. She had to concentrate on something else.

Staring up at the night sky, Carrie whispered to Jake. "Jake, do you know the names of any of the stars up there? I can see a large reddish-colored one that I think might be the planet Mars."

"I know the names of a few of them from looking at them pass overhead my whole life. You're right about the red one being Mars. See that really big one over there? He asked, pointing to a large star in that he knew to be in the north part of the sky.

"I think I know the one you are talking about. It's bigger than the others, right?"

"That one is called Polaris, commonly known as the North Star.

As long as you can find that one, you'll always know which direction is north and won't get lost. Its been used for navigation by people for eons. Now look at that huge one directly over us." Jake pointed straight up. "Notice there are two other large ones fairly close to it, which sort of together form a giant triangle. The big one is called Vega, and the other two are named Altair and Deneb. You can always see them directly over head this time of the night during April, from this part of the country. I would guess from their position right now that it's about four o'clock in the morning. Dawn will begin breaking about six o'clock."

"How do you know all that, Jake? You sound like an astronomer!" Carrie was impressed with his seeming knowledge of the heavens, which she half jokingly considered to make sense, since he was so heavenly himself.

"I took a couple of astronomy courses in college. I've always loved looking at the bright clear Texas night skies, and I decided to find out more about what I was seeing. They helped give me some science credits, besides," he joked.

"What else did you study in college? Did you graduate with a degree in something particular? Carrie was hungry to know more about Jake's life and his past.

"I finally got a degree in agriculture, in animal husbandry, actually. I figured that would be of the most value in running the ranch. We raise mostly cattle and a few crops on the part of the ranch where there are some water wells. We raise feed for our own cattle, since range land grazing often needs to be supplemented with hay or alfalfa."

"How big is your ranch?"

"We have twenty-thousand acres here on the main ranch, which adjoins Big Bend National Park. We also have some scattered acreage further west of here, in some two-thousand to five-thousand acre parcels. We have oil wells on those, but only a few cattle. Its even drier out there than it is here, and the range won't support many animals at all."

Carrie was stunned. She had never heard of anyone owning that much land. Being from the east, where people were lucky to have a small lawn to mow, the number of acres Jake talked about sounded like small states!"

"It sounds like you own most of Texas, Jake! How many cattle do you have?"

Jake laughed. He was used to eastern people having trouble comprehending the large size of Texas ranches. His was much larger than most, though, even for Texas.

"Only about twenty-thousand right now. The cattle market goes up and down and right now its starting to go up again. We had a lot of good calves this spring, so our herd is growing. We'll probably sell off quite a few next fall, so we won't have so many to feed next winter."

Carrie shook her head in disbelief. She didn't think she'd seen twenty-thousand cattle in her whole life! How could anyone possibly own or keep track of so many animals? It was beyond her.

"My turn, Carrie. I'm sure you have an education, so tell me, what was your specialty?"

"I got my MFA in Fine Arts from the University of New Hampshire, with photography being my emphasis. I've always loved to take pictures so when I graduated, I got my job where I work now. I've worked my way up the ladder, so to speak, so now I get some really great assignments, like the one I'm doing now." She couldn't begin to explain to him how the assignment she was doing right now had changed her life, forever, she was sure.

"Do you have family? Parents, or any brothers or sisters?"

"Sadly, no. I am an only child and both of my parents died in an automobile accident just after I finished college. My boss, Diana, who is also my best friend, has been like a mother to me ever since. She sort of adopted me and I never would have survived without her. I inherited my parents small apartment in New York, which is where I live when I'm not gone on an assignment." Carrie's voice sounded sad and lonely when she spoke about herself being pretty much all alone in the world.   Jake pulled her closer to him, protectively, wishing he could shield her from some of the hurt.

"Geez, I'm sorry, Carrie.   It must feel awful when you think of being an orphan.   My own parents retired to Palm Springs several years ago, but at least I still know they are there, even though I don't see them very often anymore."

Neither one of them asked the other the questions they really wanted answers to.   Jake wanted to ask if there was anyone special in Carrie's life at the moment, and Carrie wanted to know the same about Jake.   They both suspected that there wasn't anyone the other one was currently involved with, based on general comments they had made to each other in prior conversations.   But each of them was curious about whom had been important to the other in the past, and why they were unattached right now.

Jake knew that someday he needed to tell Carrie about Rachel and the baby.   He could see that their relationship was deepening, and he'd need to put that story behind him.   But he worried about what she might think about him after hearing the story.   Would she blame him for what happened, as he still sometimes did himself?   Would she wonder why Jake couldn't keep Rachel safe?   Was there something more he could have done to save them that he failed to do?   He just couldn't deal with that right now.   As he had said to Carrie earlier, it was time to try to get a little more sleep.   He noticed Carrie's breathing even out into the regular pattern of someone whom had drifted off to sleep.   He prayed he could do the same.

He must have fallen asleep himself, for when he next became aware, the stars had faded and the sky was getting light.   He lay still and watched Carrie sleep.   God, she was beautiful!   And just as beautiful on the inside as she was on the outside.   What a rare and priceless combination, he marveled.   He was determined to figure out how to make her his own, whatever it took.   He didn't want to own her like a possession, but to have her share her life with him.   He wanted to wake up with her in his arms like this every morning, for the rest of his life.

Jake slipped out of the sleeping bag, gathered his clothes and headed down to the spring to relieve himself, wash up a little, and take a look around the area. Bart rose and followed him outside and down the stone steps. Jake could immediately see the tracks of the men and their donkeys in the sand around the pool. He washed up and dressed and followed their tracks for a ways back up the trail to make sure they were really gone. Bart nosed around the area and Jake could tell from his reaction that the men were no longer nearby.

Jake turned and went back down the trail to the spring and was surprised to see Carrie standing next to the pool, already dressed. He must have been gone longer than he thought, intent on making sure the drug runners were not still in their area.

"Where were you, Jake? I woke up and you were gone. I came down to the pool, washed, and quickly dressed to go looking for you. Then I realized that I had no way of knowing which way you went. I was worried that something awful might have happened to you, after what happened last night."

"I'm sorry, Carrie. I guess I was gone a little longer than I had intended. I wanted to be sure those guys were really gone, and I found out that they are, really gone, that is." The sky was totally light now and the sun was beginning to rise over the east ridges of the canyon.

"We need to eat our granola bars, pack up our gear and hit the trail." Jake took off up the stairs to get their packs. Carrie followed after him.

"I can help. I'm sure you could use help rolling up the sleeping bag and folding up the ground tarp." She followed him into the little stone room and looking around, thought to herself that she was really going to miss the place. It was where she had spent the most thrilling and exciting night of her life. She could see by the look on Jake's face that he was thinking similar thoughts, and this pleased her enormously. He smiled lovingly at her.

"Hey, I thought this was the best motel I've ever had the privilege of staying overnight in," he said half jokingly, and half seriously.

"I was just thinking the same thing myself. And you'll have to agree, the price was right," she added with a jaunty smile.

They shared the job of getting the bedding together and Jake put everything back into his pack. Carrie picked up her daypack, took one last fleeting look around, and started down the stone steps. Then Carrie hesitated before stepping out the door of the little room.

"Wait a minute, Jake. I just want to get a few more shots of our little room." Carrie wanted these photos for her own private collection of memories. She wanted to be able to take them out and remember the time they shared here together when she was sitting alone in her New York apartment.

Jake waited for her and when they reached the pool, they sat on the sand together and ate the last two granola bars. Jake opened another packet of dog food and gave it to Bart. Except for the one remaining energy bar, this would be all they'd have to eat until they got to the village of San Vicente later in the day. Jake knew they'd have no trouble making it to the village long before dark, as Carrie was turning out to be a strong hiker and could clearly handle the rugged trail.

When they'd finished eating, Jake stuck their food wrappers into an outside pocket of his pack for later disposal. He got their hiking sticks out of some desert willow bushes, where he had hidden them the night before. He was more than glad he had been so careful after their unwelcome visitors in the night. The presence of their hiking sticks might have given them away. He handed Carrie her stick. She had her camera around her neck, handy for the pictures he knew she wanted to take along the trail. She had taken a few photos around the spring yesterday evening and more in this morning's light. She anticipated getting some excellent shots as they approached the river and made their way to the village for the night.

They walked steadily downhill for what seemed like hours, stopping now and then for Carrie to take photos and take drinks of water to keep from dehydrating. As the sun rose higher in the sky over them, the temperature in the canyon became almost unbearable. Jake used a canvas fold up dog bowl he carried in his pack to give Bart drinks of water whenever they stopped along the trail.

Jake spoke back over his shoulder, "Carrie, we should find a shady spot to stop and eat our last power bar and rest for a while. It's too darn hot to walk for the next couple hours. We need to hole up until the sun starts going back down. We only have about another two hours to the river and its about noon right now. Even if we stop for two hours, we'll still make it to San Vicente village way before dark."

"I'll vote for that idea. I'm beat and I need something in my stomach, even if it's half of a power bar. Poor old Bart's tongue is hanging out, and I think he needs another drink of water, too."

"This looks like a pretty good place up here. There's some shade from those boulders and some soft sand, besides."

Jake looked around the area carefully, banging on and poking around the nearby rocks with his hiking stick to make sure there weren't any snakes with the same idea they had. Suddenly, from behind one of the larger rocks, a six-foot long, two-inch thick black and white striped snake slithered out across the sand. Bart jumped after it, nipping at its tail and barking at it, as if to hurry it on its away.

Carrie leaped back away from the sandy area and screamed, "My God, Jake. That's the biggest snake I've ever seen! Is it poisonous? Yikes! We can't stay here!" She shuddered and stood stone still looking all around her, as if expecting to see more snakes crawling out from the rocks around her.

"It's a Texas King Snake, Carrie. They're harmless, even though they can grow to be quite large. That one's a doozy! I'm more concerned about rattlesnakes and Copper Heads. Those can be a serious problem. These Kings just look scary. The native peoples around here carve them onto their hiking sticks for good luck. They paint pictures of them on their houses, tourist trinkets, and pottery, etc. They are quite popular with people around here." The snake disappeared off into some brush and rocks across the trail from them.

"Well, they aren't popular with me, I can guarantee you that! I'm still pretty much a city girl and my outdoor experiences have been in areas where the only snakes like that are in zoos! They give me the willies, I can't help it. Are you sure there aren't anymore of them around? I'm scared to sit down next to those rocks now."

"I've banged all around with my stick. That's what scared that one out and I don't think there are anymore. I'll bang around some more, just so you'll feel more secure. Bart never would have fussed after that snake had it been a poisonous one. He can tell the difference, somehow, and gives the poisonous ones a healthy respect."

Jake sat down on the shady sand. Carrie made her way warily over to him and sat down beside him. Jake dug into his pack and pulled out their last power bar. He cut it in half and handing her a piece said, "Bon appetit, Carrie. Hey, I bet you never would have guessed I knew French, ouis, mon cheri?" He gave her an endearing silly grin, clearly pleased with his own teasing.

Jake got out Bart's water bowl and filled it from one of his trail bottles. Bart drained the bowl and looked hungrily at their pieces of power bar. Jake gave him a tiny piece of his and Carrie did the same. He wagged his tail furiously at them and whined. He had his big Bart smile on his face and they both laughed at him together.

"He's such a ham, isn't he? I don't know what I'd do without him. He's been such a fantastic companion for me, Carrie."

"How old is Bart and where did you get him?" Carrie reached out a hand to ruffle Bart's ears affectionately.

"Carlos and Maria's dog had puppies. They were so darn cute and one of them just sort of attached himself to me extra special. That's Bart here. I began to take him with me in the truck and pretty soon, he was going everywhere with me. We became joined at the hip, so they say, and he's been my special pal ever since. That was about three years ago, so I guess old Bart is about three."

They continued eating their last bites in silence, just enjoying sitting quietly together. Carrie occasionally sipped from her

CamelBack water tube.

"Jake, I'm so tired. I'd love to just lay down and sleep a little while, even if it's a few minutes."

Jake jumped up and pulled the nylon ground tarp from his pack. Carrie stood and helped him spread it over the sand. They both sat back down on the tarp.

"Just rest your head on my thighs, like a pillow. I'll just lean back against the rock and we'll both doze off." Bart immediately claimed his spot on the tarp next to them and closed his eyes.

Carrie lay back, turned onto her side and put her head on Jake's legs as he suggested.

"Are you sure you'll be comfortable with your back against that rock, Jake?"

"I think I could sleep standing up right now. Don't worry about me at all."

Carrie listened to the sounds of bees and canyon wrens and a myriad of other sounds humming together in the still desert air. It was so much hotter down here closer to the river. She remembered Jake telling her it was hotter down by the river. Yesterday when they were higher up, they at least had some breeze. Today there was none. She figured it was because the canyon walls blocked a lot of it. Maybe that would mean that it would be windier down on the river itself. She felt herself growing drowsier as she relaxed on Jake's leg and soon she was asleep. Jake managed to doze off as well.

Jake roused first, and noticed the sun was beginning to head down instead of beaming from straight over them. He guessed it was about two o'clock in the afternoon. He noticed that Carrie seemed to be dead to the world asleep. He hated to wake her, but they really needed to get going. There would be plenty of relaxing when they got to the village. Plenty of good food, and even some good tequila. He knew the villagers always had plenty of good tequila around. He could sure go for some of that. He couldn't wait to show Carrie the little village and have her meet his friends there. He knew she'd love it, and them. And talk about a prize photo opportunity! Well the village was probably almost exactly the same as it was hundreds of years ago. She'd think she had gone back in a time machine!

"Carrie, Honey. Wake up. We need to get going, Honey." He shook her gently and stroked her hair lovingly as he spoke to her, coaxing her awake.

"Ugh. I was having a wonderful dream about us, Jake. I didn't want to wake up in the middle of it. I wanted to see how it ended." She stretched out her legs to the edge of the tarp, disturbing Bart from his dog dreams. He stood up and looked at them as if he were trying to figure out if their nap had really ended or not.

"I'm sorry to have to wake you up then, Carrie. I'd like to hear about your dream sometime. And you know Honey; it can end up being anyway that we choose to make it. I don't like to even hear you use the word end. It doesn't have to end, you know? We can choose." Jake looked at her with such love in his eyes she almost melted.

"I suppose we'll get to know each other more and more deeply in the time we have left together. This whole adventure, as I like to call it, feels like one of those staged encounter groups, where people are forced to work together in some challenging situation which causes them to get to know each other very intently in a short period of time. Do you know what I'm talking about? They have them all the time for executives and managers in companies. They want them to develop a team feeling with each other and they need to develop the commitment over a long weekend." She smiled up at him, waiting for his take on her theory.

"Well, this past two days sure has created a feeling of commitment about us being a team in me! I'd be willing to run the company with you any day, Carrie."

He learned over and kissed her gently on the lips, then jumped to his feet and reached to pull her up with him. He reached down and began shaking out and folding up their tarp before putting it back into his backpack. He picked up Bart's bowl and added it to the top and zipped it closed.

"If we don't get going right now, I'll be lost. You weaken my resolve to go on instead of making passionate love to you right here and now. I want you and need you so much, Carrie. But I know we'll enjoy each other so much more when we're safely at San Vicente. I can't wait for you to experience it, and also what I have in mind for you tonight, my sweet." He wiggled his eyebrows at her teasingly.

"Oh, Jake! You are too much! I'll be thinking about what you just said all the rest of the way down the trail, though. I'll be expecting quite a lot from you tonight then," she teased. "You'd better not disappoint me."

"Oh, don't you worry, Carrie dear. I guarantee you won't be disappointed. I'll stake my life on that."

He turned and started back down the trail. They walked another two hours as the sun set more behind Mariscal Mountain and the shadows continued to lengthen up the canyon walls. Soon, the brush in the bottom of the canyon began to thicken and change as it had up near the spring yesterday. There were more desert willows and as they got closer to the river, the trail got sandier and the willows began looking more tree-like. Suddenly, they rounded a bend in the trail and the Rio Grande River was right there in front of them. They both stopped and stared at it and smiles lit both of their faces. Jake turned and gave Carrie a high five.

"We made it, Babe! You're incredible, you know? This wasn't an easy thing to do. I want you to know I'm awfully impressed with you, being a city girl and making it clear down to the river from way up there." He turned and pointed back up the trail heading back into the canyon and snaking all the way almost to the top of Mariscal Mountain. From down her, it looked like Mt Everest!

"Well, Jake. I've done my share of hiking up and down big mountains before, just never in a desert climate. This was an entirely different experience. Look! she shouted, pointing to the river and laughing.

Bart had leaped right into the water and was splashing around like a puppy, lapping up the fresh water. They watched his antics for a few minutes, then Jake whistled to Bart to get out. He turned and started walking down a trail along the edge of the river, speaking to Carrie as she followed.

"The village is down this trail about a mile and a half. It won't be long now. We'll go past a small natural hot spring. There's another one just outside the village of San Vicente, too, on the Mexico side. The villagers use it like a big hot tub. You're going to love it."

They walked along the river and Carrie marveled at the difference in the feeling of the river area from that of up on top. There were lots more insects in the air and the bushes; big flies, and even an occasional mosquito. There were more birds, as well, and occasional plants that looked like squat palm trees. Carrie had been quite surprised to see so many colorful butterflies in the desert. She had seen some flitting from cactus blossom to cactus blossom all along the trail. She had never known that butterflies lived in the desert, and the ones she had seen so far were gorgeous. She continued snapping pictures all along the trail. Soon she could see a small adobe village on a hillside above the other side of the river.

"Is that San Vicente, Jake? It certainly isn't very big." She sounded doubtful about their prospects for the night in so small of a place.

"Why this is a metropolis for down here, Carrie! Don't you worry. You'll see what I mean when we get there."

They approached a flat rocky area closer to the river with a small, water-filled pool. It looked like someone had built the small ten-foot square pool out of flat rocks, gathered from around the immediate area. Carrie could see flat stone stairs leading down into the pool all around the edges of the little wall. It was only about two feet deep and had a sandy bottom. She reached down to touch the inviting-looking water. It was hot, like the temperature of bath water. There were bamboo plants growing thickly along one edge of it.

"This is the little hot spring I told you about. There's another one like it across the river outside of the village, only a bit farther back from the river. It's closer to the source of the hot spring and one of the pools over there is hotter than this one, almost the temperature of a hot tub instead of a bath."

Jake looked up to see a Mexican man waving at them. Jake waved back to the man and shouted something in Spanish that Carrie couldn't understand. She watched the man go over to a small boat tied up at the edge of the river, get in and start rowing it across the river toward them. He soon reached their side, beached the boat and got out to greet Jake with a huge smile. Carrie snapped several pictures of this episode.

He and Jake shook hands then Jake introduced Carrie to the man in Spanish.

"Carrie this is Manuel. We've known each other since we were boys together."

Carrie smiled at the man and shook his hand. Jake told Manuel that Carrie didn't speak Spanish, but Carrie's warm smile and the offer of her hand told Manuel all he needed to know about her friendliness and acceptance of him. Carrie found it impossible to guess his age; he was so sun-baked from living in the desert all his life. He was about five feet, four inches tall, with sparkling dark brown eyes. He had straight black, collar-length, blunt-cut hair. He wore a pair of light cotton pants and a white cotton shirt. He had on a broad-brimmed straw hat and a pair of leather sandals.

Jake loaded their packs into the boat. Bart jumped in, too.

"Wait, you're forgetting our hiking sticks, Jake." Carrie turned and picked them both up.

"We won't need those anymore, Carrie. We'll be taking one of these boats the rest of the way to the main road tomorrow."

"Well, I'm going to keep mine forever as a souvenir of this adventure with you. It'll be my most prized possession from this trip. I couldn't stand to just leave it along the riverbank here in the sand. Not with what I've been through with it," she laughed.

"Since you put it like that, I'll take mine and keep it forever, too. Who knows, if we get lucky, we may need to do this again sometime."

"I hope you're kidding," she replied sternly. I don't know that I'll ever drive off the main road again with you, Jake Stockton."

He could tell by her stance and the twinkle in her eye that she was kidding. He thought to himself, that by the time they got back to civilization, he hoped she'd drive anywhere with him. At least he was going to do his very best to coax her to that conclusion. Starting tonight. He got in the boat and held out his hand to help her keep her balance until she got seated. Manuel pushed the boat out into the river current then climbed in himself and began rowing them across to his little village of San Vicente.

Chapter Seven

The trip across the Rio Grande River took less than five minutes. During the spring, the river is only two to five feet deep. In the late summer of a dry year, a person can almost walk across without even getting wet. During the time it took for them to get into the boat and cross the river, Carrie saw many people appear out of the bushes growing along the riverbank on the Mexico side. There were laughing, curious, brown-skinned children of all ages, some burros, miscellaneous dogs, and several men from the village. The village men waded into the river and helped stabilize their little boat as Manuel guided it up onto the rocky shore.

Carrie had been taking camera shots of these scenes from the boat. As she was helped out onto the shore, children clustered around her, openly staring at the beautiful blonde, fair-skinned "señorita." They chattered away at her in Spanish and she returned their chatter by smiling warmly and saying "hola," which Jake had taught her meant "hello" in Spanish. The children giggled with gap-toothed grins at her speaking Spanish to them and reached out trying to hold her hands. One of the men shouted something to them in Spanish and they backed away a bit, giving her some room to move. They reminded her of the gypsy children that she had seen in Europe, only when these children stepped back from her, she still had her camera!

One of the Mexican men meeting them at the beach spoke

English.   Jake motioned Carrie over to where he and Jake stood talking on the shore.

"Carrie, I'd like you to meet Alcalde Jose Diaz. He is the Mayor of San Vicente and a good friend of mine for many years. We'll be staying with Jose and his wife, Carmen, at their home tonight. The Spanish word "alcalde" means "mayor."

Carrie extended her hand warmly to Alcalde Diaz.   "My name is Carrie Turner and I'm very pleased to meet you Mayor Diaz. Jake has told me all about your village on our long trip down the trail.   I'm excited to be here.   I wish I spoke Spanish, so I could talk with all of your people while I'm here." As she spoke, she gestured toward the children and the other men, busily unloading their packs from the boat.

"Don't worry, Señorita. Señor Jake speaks Spanish and a lot of our people speak some broken English picked up from tourists. With your kindness, great beauty, and Señor Jake at your side, you won't have any trouble communicating."

"You are more than kind, Mayor Diaz. I'm looking forward to meeting Carmen and the rest of your family and the other villagers, as well."

"Please call me Jose, Señorita Turner. Jake told me briefly how you two came to be down here today, but I look forward to hearing the rest of the exciting story over dinner tonight. Everyone will want to know of your adventure on Mariscal Mountain."

"Please call me Carrie, Jose. Our trip down the trail was mostly uneventful, though." Carrie shot Jake a warning glance that clearly indicated to him that she didn't want him telling people about any of their most private events along the way. She watched him grinning at her like a Cheshire cat, clearly letting her know that he knew exactly which events she was talking about. Carrie blushed furiously, which caused a fraternal grin to briefly flash from Jose to Jake.

"You must be tired from your trip. We'll go up to the village now and I'll show you around and my wife Carmen will get you settled. You can rest a while before dinner. Carmen will have a room ready for your stay with us. We have a very small guesthouse next to our house that we use for our special visitors, like Señor Jake, here. We are so happy you and Jake are here to visit with us Señorita Carrie."

Jose called to the villagers who were shouldering Jake and Carrie's packs and spoke what were clearly some instructions to them in Spanish. The men quickly disappeared up the trail from the river to the village. Jake and Carrie were led over to the burros and it became clear to Carrie that they were supposed to ride these beasts. She shot Jake an alarmed look.

"I've never ridden on a burro before, Jake. I've never even been on a horse! I don't know how to make it go where I want it to go!" She tried to keep the hysteria out of her voice and smiled graciously at the man waiting to help her up onto her burro.

"Don't worry about a thing, Carrie. The burro only goes two directions. If he's at the river, he goes home to the village. If he's at the village, he goes down to the river. The burros all know to go to the mayor's house. That's where they get fed. All you have to do is hold on to the saddle with both hands."

Carrie watched Jake climb onto his burro. She couldn't help but laugh out loud when she saw Jake's long legs hang down almost to the ground on his small burro. She gritted her teeth and accepted help getting up on her burro. She stuck her feet into the stirrups and held onto the saddle horn for dear life. When the little burro seemed to be behaving itself, she let go of the saddle horn and pointed her camera at Jake and snapped what would end up being one of her favorite photos of him. He wasn't expecting it at all and so she was able to get a totally candid shot of him. That had been hard to do but she had managed to get a few surreptitious pictures when he was busy and didn't notice her camera pointed at him. She thought proudly to herself that she didn't get paid the big bucks for nothing.

With a whistling sound from the man who helped her get on her burro, the critter was off and running. Luckily, Carrie had put down her camera a grabbed hold of the saddle horn just before the burro bolted and ran.   Jake's burro immediately ran to catch up with Carrie's and crowded alongside hers as if it wanted to race to the village.   Carrie was definitely not interested in a race!   The burro's owners trotted alongside them whistling and speaking commands in Spanish.   The burros were obviously paying no attention whatsoever to what the men were saying.

"Jaaaake! Do something!" Carrie yelled.   She was bouncing up and down on the little burro as it ran over the steep rocky parts of the trail, then it slowed a little as it plowed through the deep sandy lower areas.   Soon it headed up a steep incline leading the rest of the way up the small bluff where the village was perched.

"Just hang on, Carrie. He'll stop when he gets up the hill to Jose's house!"   Jake was laughing hard, watching Carrie clutch the little burro's saddle with all her might.   He couldn't help notice that she, too, was laughing all the way up the trail, and swearing at her beastie in her best New York cab driver language.   She was certainly being a good sport.

They were being followed by a parade of villagers laughing and chattering watching the show Carrie was putting on.   Their burros came to a stop in a cloud of enveloping dust in front of a wooden hitch railing out front of Jose's house.   Jake's burro again kept crowding against the side of Carrie's burro, squishing her leg in between.

"Get your burro over, Jake! I can't even get off this critter with yours crowding mine so closely."   One of the burro drivers pushed his way between the two burros, separating them so Carrie could dismount.   She got off and staggered backwards, trying to get her balance on shaky legs.   Her butt and thighs already felt sore, from bouncing up and down on the hard leather saddle all the way from the river. She probably wouldn't be able to move by tomorrow.

"I think I'll walk back to the river tomorrow and let the burro have a day off."   She was rubbing her pretty bottom and shaking out her leg muscles while grimacing.   Underneath the grimace, was a smile, though. Jake's heart swelled at the sight of his New York princess making the best of an authentic Mexican everyday village experience. She'd remember this, all right, he thought to himself.

Carrie stood in the street and studied the village around her. Most of the buildings were made of adobe. Some had been coated with what looked like a plaster-like substance that was a light gray color. An occasional plaster-coated building had been painted with white paint. Other small homes were built of the same native stone as the little spring house they had stayed in the night before along the trail. The streets were wide and made of small stones and dirt. She could see what looked like a bar on the corner down the block and across from it was a very small church. There were windows and door openings along the walls of the buildings, but few had actual doors and there wasn't any glass in the window frames. A couple of the doors she saw were only screen doors.

It was extremely hot in the village. She guessed the temperature had to be in the hundreds even though it was late afternoon. There was a breeze up on the bluff where the village stood, which she guessed is why they located here, above the river. She also surmised that it would be protected up here in case the river ever flooded. There were some chickens and some goats roaming around loose and she noticed that some of the houses had small gardens surrounded by low adobe walls next to them. The mayor's home was much larger than the others were, and he had some solar panels mounted on a pole next to his. There was no evidence of any other electricity, with the exception of the bar, which also had visible solar panels. There was also no evidence of any running water. She could see what looked like outhouses behind some of the houses and other buildings.

There were two more traditional looking buildings down the street in the opposite direction. She was curious about these and figured that she'd find out about them on the tour that Jose had promised to take them on after they were settled. She'd wait and take photos at that time.

She noticed lots of children running around in and out of each other's little houses. They appeared to be playing together. There was an occasional tiny child peeking shyly out of a doorway at them. She thought to herself that this was an incredible way to grow up, with the entire village essentially being your home and family. It was clear that the whole village was like one big extended family.

A short, heavyset friendly looking woman came out of the house carrying a baby. It was impossible to guess her age. Jose stepped up to her to lead her forward.

"My friends, this is my wife, Carmen, and our youngest son Pepe." He beamed proudly at her. She speaks a little English, but not as much as I do."

Carrie spoke up first feeling relaxed by the woman's warm smile. "Hello, Carmen. My name is Carrie, and I'm very happy to meet you. It is so kind of you to have us as your guests. We'll try to not be a burden on you, with your baby and all to care for."

Jake added his own greetings to Carmen in Spanish. Jake seemed to Carrie to be as at home with Spanish as he was with English. She supposed that growing up this close to the border and knowing so many Mexican people, a kid would learn Spanish at a very early age. Carmen spoke back to Jake as if she had known him for a very long time. Their conversation was easy and relaxed as any you'd expect between good friends.

"Follow me around to the guest house and I'll show you where you'll be staying while you're here. Your things have already been taken there by our friends." Jose led the way around the side of his house to a small stone room, about the size of the stone house by the spring along the trail. It didn't have glass in the windows but had screens, a real wooden door and a roof. It was a little cooler inside than out in the sun, but not much. Inside was a homemade wooden bed with a little bedside table, and a washstand holding a pitcher of water with a small mirror hanging above it. The floors were made of flat stones held together with what looked like mud grout. There were some colorful hand woven rugs on the floor and hand woven drapes which could be pulled across the windows, if desired. There was a chair made of gnarled local wood with a woven seat and back. There was an oil lamp on the washstand and the bedside table held several candles. She could see their packs and hiking sticks had already been brought into the room and deposited on one of the pretty rugs.

"This is just perfect, Jose!" Carrie exclaimed in delight. "What a charming little room. Thank you so much."

"There is an outhouse out behind that our family uses. I'm sorry that I can't offer you more modern conveniences but this is all our village has. Later, the women in the family will take you down to the hot springs for a nice bath. They go every evening before dinner. It is their special time before the men go down. I think it is an experience you will enjoy after a hot day walking down the mountain on the dusty trail. But now, let me show you our village before it starts to get dark." Jose turned and led the way out of the little guest room, closing the door behind them as they left.

Jose proudly showed Carrie around the village. He pointed out the town well, which was used for all their drinking and cooking water. They visited a small church where candles burned brightly on the altar and incense perfumed the air. It was cool inside its thick adobe walls. There was a beautiful statue of the Virgin of Guadalupe along one wall, the patron saint of the people all along the southwestern border regions on both sides of the border. Tiny rose-scented votive candles burned brightly before her, and there were vases of wildflowers amongst the candles.

"Our village is too small to have its own priest, but there is a Padre who visits here once a month. He travels around to all the small villages to celebrate Mass, marry people, baptize the new babies, and conduct funerals for anyone who has died. Everyone in the village helps take care of the church." Jose crossed himself and genuflected as they left the church.

"I'm curious about the more modern looking buildings I saw as we entered the village," Carrie volunteered. "Can you tell me about them? They seem so out of character with the rest of the village."

"The green building on the right down the street is the hospital. But we have no doctor or nurse or medical supplies, so it is empty. The government built it for us but we are too poor to have a doctor or nurse. No one could afford to pay them. This other building to your left, closer to us, is our school. We don't have any teachers, either. Again, we are too poor to pay a teacher, so none will come here to teach our children." Jose looked sad about this situation, but resigned to it. It was just a fact of life in a remote village in Mexico.

"I guess I didn't realize things could be like this just across the border from the USA. I mean, I can see our country across the river, which takes so much for granted, and here you have a church with no priest, a hospital with no doctor, and a school with no teachers! It's hard to make sense out of it for a woman from New York!" Carrie was genuinely concerned for the people living in the little village.

"We are a happy people here, Carrie. A doctor sent by our government visits us once a year to vaccinate the children and see anyone who needs care at no cost to us. You see that dirt road disappearing over the hill over there?" Jose pointed to the south. "That dirt road goes to the next village called Ocampo, 175 miles away. Ocampo is a little bigger than our village, but because it has a paved road connecting it to the city of Monclova, we are able to buy supplies there that we can't provide for ourselves. We have two pick-up trucks and once a month, some of the village men drive to Ocampo for any supplies we need. Sometimes, we take a boat down the river and across to the Big Bend National Park Rio Grande Village store. There we can buy gasoline for our generators and a few other things we might need. We can also use the telephone there."

"How do you pay for these outside supplies? I don't see any way of earning money here to buy anything." Carrie waved her hands around gesturing to nothing but small houses and buildings, no obvious factories or industry of any kind.

"We make lots of things here by hand that we sell to tourists who come down the river. There are many river-rafting companies bringing tourists down the river on adventure trips. They often stop here to eat and buy some of our handmade items. Almost all of the women embroidery blouses, skirts, and dresses to sell. Many of our girls make colorful woven friendship bracelets, which are very popular with your American young people. A lot of men carve beautiful hiking sticks out of our Sotol cactus, much like your own hiking sticks. We charge people to ride the burros up from the river and back."

Jose continued explaining their functioning economy to Carrie in an enthusiastic voice. "When the tourists are here they buy food from us. We serve them authentic homemade Mexican foods like tortillas, refried beans, fried tortilla chips, enchiladas, fresh salsas, Margaritas, chicken and roasted goat meat. They purchase cold beer from our bar and we have cold pop. We have a refrigerator that we run off of a generator for this purpose. The tourists leave generous tips. This is how we manage to buy what we need from the outside."

Carrie shook her head in wonder. "Jose, this is really amazing to me. I so admire how you have carved a working economy out of a place that seems so completely barren."

"Soon there won't be many more tourists coming along. It will be too hot down here. Then we will spend our time making things to sell again when it cools off in the fall. Our big tourist seasons are in the spring and fall." Jose explained.

"Do you mean it gets hotter than this?" Carrie asked in amazement.

"Oh, yes, Señorita Carrie. It will be much hotter than this. It will be one-hundred fifteen degrees in the daytime and ninety-five at night. Hardly anyone will visit when it is that hot. Even your National Park across the river will be mostly closed down, as it will receive few visitors except in the Chisos Mountains area, where it is a little cooler."

Carrie shook her head in amazement as they walked back to Jose's house. When they arrived, they were ushered inside. Carmen was busy cooking at their small stove and the fragrances the food produced made the house smell absolutely wonderful. Carrie's stomach began to growl noisily and her mouth watered uncontrollably. She hadn't realized how very hungry she was until now.

She watched as Jake walked over to Carmen speaking to her as he removed the baby from her hip as she cooked. "Give me that little nugget, Carmen, so you can cook using more than one hand."

Jake brought the baby over and sat down next to Carrie. He settled little Pepe comfortably in his arms and spoke to the baby gently in Spanish, then English. "Pepe, this is Carrie, a nice American lady. She's my good friend." The baby gurgled happily and used Jake's big fingers for teethers. Pepe smiled broadly at Carrie and his shiny dark eyes sparkled from is little brown face. Jake jiggled him on his lap and Pepe let out a hearty laugh in response.

Carrie reached out and gave Pepe her hand. The baby took it and immediately brought her hand straight to his mouth to taste her. She laughed and Pepe laughed with her. She was utterly amazed how Jake handled the small baby. He was affectionate and comfortable with the child. She couldn't even imagine Clayton ever touching a baby, especially what he would have considered a Mexican street urchin. She chided herself for even thinking of Clayton, but it was just that the contrast between Clayton and the kind of man Jake was, always took her by surprise at the oddest moments.

Carmen put lids on all the pots of food she was cooking and came over to Jake and Carrie. She spoke warmly to Carrie in fairly good English.

"Would you like to go with us to the hot spring to bathe before dinner? It'll help you relax and enjoy the evening with us."

"Carmen, I'd love that. But I don't have any other clothes with me and mine are filthy."

"Don't worry, Señorita Carrie. I already have a plan for you. I have a skirt and blouse that I made that you can have. We can wash your own clothes and hang them up to dry overnight while you sleep. The clothes I made are very pretty and they will look very good on you.   All the women in Mexico wear these kinds of clothes for special occasions.   You will look like a real Mexican lady at the fiesta tonight, no?"   She flashed a conspiratorial grin at Jake and he gave her an approving nod and a sly wink.

"That sounds wonderful, but I insist on paying you for the clothes. I would feel guilty taking the things you need to sell for your family's income."

"No, never!   You are our guest and Jake's special lady.   That is enough for us, as Señor Jake is the best friend we've ever had.   You might not even like these clothes, as I'm sure you are used to much finer American clothes."   I will get them for you.   She turned and disappeared into an adjoining room that looked to Carrie to be their bedroom.   She returned and placed the clothes in Carrie's lap along with a pair of hand made leather sandals.

"Carmen these are so beautiful!"   Carrie exclaimed, genuinely thrilled.   She held up the pure cotton Mexican peasant blouse and a matching ruffled skirt that was gathered at the waist on an elastic band.   Both were hand-embroidered all over with colorful desert flowers and plants.   The handwork was exquisite, and the light cotton fabric was cool and soft.   "Thank you so much.   I don't think I've ever owned anything so colorful and as finely made!"

"You are most welcome, Señorita Carrie.   The sandals are called "guaraches" in Spanish.   They will look much better with your new dress than your dusty boots, no?   Now bring your new clothes and guaraches and follow me to the hot spring and we'll all get ready for this evening's fiesta to celebrate your visit with us."

Carmen took the baby from Jake.   "Pepe needs a bath, too, Señor Jake."   The child began to cry and learned out of Carmen's arms toward Jake, clearly indicating he wanted to stay with Señor Jake.

"It's OK, little nugget.   I'll be here when you're done.   You can sit with me again later."   Jake repeated this in Spanish and Pepe seemed to understand, quit fussing and accept his fate of getting a bath instead of staying with Jake.

They left the little house out the back door off the kitchen and started down a long path, leading down the hill toward a patch of dense shrubbery. On a flat area in between the village and the hot spring, there was a huge community garden being tended by several villagers. The large garden was completely surrounded by a four-foot tall adobe wall. It had a sturdy gate made from Sotol cactus sticks tightly bound together along one side. Carrie watched other villagers hauling water in large pottery jars up from the river to water the carefully tended vegetable plants. Carrie also saw animal pens made from woven cut brush branches that had goats and what looked like rangy milk cows in them. Another pen held a small number of pigs. The ever-present chickens roamed freely about the garden area as well as throughout the village.

They entered the thick willows and desert bamboo and came to a large pool area, built like the one she and Jake had seen on the other side of the river. Other village women and girls were already there, bathing small children and babies as well as themselves. They smiled at her openly in invitation to join them. There were more flat rocks placed around this pool, which gave people a place to stand and dry off without getting so much sand on their feet and clean clothes. Further away from the bathing area some of the women were washing clothes.

Following Carmen's lead, Carrie removed her boots and socks and then removed the rest of her clothing. She felt a little shy and awkward standing there naked, being the only fair-skinned, blond American woman in the group. Then she spied the same yucca root paste as Jake had made for her, in bowls around the edges of the pool. The sight of this small familiar item, one that she recognized in this strange place, eased her awkward feelings. She stepped into the warm water and sat down, letting her whole body sink underneath.

Carmen said something to one of the women washing clothes in Spanish, who got up and came over and gathered up Carrie's dirty hiking clothes and carried them back over to the laundry area. Carrie watched her begin laundering her dirty clothes.

"Carmen, I could have done that myself. I don't need someone else to wash my clothes for me!" She protested.

"It's no problem, Señorita Carrie. It will only take her a moment and she knows exactly how to do it out here. You've never washed your clothes in a spring before, no? Americans have machines to do their laundry, is that not so? I've seen them at the campground near the Rio Grande Village store."

"Yes, Carmen. But I'm not used to having someone do my laundry for me. I use the machines myself," she laughed.

"Thank you so much," Carrie shouted to the woman now rinsing her clothes. The woman turned and smiled at her and proudly held up Carrie's hiking clothes to show her how clean she had gotten them.

"Carrie, the Spanish word for 'thank you' is "gracias." If you remain in this country, it is a word you will probably use often."

"Gracias," Carrie repeated to the woman washing her clothes. "They look so much better now." The woman smiled approvingly at Carrie's use of her native language and brought her clean clothes back and set them on the rock next to her hiking boots.

"I have a rope tied out back of our house. You can drape your wet clothes over it when we get back. They will dry quickly in the breeze." Carmen spoke as she was floating little Pepe on the warm water, after washing him down with the yucca soap. He was giggling and pretending to swim with his mother holding onto him tightly.

Carrie scooped up some yucca and began washing her hair. She then washed down her entire body, leaned back and floated in the warm pool, enjoying the feel of the hot water on her clean skin. Her muscles ached from the long two-day hike down the mountain and the burro ride about finished them off, she thought. She smiled to herself when she thought about how funny Jake looked on his little burro. She thought to herself, she should remember to ask Jose how those little burros could easily carry so much weight.

Carmen climbed out of the pool with little Pepe and began drying him off with a piece of cotton sackcloth. Carrie stepped out and

Carmen passed her a piece of the cloth to use as a towel. Carrie first dried her body and then wrapped the cloth around her wet hair, trying to squeeze out as much moisture as possible. She twisted her hair up in the cloth and tucked it inside of itself, figuring she'd comb it out when she got back to her room and could get her hairbrush out of her daypack.

Next she began putting on the blouse and skirt Carmen had given her. It was only then that she realized that she didn't have any underwear. She suddenly felt totally wanton and blushed; hoping no one else had seen her turn beet red. She looked around sheepishly and noticed none of the other women had underwear, either. Oh, well, she thought to herself. "When in Rome, do as the Romans do." It certainly was a lot cooler.

She gathered up her clean hiking clothes and began walking back up the path to the house. She stopped out back at the rope clothesline Carmen had told her about and hung up her wet hiking clothes. She then went into their guest room, pulled her hairbrush out of her daypack and unwound the cloth from her hair, letting it fall around her shoulders. She brushed it out and was amazed how quickly it was drying. She set the brush on the washstand, took a quick peek in the mirror and decided she looked presentable. She took a quick drink of water from her Camel Back, before going back into the main house to look for Jake.

Carrie entered the kitchen by the back door and found the house empty. She heard voices and laughter from the front and stepped out onto the tiny front porch area. She sucked in her breath in surprise. The men and boys of the village had set up makeshift tables all over out front of the mayor's house. There were colorful lanterns hanging from the fence rails and candles had been placed on the tables waiting to be lit at dark. A piñata hung from a pole erected next to the hitching rail out front. There were small handmade chairs made with woven seats at all the tables. The area had been transformed for a party, or a fiesta, as the Mexican people called it.

Jake looked up and saw Carrie standing there happily taking in the scene. He stopped in his tracks and whistled slowly under his breath. She looked like an angel in her beautiful peasant dress, her hair all clean and shining and hanging over her pretty shoulders. He could see her ripe breasts filling out the front of her blouse beneath the thin cotton, with her pink nipples showing around the edges of the embroidered flowers on her blouse. Her slim tanned legs were clearly visible clear up to her velvet triangle of tight curls, looking lean and shapely through the thin cotton of her skirt. He didn't think he would ever be able to stand it until he got her alone in their little room after tonight's fiesta.

Carrie saw Jake staring at her and blushed. She walked over to him and kissed his salty cheek. He continued to stare at her, rooted to the same spot.

"Jake, you look like you're in a trance. Wake up. It's time for you guys to have your turn at the hot spring bath. It feels absolutely fantastic. You're not going to believe it." She reached out and shook his arm.

"My God! Carrie, you look gorgeous. Do you have any idea? That dress is beautiful on you. You look like an angel fresh out of paradise. I'm not in a trance, I'm entranced!"

"Oh, come on, Jake. You've had too much sun, that's all," she replied coyly.

"It's taking all the willpower I can muster to keep myself from swooping you up into my arms and carrying you back to our little room and making passionate love to you all night long," he whispered huskily into her ear. "You just wait, young lady. If I can last through the fiesta, I'm going to make this a night you aren't ever going to forget, as long as you live."

Carrie's whole body reacted to this lusty promise as if a jolt of electricity had gone through all her senses. Her knees felt weak. A tingle began spreading between her legs, up her belly and she was aware of the involuntary hardening of her nipples in response to Jake's heated promise. She watched Jake's eyes hungrily roam her body, blatantly stopping at her lush breasts. She could tell he hadn't missed their hardened response to his words.

"Jake, stop it! Everyone will see and know what's happening between us. I'm so embarrassed!" Carrie was blushing furiously; a pretty, rosy pink. "You go on now and get to the hot spring and give me a chance to get hold of myself." She could see the delight and laughter in Jake's gorgeous green eyes, and his pleasure at having such an instant effect on her luscious body.

"OK. But you promise me you won't run off somewhere while I'm gone now, Carrie. I can hardly stand to let you out of my sight."

"Oh, Jake! You are crazy. Where do you think I'd be going, you silly. Go on and get out of here, right now! That's an order."

Jake quickly stole a kiss and hurried off to join the other men heading to the spring. Carrie went back into the house to ask Carmen if there was anything she could do to help get ready for the fiesta. She saw other women appearing from their houses carrying containers of food to the party area. There was a long table set up off to the side for all the food. Carrie entered the house and could see that the best thing she could do for Carmen would be to take Pepe off her hands. She wasn't sure Pepe would think that was a good idea but she decided to try anyway.

"Carmen, see if Pepe will let me hold him for a while. That'll make it easier for you to deal with the food." Carrie held out her arms to Pepe and he let her take him from Carmen without protest. He looked intently at her with wide dark eyes, staring at her golden hair. She spoke softly to him and he reached out tiny fingers to touch the pale gold silk. Carrie slowly wandered outside of the front door with him, singing an American nursery rhyme to him. He laughed at her nonsensical sounding English words but responded to her happy singsong voice. He wasn't afraid since everywhere he looked around them, he saw the familiar faces of his big extended family and the familiar scenes of his own front yard.

Meanwhile, Jake was at the pool with the other men from the village. They were carrying on a teasing dialog with Jake in Spanish, kidding him about his pretty Señorita Carrie. They splashed water on each other and told him what a lucky man he was to have such a beautiful señorita. Jake blushed and they could sense that this was a serious relationship for their beloved Señor Jake. They all asked to be invited to the wedding and if they couldn't come, they at least wanted Jake to bring his new bride back to their village for a proper wedding celebration with them. Jake told them he hadn't asked her to marry him yet, but when he did, he'd let them know.

They got out and dried off. Jose gave Jake a clean, plain cotton peasant shirt and a pair of cotton pants with a drawstring waist that was tied with a piece of hemp. The legs weren't nearly long enough for such a tall Gringo like Jake, but at least he had on clean clothes that were comfortable. All the other men were dressed identically to him. Jose told him one of the village women would wash his hiking clothes after their bath and hang them on the rope next to Carrie's behind the house. He could find them there in the morning, clean and dried. They walked back up to the village as a group, talking excitedly about tonight's fiesta.

All the women were placing pots and bowls of food along the buffet-style table. There were refried beans, black beans, fresh corn and flour tortillas, bowls of homemade salsas and pico de gallo. There were pieces of charcoal roasted chicken in mole sauce, enchiladas, squash blossom soup, roasted goat meat, napalitos salad, and Spanish rice. All made with things out of their large communal garden and from the animals they raised in the pens nearby. Carrie was amazed at what the villagers had put together for the fiesta. Everything smelled so delicious to Carrie as she held Pepe and watched all these wonderful dishes appear from the little homes around the village.

Jake came up to her and offered to take Pepe for a while. Pepe squealed in delight as Jake lifted him in the air from Carrie's arms.

"Hey, you stole my baby, Jake. No fair." Carrie made a small moue with her pretty mouth, the laughed.

"Don't worry, Sweetheart, someday maybe I'll give you one of your own that we both can keep." Jake gave her both a salacious and serious look all mixed together, watching her closely for her reaction to such a loaded comment.

"Jake! You're outrageous! You surely are kidding, aren't you?" She looked at him while a mixture of emotions washed over her face in waves.

He watched shock, hope, uncertainty, longing, and surprise, all flooding her features. He was shocked himself, that such a comment would fly out of his mouth. He felt all those same emotions he saw in Carrie. He knew what he wanted, though, and he knew that he had found the person he wanted to share his life with. Now he just needed to convince her that he was the right guy for her.

"I know. I'm pretty outrageous. Hey, let's choose us a table and sit down. The guys have a treat for us before we eat." He figured he'd better switch to a safer subject fast.

Carmen came up and took Pepe from Jake. "Its time for Pepe to go to bed, Señor Jake. He's already eaten his dinner. He'll start getting too cranky soon and I want to get him settled before we all eat. He needs a little of my Mama's milk before he goes to sleep."

Some of the village men began playing musical instruments together like the Mariachi group Carrie had seen at the Starlight Theater. The colorful little hanging lanterns were lit, as were the candles on all the tables in the fading early-evening light. The mood became more and more festive. Jose came over to Jake and Carrie's table with a jug that appeared to be made out of a large gourd. He set small pottery shot glasses in front of Jake and Carrie along with a small saucer of coarsely ground salt and a bowl of small lime halves.

"Now Señorita, Carrie, you will taste your very first pure agave tequila, no? We make it from the juice of the giant century plants that you see growing all over our desert. Most of the tequila Americans buy in the United States has very little pure agave juice in it. Pure Agave is very expensive so most of your tequila is diluted. We make our own and it is very special, we think. We would like for you to try it for yourself."

"I'd love to, Jose. I had a Marguerite in a restaurant with Jake in

Terlingua. It was delicious and I enjoyed it very much. I would love to try something as exotic as your agave juice. It should be an interesting experience. How do I do this? I notice the salt and the limes. They must be part of the drink?"

Jose sat down and filled his own little pottery shot glass with the agave from the large gourd. He rubbed some juice from a lime half on a small spot the top of his left wrist then took a pinch of the salt and sprinkled it on his lime juice-dampened skin. Next he picked up his agave and swallowed it down in one gulp. He immediately licked a bit of the coarse salt from his wrist and bit into his half of the lime, sucking out its juice and pulp. He discarded the lime peel in a small pottery bowl placed in the center of the table for that purpose.

Carrie watched with fascination. Then Jake filled his glass from the gourd and repeated the ritual, just as Jose had done. The Mariachis cheered "Ole!" and strummed some vibrant music in accompaniment. All eyes then turned to Carrie. It was clearly her turn to try the agave drink. She picked a lime half out of the bowl and rubbed a little on her tiny wrist. Next she dusted it with some salt. Jose filled her little pottery glass with agave. She was ready.

"Here goes," she said cheerfully, picked up her glass, downed the shot of agave, and the licked some salt off her wrist and bit into the lime. The Mariachis and other guests cheered her on with "Ole" from all directions. The Mariachis began strumming a lively Mexican tune in celebration.

Carrie felt a slow fiery burn spread all the way to her stomach then out through her blood stream into every cell in her body. The agave was much smoother than she had expected it to be and was surprised by the almost instantaneous warm, relaxed sensation it created in her brain. It tasted like the American tequila she had tasted before, only much richer in flavor and not nearly so harsh. Jose poured each of them another round and one after the other, first Jose, then Jake, then Carrie repeated the ritual. People were gathering at other tables as their younger children had been settled in their beds, and began enjoying their own gourds of agave that had been placed at each table.

"I think I'd better eat something before I have any more of that stuff. My brain is beginning to fog over, drinking it on an empty stomach. The only thing Jake and I have had all day is a granola bar and one half of an energy bar, and I think maybe Bart got part of that, besides!"

At the sound of his name being spoken by Carrie, Bart stood up and whined from over where Jake had told him to sit, away from the tables and the food. "You're not begging now, Bart, are you?" Jake spoke sternly to Bart and Bart immediately sat back down.

"Don't worry, Carrie. I fed Bart as soon as we got here. He's fine. He just would rather be over here sitting right next to us. I don't want him wandering amongst the tables full of food where he doesn't belong. He'll have to be a proper guest tonight." Jake gave Bart a look that clearly let Bart know without words that he should stay down and not make a pest of himself.

"Bart is, without a doubt, the most well-behaved dog I've ever encountered. I don't know how you've done it, Jake. You are so gentle and loving with him but he still knows exactly what you expect from him." Carrie sat shaking her head at her observation.

People at other tables were getting up and going to the buffet table and filling their plates with the delicious-smelling food. Carrie was starving and rose unsteadily to get in line. She held onto the backs of the other chairs a she made her way over to the end of the line. Jake followed her and Carmen came out of the house and got in line with them. Carrie picked up a plate when she got to the end of the table and began trying to decide what she would try first. Everything looked so good so she decided to take just a little of each dish and sample as many as she could. This was the best looking spread she thought she had ever seen.

"Jake, I feel so strange from the agave. I think I'd better go easy on that stuff. It's incredibly strong. I need to eat something right now!" She smiled at Jake and thought he looked a little bit tipsy, himself.

"No kidding, Carrie. If I thought I was having trouble controlling myself before, well, I'd better let up a little, too. Its erasing what little inhibitions I have left." He growled hungrily and pulled her back against him and playfully nibbled on the soft area of her neck beneath her ear.

Carrie giggled then pushed at his wandering hands, "Jake, stop it! Right now! You're going to have to go over and sit with Bart if you don't stop. Everyone is staring at us."

Jake looked around at the knowing glances and smiles being exchanged by his village friends. "You know, Carrie, you're right. They are staring at us. But they look really happy about what they see, don't you think?"

"Oh, Jake. I'm so embarrassed. What am I going to do with you?" Carrie spoke to him in feigned exasperation, blushing girlishly.

"I could offer you some suggestions of what you could do to me, Señorita." Jake's voice was all smooth teasing but the raw smokiness she heard in his tone made her shiver in the warm desert air. She had to put some physical distance between them before she dissolved into a puddle of wanton need right then and there.

Carrie took her plate of food and made her way back to their table and sat down. Carmen followed and sat down next to her. Next came Manuel then Jake. When they were all seated, Jose blessed the food and they all began eating. Carrie noticed the absence of the wonderful music and looked over and saw the Mariachi band members in the food line. Carmen read her thoughts.

"After dinner, we will clear all the dishes away and we will have traditional Mexican dancing. I think you will like to see our beautiful dancing and maybe you and Señor Jake could dance, also. The steps are quite easy for the simple dances. You could learn very quickly." Carmen looked so excited and enthusiastic, Carrie couldn't say no to her.

"I'd be willing to give it a try, Carmen, if it isn't too difficult. What about you, Jake? If you say you'll do it, then so will I." She offered a clear challenge to Jake, one he had no intention of refusing. He already knew the simple steps, as he had learned them in childhood. He'd love watching her move her lithe body to the rhythmic Mariachi music in that gorgeous peasant dress.

They continued eating in silence, as everyone was hungry. Even with only taking a little bit of the various dishes, Carrie's plate was still piled high with food. After they finished with the main meal, Carmen got up and came back to the table with a small piece of fudge-like, amber fruit substance. She sliced it into several serving pieces and offered some to Carrie.

"What is this? I've never seen anything quite like it." Carrie looked hesitant.

"It is called "dulce de cacto" which means cactus juice candy. It is very delicious and makes a nice sweet finish after a big meal."

Carrie took a small piece and tasted it. "It's delicious! Is there anything you don't use cactus plants for down here? There's soap, and salads, and potato-like roots, and candy, and fruit, and juices, and medicines, not to mention your delicious agave tequila. I'm really amazed. I had no idea about these things until I came here." Carrie helped herself to another piece of the delicious candy.

The four of them chatted amiably as the men began pouring more tequila in their little pottery glasses. The Mariachis finished their own dinners, had another round of tequila shots, and then began playing their beautiful music again. Some of the women and men got up and began some intricate dances in the area next to the tables. The women swayed and twisted and turned around their partners in time to the music. The onlookers at the tables cheered them on and whistled and stamped their feet to the music.

Carrie watched them, spellbound by the beauty of their movements in their colorful Mexican dresses like she was wearing. She felt warm and hazy and more relaxed than she ever thought she would feel among a large group of strangers. Somehow these wonderful, simple people had so openly welcomed her into their life, that they felt like old friends, and not strangers at all. Carrie found it hard to keep back tears of emotion as her heart swelled.

The crowds began calling for Jake and Señorita Carrie to dance. Jake got up and offered her his hand like a fine southern gentleman. "Señorita Carrie, would you do me the honor of this next dance?"

"You'll have to show me how. I don't know any of the steps." Two Mexican girls ran forward and took her hands and led her to the dancing area. They showed her a couple of simple steps and twirls that the women were required to do. She imitated their dance movements. They smiled encouragingly at her as she quickly mastered enough steps to do a simple dance.

Jake took her hand and led her into the group of swirling couples already dancing. He began the dancing movements performed by a Mexican male and she tentatively began the steps and flirtatious twirls and sways required by the females. The onlookers clapped and whistled and shouted their approval. Carrie became caught up in the rhythm of the music and the soft glow of the lantern light. And Jake. Her eyes were riveted by his as they moved in a primal dance between male and female, a mating ritual as old as time. She undulated her lithe form seductively in front of Jake as the other young senoritas did before their chosen young men. Her long blond hair flashed around her, catching the lantern light and looking like bright spun gold. She twirled and teased and swayed around him the way a snake charmer would move before a deadly cobra. And she knew instinctively that he could be just as deadly to her heart as the most lethal cobra, if she chose to let him possess her. But she was flirting with something she was no longer able to stop.

Jake was mesmerized by her - his beautiful gypsy woman. He couldn't last much longer. He had to get her alone in the privacy of their little room. The music stopped and Jake led her back to their little table. Jose and Carmen were holding hands in the candlelight, speaking softly to one another. Carrie smiled shakily and sat down, with Jake sitting next to her. He scooted his chair closer to hers and wrapped her in his arms. She didn't protest this time. It clearly seemed like the most natural thing in the world. Jake felt her relax against his body and they both watched the twirling dancers who had begun another round of dances. One by one, they watched laughing couples melt into the darkness toward cozy little homes. Jake couldn't wait another minute. He whispered something scandalous into Carrie's ear while hungrily nipping her lobe. He stood up abruptly, pulling Carrie to her feet along with him.

Jake spoke for both of them. "Jose, Carmen, I think Carrie and I will say good night now. We have had a very long day and we are exhausted. We can't thank you enough for all you have done for us. Everyone has been so nice to us and we appreciate your kindness so much. We will see you in the morning sometime after we have slept our fill." Jake waved to the rest of the villagers, shouting "Gracias, Amigos! Buenas noches. Thank you and good night!"

Carrie was aware of herself echoing "Gracias" to everyone and then she was aware of nothing but the warmth and firmness of Jake's hand, leading her around the side of the mayor's house to their little stone room, and toward the heated promise of a night she'd never forget.

Chapter Eight

The little stone room had cooled down considerably during the time they were at the fiesta. This was the blessing of living in a desert. The days could be blistering, but it always cooled off at night. Jake dropped Carrie's hand and fumbled in the dark for the matches to light the oil lamp on the little washstand. He got it started then replaced the globe. As the wick caught, a soft glow enveloped the room. Jake next lit the small candles on the nightstand, bathing the bed in candlelight. Carrie remained rooted to the spot where Jake left her when they came in the room, waiting for him to light the lamp. When he turned to look at her, she was standing in front of the doorframe, outlined by the light from the fiesta lanterns, making her look like some kind of mystical, ethereal apparition.

Carrie's body shivered in anticipation as she returned Jake's steady smoldering gaze. Jake came toward her and took her hand, gently pulling her inside the doorway. He closed the door and secured the primitive latch. He then pulled the drapes across the screens to give them complete privacy. Bart had already settled himself on a rug at the foot of the bed. Carrie felt the nervousness of a new bride and the thrill of discovery excited her. She had never experienced the intensity of need and emotions she was experiencing with Jake. It both electrified and frightened her at the same time. She felt hazy from the tequila, but the intoxication she knew she was feeling, was caused by being with Jake. Whatever else happened tomorrow, she wanted this night with him more than anything she'd ever wanted in her life.

Jake wrapped Carrie in a heated embrace. He tilted her chin up towards his face and kissed her lips. She responded immediately, letting out a slow groan as she let her body mold to his. As he deepened the kiss, his tongue reached out and explored her lips, coaxing her mouth to open for his exploration. Carrie could feel his swelling erection against her stomach and it excited her beyond reason. She opened her mouth and met his tongue with her own, probing at him to savor his taste. Jake groaned from deep in his chest and began slowly pulling them back toward the bed.

"Jake, I need to take off these clothes," she whispered breathlessly. He kept covering her face and neck with kisses, like a man dying of starvation.

"No, Carrie. Let me take them off, slowly." Jake pulled the spread back with one hand while keeping Carrie's lips in his full possession. He laid her down across the cool sheet. He slipped off his own shirt and stood looking at her, the burgeoning evidence of his need for her clearly visible from the placket of his thin cotton pants. Carrie shuddered and reached out for him to come to her.

"Not yet, Baby. I want to savor every minute of this, slowly." He removed her guaraches and dropped them on the floor next to the bed. He then massaged a warm foot and teasingly began to work his hand slowly up her leg, stopping at her knee. He leaned down and tenderly kissed the inside of her knee. He next let his hand begin tracing a pathway up the inside of her thigh, separating her legs and pushing her pretty skirt up as he made his way to the treasure he sought. Carrie writhed on the cool bed sheet.

"Jake, I can't stand it! I need to touch you." She stared through glazed eyes at Jake's beautiful chest. His own nipples were tight buds and his muscles alternately relaxed and contracted under his smooth skin. He had very little hair on his body, his chest and strong arms being covered by the smooth, bronzed skin of a man who often worked shirtless in the sun. She could see him covered by a thin sheen of sweat from the effort of maintaining his control until he accomplished what he intended for her to experience.

His hand crept further up, continuing to push her skirt up around her hips and trailing tender kisses along her sensitive inner thighs as he went. When he reached the top of her leg, he hesitated as she whimpered, paralyzed by her expectations and need for what she knew would come next. A sultry, confident smile crept across his beautiful features as he witnessed her responses to his fiery touch and increasingly intimate kisses. She could see his engorged penis reaching further out through the fly of his pants toward her body. She frantically clawed at his arms, trying to pull him down to her.

"Uh, uh, uh, Carrie. Not yet. Just a little bit longer now." Keeping his left hand on the top of her thigh, gently teasing at her swollen vulva with his fingers, he used his right hand to untie the bow holding the top of her peasant blouse together. He could see her tight nipples straining under the cotton cloth of the thin blouse. He separated the front of the blouse revealing her lush breasts, swelling under his touch. He moved his hand to her left nipple and gently messaged it, pulling at the sensitive, engorged areola. He then moved to the other nipple and fingered it until she was moaning and writhing beneath his touch. He leaned down and suckled on one nipple while messaging her other one.

He released her breasts and pushed her skirt completely up around her hips, exposing her completely to his view. He coaxed her thighs apart and settled himself between her legs. He sat back on his haunches and surveyed this view of paradise found. She lay with her golden hair spread out across the pillow, her beautiful breasts ripe for his suckling. He stared at her erotic pink vulva, swollen with her need for him under the beautiful blond curls. She was shining wet with the dew of her readiness for him. He had to sample her before he allowed his body to ravage her completely.

"Oh, Jake. My God, Jake! What are you doing to me? Touch me, please, touch me, Jake." Her eyes were bright with the unshed tears of passion as her head rolled back and forth across the pillow. He thought he was going to completely lose control, but he steeled himself, wanting to give her the maximum pleasure before he plunged into her and was completely lost to his own.

He reached out and separated the dewy lips of her vulva revealing the pulsing bud of her womanhood, erect and tight in her need. He leaned slowly over and reached out his tongue and began caressing and nibbling gently on her. Carrie cried out and reached for his head, tangling her hands in his hair. He continued exploring her with his tongue as he reached one hand up to fondle a heavy breast while he guided the fingers of his other hand into her passage. He inserted first one finger, then two, then three stretching her passage walls while drawing her clitoris into his mouth and suckling it. Carrie screamed out and Jake felt the spasms of her climax begin deep inside her around his fingers and work outward until she was pulsing in his mouth and thrusting her hips toward his tongue in the primal movements of her frantic need.

"Now my Sweet Carrie. Now!" Jake untied his drawstring and shoved his pants over his rigid length and down his hips and onto the floor. He stretched forward between her splayed thighs and eased his throbbing member into her opening and then plunged into her to the hilt. Carrie was writhing and thrusting beneath him driving him completely mad. He set up a steady rhythm of pulling out and plunging back in, deeper each time until he began to feel the spasms of the beginning of another orgasm beginning again deep inside her, massaging his length with her internal muscles until he was lost in oblivion. He slipped violently over the edge along with her, pumping his life's essence into her, in the perfect harmony of their togetherness.

She pulled his face close to hers, covering him with tender kisses. He had never felt so totally at peace and at one with another person in his life. He raised his head and looked into her passion-glazed eyes, and kissed the tears of release from her cheeks.

"Carrie, I love you. I know it's only been a short time, but these have been the most intense days of my life. My heart is sure -

without a doubt - and I know that you are the person who I've been waiting for all these lonely years. I knew there had to be a reason why it was never right with anyone else. My spirit was waiting and longing for you." He rained loving kisses over her face and eyes.

"Oh, God, Jake. How can we be this sure, out here where the rest of the world feels like it doesn't exist? I believe I love you, too. But what's going to happen to us when we go back to our own worlds and have to sort all this out? Part of me wishes we could stay here forever, in this simple village, living a simple uncomplicated life with these dear, sweet people. But we both know, our world isn't like this." Carrie clung to him tightly, her feelings speaking louder to him than her words.

"Carrie, listen to me. There is nothing we can't work out together, if we both want the same thing. The problems we have are not even problems, but solvable issues. I don't want to own you, well, that's not exactly true, I do want to own you." His eyes sparkled mischievously. "But not own you in a confining way. I want you to continue your career doing your wonderful photography work. You are so very talented, and I don't see why you couldn't keep doing that and be with me, too."

"Jake, you make it all sound so reasonable and simple. I'm just worried about how you will feel tomorrow in the cold light of day when we have to go back to our real world. Maybe you won't want me at all then."

"Hush Carrie. Don't even think something like that. I'm old enough to know my own heart and feelings, and I guarantee you, I'm sure about us. I think, in your heart, you are sure, also, Carrie. Enough of this discussion for now, Carrie. This is our night to own and remember for the rest of our lives. There will be enough time in the tomorrows to sort out the rest."

Jake kissed her lips and she could feel his body already beginning to awaken inside her again. She caressed his arms and ran her hands down the rippling muscles of his smooth back, teasing him with her nails. He began his rhythmic movements inside of her and felt the muscles of her vagina pulse and caress him in return, spurring him on to greater heights. He covered her with kisses and bent his head to take a breasts in his mouth and suckle on her, drawing her nipple in deeply causing a tightening coil down her belly to her womb. They moaned together and brought each other to higher and higher peaks, each gaining momentum and impetus from each other's fevered responses. Soon they were lost in the netherworld of each other's consuming orgasms, until they both lay prostrate on the damp sheets.

Jake blew out the bedside candles and then got up and extinguished the little oil lamp. He pulled the drapes back from the screened windows to let some of the night breeze blow through and cool the room. They lay in each other's arms, shielded by the darkness. They listened silently to the night sounds of crickets and spring peeper frogs down by the river. In the distance came the soft murmurs, and laughter of other couples enjoying each other on this warm spring night after a fiesta. Somewhere a baby cried, and they could hear a mother gently quiet its hungry cries, probably with a full breast. The village pulsed with the night sounds of people living their lives, carried on the night air around the village through open windows. Carrie dozed off thinking she had never felt so close to the intimate life forces of other people in her life. She had spent every minute of her life locked behind solid doors and closed windows, careful not to hear the sounds or smell the smells of life that surely had always been around her.

They slept for several hours, awoke and made love again and fell back asleep, still joined together as one. There was a shuffling sound outside their window and Bart jumped up and growled. Jake leaped to his feet to go to the window and Carrie sat up with alarm.

"What is it, Jake?" she whispered. She jumped out of bed and stood next to Jake, straining to see out the window at what was making the noise in the semi-darkness of early dawn.

"Look over there next to the garden wall," Jake pointed out to her. "It's an armadillo, that's all."

Carrie saw the animal he was pointing at, as it shuffled along the garden wall looking for an opening so it could get at the lush plants it could smell inside. It stopped here and there and dug furiously at the bottom of the adobe wall, trying to tunnel its way underneath. It looked like a big rat, only with armored plates all over its body. It had a sharply pointed little face, which was covered by protective scales, and it had a long, pointed rat-like tail. Carrie had never seen one in the wild before. She laughed at the sight of this bizarre little creature and Jake laughed at her reaction to it.

Soon a village dog heard the commotion and ran over and began nosing the armadillo away from the garden. It hissed and fussed at the dog which nosed and nipped at it, making sure it was leaving before it came back over to investigate where the armadillo had been trying to dig under the wall.

"Those things can make a mess of a garden in a hurry. They are terribly destructive, and just one can ruin an entire garden full of vegetables in one night. They like to eat the tender roots of plants, and will dig them up and eat the roots completely off of them. You've probably noticed the walls around all the gardens? Well that's to keep out armadillos and Javelinas. The village dogs are depended on to scare these critters away or at least warn people when they come around.

"I've heard of Javelinas, but I've never seen a wild one. Are they really around here?" Carrie strained to look out into the yard as if a Javelina might appear at any moment.

"They sure are. They run in packs of twenty to fifty. They can destroy a large village garden in one half hour or less. They look like wild pigs or boars, but they aren't pigs at all. Their true names are Collard Peccaries because they look like they have on a white collar. They are black with very coarse, bristly hair. They can weigh anywhere from 35 to 60 pounds, and they eat cactus, roots, prickly pear fruits, lizards, bugs, etc. They are called Javelinas because that is the Spanish word for javelin. The Spaniards named them that because of their long, pointed sharp teeth that they thought looked like little javelins. They have a terrible skunk-like odor and can be mean as hell. Some of them have sharp tusks that curve downwards which they use to fight and root up food. They aren't at all nice, and people give them a wide berth, if they're smart. The village dogs are important in keeping them out of the village. They could be a great danger to small children."

"I'd sure love to see one, Jake. From a healthy distance, that is. Do you think I'll get a chance? I'd love to get some pictures of some." Carrie leaned her body back into Jake and continued staring out the window at the breaking dawn sky.

"We might see some on our boat trip down the river to the road tomorrow. Or else, I guess I should say, today. It's getting light out fast." He held her close against the length of his body and ran his hands up her belly and held one of her full breast in each hand. His thumbs began toying with each nipple, rubbing them until the friction of his touch caused them to tighten into hard buds. Carrie could feel his arousal probing against her buttocks. She moaned and tried to turn in order to find his mouth, already hungry for him again.

Jake held her in her same position with her back pressed tightly against his erection. He walked her over in front of the mirror hanging over the washstand. Carrie was twisting her body, trying desperately to turn in his arms to kiss him and wrap her arms around him. She stopped squirming and reached behind her back with her hands to stroke his hardened length.

"Carrie, stop squirming and open your eyes and look in the mirror," he commanded in a husky whisper, breathing heavily in her ear.

She opened her eyes and froze, mesmerized by the sensuousness of watching the reflection of him playing with her erect nipples in the gathering light. He teased them and pulled on them while both their eyes were riveted to the erotic scene of watching him arouse her to a fevered state. It was wanton and voyeuristic and totally captivating, compelling her to continue to stare helplessly. He slid a hand down her belly and reached a finger between her legs to massage the erect bundle of nerves swelling under his fingers. Carrie moaned and parted her thighs allowing him easier access to her while he continued toying with an engorged, overly-sensitive nipple.

"Jake, no, no, no more, she cried out." She remained rooted to the spot in spite of her protests. Her eyes involuntarily closed in a near swoon.

"Carrie, open your eyes and watch, now!" She obeyed him. She stared at the erotic scene of him arousing her, kissing and nipping her neck and shoulders hungrily, while pulling hard on her taut nipple. Their eyes met and held in the mirror, and she came in a violent explosion like nothing she'd ever experienced in her life. She cried out and whimpered in his embrace, while he continued to finger her until her knees weakened and he had to hold her up to keep her from collapsing on the floor at his feet. He swooped her up in his arms and deposited her on the bed. She opened her legs for him, beside herself with a hungry need for him to be inside her. He settled himself between her creamy thighs and drove furiously into her, feeling the tip of his erection bumping up tight against her very womb. He thrust in and out of her in a fever, then threw back his head, cried out and came in her in a seemingly endless series of pulsating throbs.

He collapsed over her, showering her with loving kisses while whispering her name over and over again. "Carrie, Carrie, my beautiful Carrie. I love you so much, I can hardly stand it."

"Jake, I can't believe what you do to my body. I lose all control. This has never happened to me in my life! What you do to me doesn't have words."

He rolled off of her and pulled her along with him so he could stay inside of her. She threw one leg over him to keep them joined and they cradled each other as the daylight brightened the corners of the room. A slight breeze began stirring through the windows, which felt wonderful blowing across their sweat-glazed naked bodies. Carrie stared up at the crucifix hanging over the bed and thanked a benevolent God for Jake. Now if only they could figure out a way to have it never end. Then she'd be in heaven for sure.

They must have dozed off for a while, as the next time Carrie opened her eyes, the room was completely filled with sunlight, heating up in the little room. She could hear the sounds of the little village waking up. Children began stirring in the streets, waiting for their breakfast. She could smell smoke from cooking fires and the fragrance of fresh tortillas being baked on griddles. Her stomach growled in response to the aroma. The voices of villagers combined with the sounds of tables and chairs being taken away from the fiesta area out front of Jose and Carmen's home.

She looked over at Jake. He was staring at her adoringly with those gorgeous green eyes and smiling. He had clearly been watching her for a while.

"Good morning, Sweetheart. How was your night?" He grinned at her puckishly and she didn't fail to catch the double meaning of his seemingly innocent inquiry. He stole a quick kiss from the tip of her nose.

"Well, Mr. Stockton. Let me see. I seemed to have had this incredible, shameless dream about the two of us. Our behavior was utterly shocking." She smiled broadly back at him and stole a kiss of her own. Jake reacted to her mention of their shocking behavior by reaching out and cupping one of her pretty breasts.

"Oh, no you don't! The curtains are open and it sounds like the whole village is up and about. People will think we've died in here and come looking for us. We need to get up right now." She giggled and tried to push his hand away and roll out of his grasp.

"Ah, come on Carrie, they'll be able to tell from the sounds coming from here that we certainly aren't dead. Just a few more minutes, please?" Jake grabbed her around the waist to pull her back into his arms before she could escape off the side of the bed. He began sliding a hand up between her thighs and began slowly stroking her dampening vulva. She could feel his erection pushing against her side.

"Jake, No! I'd be too embarrassed. I couldn't look anyone in the eye knowing they heard us making love in here. We'd probably look up to find curious kids looking in our windows!" She was squirming and laughing, trying to get away from him. She knew that if he slipped inside her she'd be lost to reason. Jake teased at her opening and clitoris feeling her body readying for him, as she was warm and slick with her womanly dew. He slid an exploring finger up inside her and heard her swallow a ragged moan. Her nipples tighten into stiff peaks under his other roving hand. Then he suddenly withdrew his finger and released her.

She jumped off the bed and stood staring at him, breathless and flushing a rosy pink, her blue eyes darkened and glazed with desire. She stared at his huge erection, laying stiffly up his belly reaching almost to his navel. He boldly maintained eye contact with her while reaching down and taking himself in his hand and suggestively stroking slowly up his magnificent length.

"Carrie, I'm lonely for your body. Can't you tell how much I need you?" Jake's blatant sensuousness was almost her undoing. He could see the battle going on inside her between arousal and hesitation. Pearly fluid dampened her thighs. He saw her suck in her breath and it looked like she was going to reach out and touch him.

"Jake, you've got to stop that right now! We can't do this now. Come on, you're driving me insane. Please? I can hear Manuel and Carmen just outside. Be reasonable, Jake." She backed further away from the bed as if unsure of her own control.

"OK, Baby. I know you're right, but I can't look at you without wanting to make love to you every minute, Carrie. You've cast some kind of spell on me, my lusty little witch."

Jake leaped off the bed, gathered her into his arms and kissed her. He let her go, went over to the washstand and poured some tepid water from the pitcher into the wash bowl. He handed her a piece of cloth to wash up with. He washed himself and looked in the mirror at his three-day stubble and groaned.

"Hey, Jake. You look like one of those sexy movie stars with those whiskers growing out." She shot him a teasing look and he smiled back at her.

"I guess there's nothing to do about it until I get back to the ranch. Carrie, I've been thinking. When we get back to town, maybe we could go get the rest of your stuff from the motel and you could come stay at the ranch with me until you need to go back to New York. I really want to show you the ranch and you'd be so much more comfortable there. Besides, you'd be closer to Alpine from the ranch. I've got a phone and FAX and satellite TV so you could make all the calls you need to without any problem." He looked pleadingly at her, hoping she'd seriously consider his idea.

"I'd like that, Jake. I'd love to see your ranch, but as soon as we get to a phone, I need to call Diana. I'm sure she's frantic by now since she hasn't heard from me in more than three days. I need to let her know I'm alright and tell her where she can call me if I leave the motel." She watched a huge smile of relief break out on Jake's handsome face when she agreed to stay at his ranch with him. She just couldn't bear to have the dream end so soon.

Jake pulled on his peasant pants and went out to the outhouse, stopping at the rope clothesline on his way back to get their clean hiking clothes. They both dressed in their clean hiking clothes and Carrie headed out to the little outhouse for her turn. They met back in Carmen's kitchen.

"Good morning, Amigos." Carrie and Jake exchanged pleasantries with Jose and Carmen while Carmen put some fresh, warm tortillas on the table and a pot of refried beans. She added a bowl of scrambled eggs and chorizo, and another bowl of Jalapeño pepper slices mixed with pickled carrots and onions. They sat down and began making breakfast burritos using the tortillas and fillings.

"Jose, we need someone to take us down the river this morning in the boat. Do you think you'd be able to do it, or should I ask someone else?" Jake was busy adding more of the pickled vegetables to his burrito as he spoke.

"No problem, Señor Jake. Manuel can take you. He needs to bring back some gasoline for our generators, so he's going today, anyway. You can leave right after breakfast, if you'd like."

"That would be good. Carrie really needs to get to a phone and call her office in New York. They will be very worried about her since we've been out of touch for three days. I need to call Carlos and get him to send some of the men out to the old Mariscal Mine to fix my truck and get it back to the ranch. I also need to have him drive down to Rio Grande Village to pick us up. All that will take a while since its over seventy miles from the ranch to the village store. We'll be doing well to get back and settled before dinner tonight."

Carrie listened to their plans as they were speaking in English. She imagined Jake spoke with Jose in English so she could get an idea about how their day would go. It was easier than Jake having to translate their conversation back to her if they had spoken in Spanish.

"Carmen, I don't know how to thank you for all you've done for us. This has been the most memorable experience I've ever had. I don't know how to ever repay you. I love the beautiful clothes and sandals and I will always treasure them." Carrie reached out and squeezed Carmen's hand.

"You are very welcome, Carrie. I hope you will come back and visit us again. It would be a good reason to have another fiesta, and you would have a place to wear your pretty new clothes again, no?" Carmen laughed and squeezed Carrie's hand affectionately in return.

Jake got up and walked over and picked up Pepe off the floor where he was playing with some tiny trucks. "Well, little nugget, you be a good boy while I'm gone." He kissed his tiny brown cheek and set him back on the floor. Pepe was more interested in his trucks than Jake's good-bye.

Jake and Carrie went back to their room and gathered up their packs and hiking sticks. Carmen had given Carrie a straw bag to put her new clothes in as being stuffed in her daypack would ruin them. They stopped by the town well and Jake used his Sweetwater filter to fill their trail bottles and Carrie's CamelBack. Carrie took photos of Jake by the well and Carmen, Jose and Pepe in front of their house. They were ready to go. They told Jose they would enjoy walking back to the river rather than riding the burros. Carrie wanted the chance to take photos along the way, something she had been unable to do while hanging onto the bouncing burros on the way up.

Carrie and Jake walked down to the river in virtual silence. They both seemed lost in their own thoughts, knowing they were going to be back in their own worlds too soon. They each wondered what the future held for them as a couple.

Manuel was already down at the river waiting for them. He handed Carrie a large straw hat to wear to keep some of the intense sun off of her pretty face. They climbed in the boat and Manuel let the river's current carry them down toward the Rio Grande Village landing. The sun was climbing high in the morning sky and the temperature climbed right along with it. There was a nice breeze out on the river, though.

Carrie dug in her pack and got out her sunscreen. She applied it to her arms noting their deep golden color from being out in the sun so much the past few days. She was very glad to have the hat today. She wished she had had one the whole time. But how could she have ever known what was going to happen to them when she left her motel room that morning with Jake, going out on what was to be a routine photo shoot?

She marveled that it had really only been a couple of days, as it felt like it had been weeks. So much had changed in her life. She stared off into the distance, lost in her thoughts about everything that had happened to her. She knew deep in her soul that her life would never be the same. Something extraordinary had happened to her heart.

Jake was lost in his own thoughts. He watched Carrie from the back of the boat and just looking at her caused his heart to contract in his chest. She was so beautiful and such a wonderful person. He thought about her genuine acceptance and kindness to his friends in San Vicente and thought that she would fit in very well living in this country. He worried that she would miss the big city too much to stay with him, but he knew he could solve that problem by not making her feel like a prisoner out here. No, he would be sure she had her freedom to pursue the career she loved. He thought about life being different for women these days. Why couldn't a woman continue doing what she loved to do even if she married and had children? Why did it seem like they should have to choose? Men could do both and had done both, for eons. No one thought a man should give up a career when he married and had kids.

"Jake, Manuel, look! Carrie pointed excitedly at a herd of about 20 small black pig-like animals along the shore of the river. There were large ones with curving tusks and some little baby ones following closely behind their mothers. They were rooting up plants along the riverbank and drinking from the river.

"Carrie, those are the Javelinas I told you about last night. You can get some good pictures of them out on the riverbank like that. You can probably see what I meant about them ruining a garden in minutes. The people of the village would be in dire straits if they lost their gardens. That is about their only source of fresh vegetables."

Carrie already had her camera out and Jake watched her whirling away with it. She zoomed in for some close-ups of individual Javelinas as well as snapping group pictures. Most of the Javelinas paid little attention to the boat full of people, but some of them stared out at them, making sure the boat kept on going.

Carrie turned and smiled broadly at Jake. "Well now I've seen my first real wild Javelinas, Jake. The wildlife down here in the desert is so different from any other in my experience. It's been such a treat to see and experience so many new things."

Jake beamed back at her and their eyes locked as they shared a silent tender exchange. Bart stood up and whined at the Javelinas causing the boat to rock back and forth.

"Bart, sit down and be still!" Jake spoke sternly to Bart who immediately sat down. "You're going to turn us over in the river, Bart, you crazy dog!" Bart put his ears down and looked sheepishly up at Jake. "That's OK, Bart, you're a good dog." Jake's voice softened when he saw the repentant look Bart gave him.

"Jake, look. There's another little village like San Vicente." Carrie pointed across the river up a small bluff. "It looks almost exactly the same."

"That village is called Boquillas del Carmen, Carrie, and it is very much like San Vicente. We are almost at the landing at Rio Grande Village. It's right across from Boquillas."

Carrie watched villagers and burros along the river just like she saw at San Vicente. They all waved and hollered and Manuel shouted something in Spanish back to them. They also had some small rowboats. Manuel then began turning their boat toward the American side of the shore and Carrie could see a stony beach area with a couple other boats pulled up out of the water. A road led from the landing area through thick stands of desert willows and river bamboo.

They unloaded the boat and began walking up the road toward the store and the National Park Ranger Station. The road was paved and meandered through a campground. There were tents and some Recreational Vehicles occupying different sites. The heat was stifling. Soon they came to a wooden building with an American flag fluttering in the hot breeze. There were two gas pumps and several large ice freezers out front. Manuel set his gas can down next to the pumps and they all went inside the store.

"I think we should gather up some food from the coolers for lunch. They always have some sandwiches, yogurts, milk and different kinds of things like that, as well as chips and pop and canned goods. Maybe we could grab a bag of some kind of cookies, too. I'm starving." Jake looked around the store hungrily and began gathering up food that looked good to him that would be easy to eat at a picnic table. "We can sit out at one of the picnic tables off the other side of the building where it is shady. There are a couple of pay phones we can use on the outside wall there, too."

Carrie raided the coolers and found a carton of yogurt, a tuna sandwich and some hard-boiled eggs. She picked up a bag of potato chips and a large plastic bottle of diet Coke and went over to the meager produce cooler and selected some oranges. She saw that Jake already had a large bag of Oreos. She found plastic spoons and some salt and pepper for the eggs over at the condiment counter.

"Manuel, get whatever looks good to you and put it up here with ours. Lunch is on me." Jake began fishing money out of his wallet in his backpack. He made small chitchat with the clerk at the register while Manuel and Carrie finished gathering up lunch items.

"I'm going out to use the pay phone, Jake. I've got to check in with Diana. She'll be frantic, I know. I'll meet you guys at the picnic table." Carrie left the store and went around to the side where the phones were located. She got her calling card out of her wallet and called Diana's office.

"Diana, it's Carrie. I'm calling from Big Bend National Park."

"Carrie! Where have you been? I've been calling and calling you at the motel and that Pearl lady says you guys just disappeared! She said you went off into the desert to take pictures and didn't come back! I've been crazy with worry. What happened?" Diana spoke in a breathless rush. Carrie could tell from her tone of voice she was clearly upset.

"It's a long, long story. I can't tell you about it now. I just want to let you know that I'm fine and that I got some really good photos for the layout. Unbelievable, actually."

"Well, I need you to get back here as soon as you can. Those travel guys are all over my butt wanting those pictures for their June issue. They want you to show them the shots and help them figure out which ones would be best for their spread. They'll only work directly with you, so you've got to get your sweet little ass back to New York."

"I can't possibly get out of here until the day after tomorrow at the earliest. Can you get my flights for me? I can call you back tonight at your apartment and find out what you've arranged. What is today, anyway? I've completely lost track."

Carrie was trying to keep the weariness from showing in her voice. It would only worry Diana even more. She felt so removed from

New York and the world right now, disoriented, actually.

"Carrie, this is Tuesday, for Christ sakes. You sound so different. Has something happened to you out there?"

"Diana, try to get a flight out of Alpine for Friday morning. Try to get the Tree House Room in the Corner House in Alpine for me for Thursday night. I loved that little place. I'll get back to New York Friday evening, and you can count on me working all weekend. I don't have anything else to do. And don't worry, Diana. I've worked with magazine people before. I know that they want everything done yesterday. I can handle them."

"OK, Carrie. But promise me you aren't going to up and disappear on me ever again. I can't take that. I'll expect to hear from you later this evening. And Carrie, are you sure you're all right? There's something really different about you. I can feel it. You didn't go and get yourself abducted by aliens or something, did you?"

Carrie laughed for the first time in their conversation. "No. I'm fine, Diana. Just hot and tired. The thermometer on this building says it's one-hundred and four in the shade and I need to eat some lunch. Please don't worry about me. I've got tons to tell you about when I get back. Amazing stuff, actually, and I've got the pictures to prove it." She laughed again just to put Diana at ease.

"Well, then, I'll wait for your call. I should be home all evening. Bye, Babe."

Carrie hung up the phone and spotted a women's room across the breezeway. She ducked in for a minute to pee and wash her hands before lunch. She felt like it had been years since she had used a modern restroom. How could so much change in a person's life in three days, she wondered to herself?

When Carrie came out of the bathroom, she saw Jake on the phone. She figured he was calling Carlos to come get them and have someone go get the truck. She walked over to the picnic table where Manual was already eating lunch.

Carrie watched Jake walking back toward the picnic table after finishing his phone call. He carried Bart's water bowl full of water from the drinking fountain and had a small bag of dog chow under his arm. She was glad to see the relaxed look on his face indicating the transportation arrangements must have gone well. She waited anxiously to hear what he had to say about their plans.

"I just spoke to Carlos. He's sending a couple of the guys out to get the truck. They'll take a new lower radiator hose and a couple of gallons of coolant with them, as well as a few extra parts that might be necessary to fix it. Carlos will head over here to get us, Carrie, but it'll take a couple hours for him to get here. Maybe a little less, but it's a long way from the ranch to here." Jake set Bart's bowl down in the grass and dumped some of the dog chow on the cement pad under the picnic table for Bart.

"That's OK, Jake. After we finish lunch, I'd like to stroll around this area and take some photos. The scenery here is very different than what we've seen so far. How come all these trees around here are so tall? I haven't seen trees this tall since I got to Texas. And some of them that are back from the river a ways, aren't as tall and look old and gnarly, like they've been here for eons."

"These really tall trees right around the campground area along the river are Cottonwoods. They can grow 40 to 60 feet tall where they get consistent water. You'll find Cottonwoods growing along riverbanks where rivers flow consistently, even in a dry season. There are lots of small natural seeps and springs along this part of the Rio Grande River. This creates ideal conditions in which the kinds of trees growing around here can flourish.

The old gnarly ones further back from the river are mainly Live Oaks, Red Oaks, and Pin Oaks. They are very old, some maybe 150 years or so. Being further back from the river, the amount of water they get varies from year to year. They get their squat, gnarly shapes because in the years they get plenty of water they grow a lot. Then during the years that are really dry, they grow very slowly, if at all. That way, they never get tall and straight like the trees down here next to the river, that consistently get plenty of water every year."

"Holy smoke, Jake! Is there anything you don't know about this area? You seem to know all the plants and animals and trees and snakes, etc."

"Think about it, Carrie. Don't you know those kinds of things about the places you are familiar with? You probably know the names of the plants and animals and trees that grow in Central Park? It's the same for me here. This is my home and environment. It's just seems difficult to you because all the things you are seeing are foreign to you. Besides, I do have a degree in agriculture where I was required to learn many more details about what kinds of flora and fauna exists in this area and why.

Did you know that there are five-thousand species of flowering trees in the United States? About forty percent of those can be found somewhere in the state of Texas. Most of them are found over in the eastern part of Texas, where there is a lot more rain. Texas has climates that range all the way from tropical, in the extreme southern area near the Gulf Coast at Brownsville, to the dry western Texas deserts you've seen around here. We even have a few mountain climates. The Davis Mountains, north of Alpine, and the Guadalupe Mountains, way over on the New Mexico border, have pine trees and snow."

"I suppose you're right. This is the only part of Texas I've seen so I just ignorantly assumed it was all like this. When we're finished with lunch, I'd like to wander around a while with my camera and get some photos of this area. These photos will be quite a contrast to the other ones I've taken, even though this is still clearly a desert area. It's just more like an oasis."

"That sounds good. We can leave our stuff here on the picnic table. Don't leave it on the ground. You don't want to pick up any hitchhikers in your daypack or bag of clothes." Jake began piling some of their things onto the tabletop.

"What are you talking about? Hitchhikers? What exactly does that mean?"

"There are fire ants around here and scorpions. I've also seen centipedes and tarantulas, too. But you're not too likely to pick up a tarantula. You don't want to reach into your pack later this afternoon and find one of those critters! They sting like the devil and they're poisonous to boot. They can give you a real nasty time of it. The worst we'll get up on top of the table will be some pesky crows investigating our stuff. We'll throw all the food related trash away up at the store, so the crows won't find anything that interests them. It looks like Bart ate all the dog chow off the cement under the table, so there's nothing left there to attract anything."

"Good grief! I thought all I had to worry about were rattlesnakes, copperheads, Javelinas, and mountain lions. Now you're telling me there are man-eating insects as well? I don't know, Jake. Will I be able to fight these new critters off with a hiking stick?" Carrie looked at Jake with a half serious, half-teasing grin.

"You may not have noticed these past couple of days, but every morning I shook out our hiking boots before we put them on. It becomes an ingrained habit from childhood in Texas. You never put on a shoe or boot without shaking it out first, even if you get it out of your own closet at home. These kinds of insects live here with the rest of us and we just learn to live with them. Once you get used to it, you don't even think about it much. It just becomes something you automatically do to protect yourself.

I imagine you do similar things in New York, only you do them to protect yourself against two-legged poisonous critters. Like not walking alone down dark alleys, and parking your car where it is well lit and where there are lots of other people around. I bet you look around carefully before you step into an elevator alone with a strange man."

"You're right about that, Jake. Those are things we all do in the city without even thinking about them. I can see your point. I suppose there are hazards in life wherever a person lives."

"While you go for your walk, I'm going to help Manuel get his gas cans and supplies back down to his boat. I'll meet you back here in a little while. I told Carlos we'd be here at the picnic area next to the store. We'll be back here long before Carlos shows up, however.

Bart! You go with Carrie."

Carrie decided to take her hiking stick with her, just in case. Bart followed along with her, which was surprisingly reassuring to her. She wandered over to a small estuary surrounded by reeds and cattails. She was surprised to see it was a natural lily pond. Beautiful pink and white water lilies covered the surface. Growing close to the water were pink primroses, feathery white fleabane, and black-footed daisies. More colorful butterflies fluttered amongst the blooms here, too. She watched a Texas Horned Toad race across the sand.

Carrie found her thoughts returning to Jake. She had never before felt anything for any man like what she felt for Jake. Not that she had had many men in her life. Except for a couple of boyfriends in high school and college, there had only been Clayton. Clayton was the first man who claimed her virginity. Clayton was dependable and comfortable and they shared a lot intellectually and socially. But, Carrie couldn't help feeling like there was something deeper missing from their relationship, something that she couldn't put into words. Now she knew. It was unbridled passion and joy. Her sex life with Clayton was sterile and perfunctory. He wanted the lights out and was uncomfortable with nudity. He'd satisfy himself quickly, get out of bed and put on pajamas immediately. She was left frustrated and unfulfilled.

Jake was unselfish in every way. As a lover, he showed her sensitivity beyond her wildest imagination. He was uninhibited and loving and clearly put her pleasure above his own. He was the kind of person who derived a lot of his pleasure from giving to others. He was that kind of person in bed and out of bed as well. Finding a jewel of a man out here in the middle of nowhere had taken her completely by surprise. Now she would have to see if their magical love would survive when they were back in their own worlds.

Carrie got back to the picnic table before Jake returned. Thank God, it was still shady where their table was located. There was a stiff breeze blowing though the trees. She rearranged their stuff on top of the picnic table and lay down on top of it using one pack as a pillow and putting the other one under her knees. She was surprised at how comfortable she was. Bart stretched out on the cool cement pad underneath. Carrie stared up into the clear sky watching wispy Cottonwood tree seeds floating on the breeze. This time of year, they were dispersing their seeds, which covered the area with what looked like cottony snow. Each tiny seed had a giant kite of fluffy white fibers attached to it, which floated easily in the stiff river breezes. She fell asleep instantly.

Jake returned after a while and saw that Carrie was sound asleep on top of the table. He sat down at another picnic table nearby so as not to disturb her and watched her sleep. He thought about all that had happened to them during the past few days. He recalled the instant attraction they felt for each other at their dinner together at the Starlight Theater. God, but that felt like it happened years ago! How could so much change in a person's heart and soul in only a few days? He felt like he and Carrie had always been a couple. He liked to think that it felt like that with her because their spirits had known each other forever and it took a long time for their physical beings to finally catch up to each other.

He knew that seemed a bit metaphysical, but he was familiar enough with Eastern religious philosophy to understand that there were some things that defied scientific explanation. Here was a prime example. He and Carrie finding each other in one of the most unlikely places he could imagine. It felt like fate. The truck breaking down, completely stranding them, necessitating their hike to the river. The forced time alone together allowing them to compress years of learning about each other's character and nature into three short days. It couldn't be explained by any logical reasoning. He wasn't even going to try. All he knew for sure was what he felt in his own heart and soul, and that was that Carrie was the person he wanted to spend the rest of his life with. Now he just needed to convince her that they belonged together, no matter what.

Jake stretched out across his own picnic table and slept. He awakened when he heard a familiar-sounding truck pull up in the lot closest to their tables. He rolled off the table and saw that it was Carlos. He had brought the larger crew-cab truck that had the extra room inside since there would be three of them and Bart. He strolled over to Carlos with a huge smile on is face.

"Boy, Amigo, am I ever glad to see you. Are the other guys on their way to get my truck? I hope they have some extra parts with them, just in case. It looked to me like just a torn up radiator hose. I didn't see anything else wrong. I lost all the coolant out the bottom pretty fast." Bart had jumped up as soon as he heard the familiar truck and run over to greet Carlos, too.

"They left when I did. Don't worry, they'll have it back by this evening, I'm sure. Those guys can fix anything, Jake, you know that."

"Carlos, that pretty lady asleep over there is Carrie Turner. She'll be staying with us back at the ranch for a couple of days, but first we need to stop in Terlingua and get the rest of her stuff from the motel."

"Aha, Señor Jake, are you telling me that you had even more of an adventure than you said on the phone, no? You rascal. Maybe you have found a señorita for yourself out here in the desert, no?"

"I have found a señorita for myself, yes! And this is serious, Carlos. I mean it. I'm going to do everything I can to convince her to stay. It may take some doing, though. I think she still has some worries. I expect you and Maria to help me out here, OK?"

"You can count on us. Maria will be so happy and excited. She's prayed to our Holy Mother for a señorita for you for years, Señor Jake. She loves you like one of her own sons. She will be sure our Blessed Virgin of Guadalupe has answered her prayers." A wide smile filled Carlos's face and his eyes sparkled at the thought of Jake having a woman to love.

"Let's go over and wake her up and get going. It's still a long way back to the ranch with the stop in Terlingua. You're going to like her Carlos. She's a real keeper."

Jake gently shook Carrie's shoulder. "Wake up, Honey. Carlos is here and we can start back now."

Carrie sat up and slid off the tabletop and shook herself awake. She immediately offered her hand to Carlos. "I've heard so much about you, Carlos, and I'm so glad to finally meet you. Jake has told me how much affection he has for you and Maria and your whole family. I'm excited to meet the rest of them, too. Thank you so much for coming to get us." Her warm smile and firm grasp conveyed her genuine happiness to know him even without her words.

"I am happy to meet you, too, Señorita Turner. Jake says you will stay with us at the ranch, no? That way you'll get to meet everyone else, as well."

"Please call me Carrie, Carlos. We'll just get our stuff off the table here and we can get going. I'm excited to get to the ranch."

They each grabbed something and soon were settled in the cab of the truck. Carlos put the air conditioner on high, and Carrie luxuriated in the cold air blowing across them. She insisted on sitting in the back seat with Bart so she could load new film in her camera from her daypack. In the front seat, Jake told Carlos excitedly about the adventure he and Carrie had shared. An hour later, they were pulling up in front of Room 18 at the motel in Terlingua.

Carrie dug her room key out of her daypack and opened the door. "It'll just take me a minute to gather my things. I just have the one suitcase and a couple things in the bathroom." Carrie went into the bathroom and closed the door to pee. Then she washed her hands and grabbed her birth control pills out of the cabinet. She opened the packet. There were only three left. She figured she must be safe since she had taken most of them anyway. How could it hurt only missing the three of them at the end of the cycle? She'd probably get her period in a few more days but she prayed it would hold off until she had another night or two with Jake. The thought of a night or two more with him sent a thrill through her like an electric shock. She took one of the pills she had missed. Now there were only two left. That should hold her period off a few more days.

She wondered briefly why she continued to take them after her break-up with Clayton. She had been on them for a few years and they helped keep her periods so predictable that she just kept taking them. It made it much easier to plan wilderness shoots when she had her menstrual cycle under tight control. God knows she hadn't needed them for any other reason! Until now. Well, she wasn't worried about being pregnant with most of the pill cycle over with anyway. She gathered her toiletries and put them back into her little case and left the bathroom and put it in the suitcase with the rest of her things. Jake closed the suitcase for her and took it out to the truck. Carrie headed down to the office to check out of her room.

Pearl greeted her at the office door. "Well, for land's sakes, child! Where have you two been? Your secretary has called everyday, several times a day, mind you, frantic about you. What in the world happened to you?" She looked from Carrie to Jake and back, her keen eyes searching carefully for any little clues.

"It's a long story, Pearl. Jake will tell you later, I'm sure. I need to check out of my room." Carrie looked a little sheepish in Pearl's estimation, and Jake there, well he looked downright shifty as sin to her.

"Oh? I thought you didn't have to be back in New York for several more days?"

"Pearl, Miss Turner will be a guest at the ranch until she goes back to New York. We'll be leaving the keys to her Jeep here at the office with you. One of my men will pick it up tomorrow and drive it out to the ranch for Carrie, if that's Ok with you?" Carrie blushed and Jake kept continuous eye contact with Pearl as if daring her to say anything that would embarrass Carrie.

"That'll be just fine to leave your Jeep here until tomorrow. I'm sure you'll love the ranch, Honey. It's quite a place and you'll probably get some nice pictures out there, too. If you ever come back this way, I'd love to have you stay here and I'd much appreciate it if you'd tell your travel magazine friends about my place here, too." Pearl was obviously fighting hard to refrain from asking any more questions. The look Jake was giving her precluded that. Diana had already taken care of the bill in full when she made Carrie's arrangements for her stay. Carrie just needed to sign the check-out statement.

"Thank you very much, Pearl. It's been a pleasure knowing you and I certainly will tell everyone about your nice motel down here. I've enjoyed my stay a lot. I hope I see you again sometime." Carrie smiled at her and she and Jake turned and left the office.

Jake paused a second before he closed the door and turned to wink at Pearl with a sly grin. "Bye, Pearl. I'll see you when I come to town next."

The minute Pearl saw Jake and Carrie get back in the truck, she picked up her phone. The phone lines were going to burn right up with the news that she had to tell everyone this time.

Chapter Nine

They drove back to the junction of Highway 118 at Study Butte and turned north. After going north about fifteen miles, Carlos turned right onto a well-maintained dirt road. They drove under a wrought-iron arch with the name Stockton Ranch spelled out in the ironwork in the arch. A cattle guard completed the gate entrance, and they drove eastward toward some low craggy mountains.

"The tallest mountains you see up ahead, Carrie, are called the Corazones Peaks. 'Corazone' means 'heart' in Spanish. The ranch house is on the other side of those mountains in a small valley. It won't be too much longer now."

Jake turned and exchanged an excited smile with her. Carrie couldn't help but believe she was going to learn a lot more about this man, Jake Stockton, over the next couple of days. Being able to see where he grew up and meet people who had known him his whole life was bound to fill in a lot of details for her. His excitement at showing her this private part of his life was contagious. She reached out and affectionately squeezed his shoulder. He gently kissed her hand.

As their truck came over the pass between the highest Corazones Peaks and began descending into the valley below, Carrie got her first glimpse of where Jake had spent most of his life. She could see a large area of trees clustered around a very large hacienda-style main house and several outbuildings in the bottom of the valley. Even from this distance, it appeared to be beautifully landscaped and cared for. As they drew closer and closer to the ranch house, more details came into view. Carrie noticed several windmills whirling rapidly in the windy valley. There were corrals attached to some of the outbuildings. She saw horses in some and cattle in others. A large fenced grazing area contained a herd of goats. There were several small homes on the grounds, which appeared to house families of the ranch hands and a small chapel. She saw a building that reminded her of one of those small portable classrooms often seen next to older schools.

As they got closer to the ranch itself, Bart stood on the seat, restlessly wagging his tail furiously and whining. "We're almost there, Bart, but it looks like you already know that, though." Carrie stroked his back.

Soon, Carlos pulled up in front of the hacienda on a broad circular drive made of beautiful paving stones. The hacienda was a gorgeous white stucco Spanish-style, two-story mansion with a red tiled roof. Bright red and purple Bougainvillea grew around the outside of the home in an explosion of color. Some of the tall upstairs windows opened out onto small decorative wrought iron balconies holding colorful Mexican clay pots full of profusely blooming flowers. The front door was almost four feet wide and made of a beautifully hand carved dark wood of some kind. The top center section of the door contained an elaborately crafted stained glass window.

The door suddenly burst open and a short, stout Mexican woman came out to greet them. She had salt and pepper colored hair pulled back into a neat bun. She had on a colorful cotton Mexican-styled dress much like the ones Carrie had seen in the little village in Mexico. She had beautifully bronzed skin and dark brown expressive eyes that sparkled with life. She had on a pair of comfortable well-worn guaraches like the ones Carmen had given to Carrie for the fiesta. Maria gave Jake a familiar hug and spoke to him in softy in Spanish. Jake affectionately returned the hug.

"Maria, this is Carrie Turner. Carrie, this is Maria. She is Carlos's wife and has been part of our family almost forever. She was born and raised here on the ranch. She runs this place, actually." Jake laughed as Maria protested this last statement he made about her.

"Maria, I'm so delighted to meet you. Jake has told me much about you and I've been so excited to finally meet you." Carrie was surprised when Maria gave her the same kind of warm hug that she had given to Jake.

"Welcome to the Stockton Ranch, Carrie. We've all been excited anticipating your arrival. Come in, come in. I'll get you settled and then Jake will show you around." She took Carrie's hand and pulled her along with her to the inside of the front foyer. Carrie was surprised that Maria's English was so good. She spoke with a Spanish accent but her diction and vocabulary was that of someone who had been well educated.

The interior of the house was magnificent. Carrie sucked in her breath when she saw the handmade tile floor gleaming spotlessly in the soft light. It was cool inside, from a combination of air conditioning, surrounding shade trees, and the foot-thick walls of the house. A long staircase made of carved bola wood led to the upstairs. There was a large intricate wrought iron chandelier hanging in the front foyer, with matching wall sconces along the walls of the foyer and up the staircase. The wall sconces and the chandelier held soft electric bulbs but it was clear to Carrie that they probably used to hold candles at one time. They appeared to be antiques converted to use modern electric lighting.

She followed Maria up the staircase and into a large bedroom decorated in soft yellows. Carrie looked out of the tall window with French doors and saw that it opened on to a small balcony that overlooked a walled patio below. A small wrought iron staircase led from the balcony to the little patio below. The patio had a variety of colorful pottery jars holding a profusion of brightly blooming shrubs and flowers all around its inside walls. It was paved with interlocking paving stones designed in a circular pattern, and featured a bubbling stone fountain in the center. The walls surrounding the patio were overgrown with the brightly blooming Bougainvillea and there was a tall iron gate off to one side leading down a stone path around to the back of the hacienda. Two comfortable looking wrought iron chairs and a small table on the patio completed the tableau of a private little retreat from the world where two could have a breakfast or pass an evening together in privacy.

Carrie turned her attention to the bedroom. It had what looked like a king-sized carved four-poster bed with a beautiful intricately carved headboard. There was an enormous matching armoire and a dresser along another wall. There were two matching nightstands, a private sitting area with a butter-soft leather sofa and two large wing chairs arranged in front of an enormous fireplace. The fireplace was faced with colorful hand-painted tiles containing small Mexican scenes and flowers all reflecting the overall yellow décor of the room.

Along another wall was a beautiful antique desk holding a multi-line phone, a FAX machine and a computer. Another large cabinet with double doors sat near the writing desk. Maria walked over and opened the doors of the cabinet to reveal a large television. The lower doors contained a VCR, a compact disk player, stereo system, and other components of a surround-sound equipment. Carrie looked closely at the high ceilings and could see the small Bose speakers cleverly hidden in the carved ceiling molding. She thought that Jake sure wasn't just kidding when he suggested that she would be more comfortable here than at the motel in Terlingua!

Maria led her over to an adjoining room, which turned out to be the bath and dressing room. It had a room-sized walk-in closet, which already held her pretty Mexican clothes, neatly hung up. Her only outfit looked lost in the vastness of the closet space. Her guaraches sat in their own little cubical of a built-in shoe storage area, and her straw bag in another. The bathroom was decorated in the same pretty yellows of her bedroom. It held a large whirlpool tub, a walk-in shower area, a double sink, both a toilet and French bidet, and there was a make-up area with a large lighted mirror and small upholstered bench. She noticed scented soaps and shampoos and conditioners sitting in small baskets on the counters. There were bath towels, hand towels and washcloths neatly arranged in wicker shelves conveniently placed within reach of the tub and shower area. Carrie marveled that just this bathroom, dressing room, and the closet area was larger than her entire New York apartment!

"Maria, where does the door on the other side of the room lead?" Carrie pointed across the room to a carved wooden door near the fireplace grouping of furniture.

"That door opens into Señor Jake's room, Carrie. His room is similar to this one, only it is arranged more for the convenience of a man. This room is part of the original master suite of the hacienda. Since Jake's parents moved out, this room has remained empty until now. Jake thought you'd be more comfortable here as it is much larger and better furnished than the other guest rooms."

Carrie felt a heated flush creep up her body, beginning in the lower part of her belly and rapidly spreading to her beautiful face. She was afraid her voice would betray her flustered state to Maria. Maria immediately picked up Carrie's reaction, smiled to herself, and had the good sense to quickly change the subject and move on.

"Now that you know where your room and your things have been put, lets go find Jake. I'm sure he'll want to show you the rest of the hacienda himself." She led the way out of the magnificent bedroom and down the stairs, with Carrie following behind her, unable to conceal her excitement.

Jake was in the main room off of the foyer. He was talking with Carlos about ranching matters. Having been gone for three days, he probably had much catching up to do. He told Carlos they'd talk again later and Carlos excused himself. Carrie looked around the room furnished in hand carved antique furnishings. There were three large leather sofas arranged in a grouping in front of a fireplace along the far wall. The fireplace in this room was faced with similar hand-painted tiles to the one upstairs in Carrie's room, but this fireplace was much larger. Portraits of what she assumed were Stockton ancestors adorned some of the walls. She noted the beautiful resemblances to Jake in their faces. There were groupings of leather chairs, pretty carved tables holding beautiful lamps here and there around the room, which could clearly seat many people comfortably.

A double door led off the side of the great room into a cozy library. The walls were lined with floor to ceiling built-in wooden bookshelves filled with a fantastic collection of the classics, travel books, art books and beautiful carved figurines and interesting rocks, and what looked like ancient bones. Off to one side was an enormous wooden desk next to a computer console center containing a combination FAX machine and photocopier. A multi-line telephone sat on the desk. Next to the computer console sat two matching wooden file cabinets. There were comfortable chairs and lamp tables, and library tables around the room encouraging sitting and reading comfortably. At the back of the library, beyond the desk area, the library opened out onto the main patio that Carrie had noticed at the back of the great room.

"This is where the business of the ranch is handled. I use this room a lot, and encourage the others living here on the main compound to use it too, including the children. I have a special area in the far corner over there set up just for kids. It has small tables and chairs. All the children's books are within easy reach on the lower shelves." Jake picked up a large book off his desk, smiled broadly, and handed it to Carrie. "Do you recognize this? He asked.

"Of course, I do! This is my photo book of Alaska that was published a few years ago! I loved doing the Alaska shoot. It is such an incredible place." Carrie was pleased and flattered that Jake owned a copy of her book. "When did you get this?"

"I bought it a couple years ago at the bookstore in Alpine. I just happened to see it in there and I couldn't put it down. Can you believe the irony of it? I felt compelled to buy the book, and now, here you are in my life, the author of it! This is the fate kind of stuff I was talking about down in San Vicente. I took it out and looked at it again when I knew you were coming here to photograph Big Bend." Jake smiled tenderly at her, took the book from her and placed it back on his desk before leading her out of the library.

He led her back into the great room and over to a double set of French doors that led out onto a beautiful large walled patio. It had a large stone fountain and pots of blossoming shrubs and flowers much like the tiny private patio off of her bedroom. He opened the doors and she inhaled the fragrances of Jasmine, Gardenia, and Honeysuckle. She could see that the sun was setting rapidly and small glass globe lanterns had been lit around the patio. There were wrought iron furnishings conveniently placed in this patio, too. The same swirling paving stones formed a circular design with the fountain as the centerpiece.

Jake closed the door to the patio and explained to Carrie. "It'll be surprisingly cooler out there later in the evening. You'd be surprised at how much a fountain will cool down an area. The splashing water really removes a lot of heat from the air through evaporation. We're fortunate to have two deep water wells tapping directly into an underlying aquifer, so we always have plenty of water here, even in dry years." He placed his hand on her waist and guided her out through a doorway off the back of the great room, speaking as they walked through a rear hallway.

"Now I'll show you the kitchen and dining areas, then I'll give you a chance to rest for a while, Carrie. I know you need to make some more phone calls. Everything you'll need is on the desk in your room. Feel free to use the FAX and the computer for email. There are office supplies in the desk drawers and if there's anything else you need that you don't see there, let me know and I'll get it."

"I can't imagine I'll need anything else. That room is gorgeous, like a fairytale dream. I've never stayed in anything so beautiful in my life. I just love it! I'll never be able to look at my little New York apartment the same. You're spoiling me rotten, Jake." Carrie gave him her bright smile that always melted him through and through.

"Well, Carrie, my love. I can't say that I don't have my ulterior motives. I want you close and available to me both day, and especially, night." He lowered his voice and breathed close to her ear when he said the word night.

He then continued in a near-normal voice. "You can relax and bathe and change if you'd like for dinner later. Whatever would make you the most comfortable. First we'll have refreshments on the patio and eat dinner later, if you're not too hungry to wait a little while. We usually eat the traditional late dinners that are common in Mexico. That gives all of us time to finish our chores, get back to the main house, cleaned up, and have time to relax with a drink before dinner."

They entered a large kitchen. It had an enormous central island made of wooden butcher block. A hanging wrought iron pan rack held all different sized pots and skillets. One wall had a large six-burner gas stove and next to that were a double oven and a large warming oven. A giant range hood vented the heat away from the cooking area. Another wall had a double sized, four-door stainless steel refrigerator. Next to the refrigerator was a tall, wine cooler with a glass door. There were large sinks and counter spaces for preparing food. Three women worked away at preparing the evening meal.

Jake spoke to the women in Spanish and they turned and smiled at Carrie. Carrie heard Jake speak her name in his stream of Spanish.

"Carrie, this is Consuela, Rosa, and Carmelita. They are the wives and daughters of some of my ranch hands. They live with their families in some of the houses you saw as we drove in."

"Hola," Carrie responded, proud that she remembered the word for 'hello' that Jake had taught her down at San Vicente.

Jake next led her through a swinging door into the main dining room. It was at the front of the hacienda, off the foyer from the other side of the great room. It had a long carved wooden table and enough chairs to seat twenty people. As they passed through the formal room, Jake explained. "We only use this when we have lots of people over for something, or the other. I usually eat on the private patio off of your room or down on the big patio. I like it so much better than this monstrous empty room. It serves its purpose when necessary, but I avoid it when I'm eating alone."

They had come full circle through the house and now stood back in front of the staircase in the foyer. "I have some business I need to take care of, Carrie. You can go up and make your phone calls and do whatever you'd like to for an hour, or so. I'll be up after I finish in the library, shower, and change. Then we'll come down and relax on the main patio where we can have our dinner."

"Tomorrow I want to show you around the rest of the main compound surrounding the house. There is no way we have time for me to show you around the entire twenty thousand acres! That would take a week, or more. I'll have to do that when you come back from New York." Jake spoke confidently, as if Carrie's return to the ranch was a foregone conclusion.

He pulled her into a tender embrace and kissed her deeply with all the lingering promise of more to come later. "Go on, girl, right now, before I lose my good sense and chase you up the stairs and ravish you."

Carrie giggled, teasingly pushed away from him, and ran up the staircase feeling happier than she could ever remember feeling in her life. She replied in a smoky voice over her retreating shoulder, "I'll see you later then, Jake. Don't work too hard. I'd hate for you to fall asleep early tonight."

Jake watched her until she disappeared into her room and closed the door. He loved the way her ponytail bounced around her shoulders as she ran up the stairs, making her look like an excited little kid. He watched her strong shapely legs take the stairs, two at a time, and found himself remembering what they felt like, wrapped around him when he was buried deep inside her. She was so full of life and fun. He couldn't remember the last time his home had been so alive and full of laughter. His very soul was singing he felt so happy. He headed across the room to the library to finish some ranch business as quickly as he could. He could hardly wait until he could be with her again in an hour.

Carrie sat down at the desk in her room and found a notepad and pen in the top drawer. She picked up the phone to call Diana. The little clock on her desk said five-thirty, which meant it would be six-thirty in New York. Diana should be home by now. She answered on the second ring.

"Diana, this is Carrie again. What's up? Did you get my hotel reservation in Alpine and my flight on Friday morning?"

"I sure did. You are all set. You need to be over at the Alpine airport by ten on Friday morning. Your flight leaves at eleven-thirty in the morning. That flight goes straight to Dallas, after a couple of stops, of course, then you'll fly from Dallas to JFK direct. You'll get into New York at ten at night. Sorry, it's so late, Carrie, but it is the best I could get for you."

"Diana, that's fine. I'll be into the office about ten on Saturday morning. The guys in photo can develop all my film and we can meet with the magazine people at three o'clock. That'll give us time to look them over first. You'll be in on Saturday, too, won't you?"

"I was planning on it. These people are willing to work Sunday, too, just as long as they get what they want as soon as possible. Any chance you have a FAX machine near where you're calling from? I could FAX your travel arrangements, that way you wouldn't have to try to write this all down."

Carrie looked over at the FAX and noticed that the phone number for it was on the front. It was clearly on a different line than the phone she was using. She gave Diana the number to the FAX. She could tell by the lights on the buttons of her phone that someone was using yet another line, as well. She figured it was Jake downstairs in the library. Jeeze! She wondered how many different phone lines came into this place, anyway? She could see at least five from looking at the buttons on her phone. The FAX next to her started up and she could see the printout of her itinerary coming out the front. You sure couldn't beat this place for convenience, she thought to herself.

"Your FAX is here. I have it in my hand. The arrangements look fine to me. Thanks so much for taking care of it for me."

"Well, you can thank Sandy. She's the best secretary I could ever hope for. There's nothing that woman can't accomplish and I'd be screwed without her. Hey, Carrie, it doesn't sound like you're calling from your motel room. You must be calling from the motel office where there's a FAX."

"Well, Diana, not exactly. I'm out at Jake's ranch. I'll be staying here until I leave. I can give you the number here where you can reach me."

"Really? Carrie, I think there is an awful lot going on with you that I don't know about. I thought you sounded different this afternoon and you still have a strange quality to your voice. I don't suppose you're going to tell me anything now, but you better be ready to spill everything later. I'll want to know what's happened to you down there, you hear me, Babe?"

"I promise, Diana. I'll tell you absolutely everything over dinner on Saturday night. It's pretty unbelievable, actually."

"Good unbelievable, or bad unbelievable, Carrie? You better not say it's bad unbelievable, either."

"No, it's good unbelievable. I think? Oh, God, Diana. I need to talk to you about all this. But we'll just have to wait until Saturday. If you don't hear from me sooner, I'll see you Saturday at the office about noon. 'Love ya, Bye."

Carrie hung up and stared at her itinerary. Two days. That's how much time she had left with Jake before she had to leave. And three more nights, assuming he'd go with her to Alpine on Thursday afternoon. She had the strongest feeling that he'd be in that lovely Tree House Room with her on Thursday night. A thrill ran through her at the thought. She set the printout on the desk and went into the bathroom to take a shower and put on some clean clothes. She noticed that someone had brought her suitcase upstairs and placed it on a fold-up luggage holder in the walk-in closet. She took out her toiletry case and placed it on the counter next to the bathroom sink. She took off her hiking boots and placed them in one of the little shoe cubicles. She dropped her sweaty sox into a laundry hamper. She stripped, adjusted the water temperature, and stepped into the luxurious shower.

When she was finished with her shower, she stepped out onto the thick pile rug in front of the shower. She dried off with an oversized Egyptian cotton bath sheet. She went to her suitcase and chose a pair of white cotton knit shorts and a powder blue knit tank top. She decided to wear her comfortable guaraches sandals. She sat down on the bench in front of the large mirror and brushed out her pretty blond hair. She pulled it back into a ponytail and secured it with a blue silk-covered elastic band. She added a touch of pale rose lipstick, just enough to give her a little color. She found a bottle of Jasmine scented body lotion on the counter and rubbed a little into her chapped elbows, hands and knees. It smelled wonderful and soothed her desert-dried skin.

When she went back into her bedroom, she thought she could hear the sound of a shower running on the other side of the door leading to Jake's bedroom. She decided to go downstairs ahead of him and look around in the library some more. She had seen so many fascinating mementos on some of the shelves that had obviously been brought home from world travels, and she wanted to look at them more closely.

Jake arrived before long and found her in the library. He was clean-shaven and his hair was still damp from his shower, curling attractively around the back of his neck. He had on a pair of khaki shorts and a green sleeveless knit shirt, which only emphasized his fantastic physique. He looked gorgeously handsome to Carrie.

"Why don't we go out to the patio, Carrie, and enjoy the wonderful evening? The girls have some cold drinks for us already on the table and a plate of snacks to go with the drinks." He held out his hand to her, beckoning her to take it.

"That sounds great, Jake. I'd really enjoy that." She took his hand and they walked outside to the table and chairs by the fountain. It was still warm out, but not unpleasantly so. She sat down and Jake poured her a tall glass of Sangria. Fresh orange and lemon slices floated in the delicious wine punch. There was a plate of fresh cheeses and crackers on the table. Carrie helped herself. Jake poured himself a glass of Sangria and sat down next to Carrie, propping his feet up on one of the extra chairs. Carrie sat back with her glass of Sangria and inhaled the fragrances of the night-blooming Jasmine and the gardenia. The honeysuckle blossoms had closed up as soon as it got dark, but she could still smell their lingering aroma on the night air. The fountain gurgled pleasingly, sounding every bit to Carrie like the small creeks she had heard when she was in the mountains in Alaska and by the little spring in the desert on their hike down Mariscal Canyon. Candles and small lanterns flickered from around the patio area casting a romantic glow over the whole area.

"Were you able to talk to your office earlier? I hope you didn't have any problem getting hold of Diana. Did she have your flight schedule figured out for you?"

"I forgot to bring my itinerary downstairs with me. It's sitting on the desk in my room. I had Diana FAX it to me. I leave Friday morning at eleven-thirty from the Alpine airport. She booked me into the Tree House Room again at the Corner House for Thursday night. I plan to drive up to Alpine late Thursday afternoon so I'm there before dark." Carrie had her fingers crossed hoping Jake would say he'd go with her to Alpine. She wasn't disappointed.

"I'll go with you up to Alpine on Thursday, Carrie. At least if that's OK with you. That way we'll have one more night together before you have to leave. I'll follow you up in my truck and then we can drop your rental car off Thursday night. I'll take you to the airport Friday morning." Jake got up and walked over to the fountain, keeping his back to Carrie so she wouldn't see the difficulty he was having keeping himself composed while talking about her leaving.

"I'd love that, Jake. I'll greedily take every last minute of time with you I can get," she replied softly.

Jake whirled around to face her. "Carrie, do you really mean that? If so, then stay here with me. Don't ever go away. Oh, God, Carrie. Listen to me! I'm such an idiot! I know you have to go back for this project, but please come back to me here when you're finished with it."   Carrie could see that Jake's face was tortured with unspoken thoughts and emotions.

"I think we'll just have to see how we still feel when we are both away from each other for a while.   Maybe our feelings will change when we're not together.   The last few days have been so intense and everything has happened so fast.   How can we be sure, Jake?"

"Do you really believe in your heart that what you are saying is true, Carrie?   Do you really believe in your soul that we'll feel differently a week, or a month from now?   I know I won't.   Of that much, I'm positive."   Jake came over and knelt beside Carrie's chair and took her chin in his hand and gently tilted her face toward him so she had to look into his eyes.   "Look at me, Carrie, and tell me you won't still love me when you are back in New York.   You can't do it, can you?"

"Jake, I'm afraid.   I've been hurt in the past and I want to be sure that what you are saying and feeling is true.   I want to be absolutely sure, and I need to really know that you are, too.   This is such a major decision for both of us.   Especially for me.   We need to take this time and be sure our feelings will exist outside of this magical place."   Carrie leaned forward and kissed Jake's trembling lips.   "Let's just enjoy the time we have left and let the future fall into place naturally.   If this is meant to be, then we'll both know it soon enough."

"I know you're right, Carrie.   But the thought of you leaving here grips my heart with such powerful feelings of despair I nearly go crazy!   I'll try not to think about it and be more patient.   But I can't make any guarantees, Sweetheart."

Jake sat back down and refilled both their glasses with more of the fruity wine punch.   They were both beginning to feel the heady wine work its magic on them.   They relaxed and laughed together talking about their adventurous past few days.   Jake made Carrie promise to send him copies of some of the pictures she had taken.   Soon Rosa appeared and asked Jake if they were ready for their dinner.   He and Carrie answered "yes" in unison, as they were both starving.

Rosa brought them a simple flavorful dinner of roasted chicken, fresh grilled vegetables, savory black beans, fresh tortillas and salsa. They laughed together enjoying their delicious meal and when they were done, Rosa served them each a dish of a cold caramelized Spanish custard called 'flan.' After dessert, they sat sipping coffee laced with brandy, talking together softly into the night while watching the moon rise in the sky over the garden walls.

Hand in hand, Jake walked Carrie up the long staircase to her bedroom. He followed her inside and closed her heavy bedroom door. He took her in his arms and began a kiss that felt like it would never stop. It was slow and deep, a melding of more than their mouths, but their hearts and souls as well. He deepened the kiss, plundering her mouth and probing its depths all the while moving them ever closer to the large bed. Carrie began tugging on Jake's shirt, pulling it free from the waistband of his shorts. She ran her hands up under his shirt, desperate for the feel of his warm skin covering his taut male muscles. He broke off their kiss long enough to slip his shirt off over his head, and reached to pull her back into his embrace.

"No, Jake. This night will be my gift to you. I'm going to undress you myself and have my way with you. And you're going to let me."

Carrie reached for the top button on his shorts and slowly unbuttoned it. Before unzipping his shorts, she ran her hand down his burgeoning length bulging beneath the khaki fabric. The tactile sensation of her teasingly stroking the outside of the fabric over his imprisoned erection caused a ragged groan to escape from his lips. Carrie pulled back the pretty yellow bedspread and told Jake to sit back on the edge of the bed. She stood in front of him and eased the top of her tank top down, freeing her breasts directly in front of his face. He leaned forward and sucked a peaked nipple into his mouth, reaching to try to pull her down on the bed next to him.

"Not yet, Jake. Two can play this game and I'm a fast learner. I think you're going to like my rules even better than your own." She smiled wickedly and gave him a sly wink.

She pushed him back indicating that he should lie down on the bed. He kicked off his sandals, letting them drop to the floor next to the foot of the bed. He looked up at Carrie standing over him next to the bed. He was mesmerized watching her pull the elastic band out of her ponytail allowing her hair to fall around her shoulders. She leaned her head back and shook out her hair, a motion that caused her breasts to sway seductively over him. He moaned and reached out for her and she gently but firmly pushed his hands away.

She reached down and began to slowly unzip his walking shorts, stroking him as the zipper descended. She slid his shorts down his hips, which was a movement he was happy to assist her in doing. They dropped them off the foot of the bed along with his sandals. She gently pushed him back flat on the bed still in his silk undershorts. She ran a fingernail slowly up his leg from his ankle to the top of his thigh. The slight grating sensation her nail created as it slowly drew through the hair on his legs was excruciatingly sensuous. She left her hand on the edge of his groin just under the silk of his shorts while she leaned down and kissed his lips tenderly. Her full breasts brushed against his chest as she did this. Next she began trailing slow, tender kisses down the side of his neck and onto his chest. She stopped at a nipple and reached out her tongue and circled the taut bud several times. Jake arched up off the bed, his hips thrusting upwards.

"No, Jake. Be still. I not finished yet." Carrie put a hand on his chest indicating that he should lie still.

"My God, Carrie! I don't think I can take anymore of this. You're making me crazy."

He writhed beneath her firm hand on his chest, her thumb continuing to worry his erect nipple. His erection was straining against the fabric of his undershorts, threatening to burst through the thin silk. His head rolled back and forth across the pillow, his eyes trained on the sight of her naked breasts and her sensuous hair cascading around her shoulders. It was the most arousing scene he could have ever imagined - only it wasn't just his imagination. This was real and happening to him. He feared that if he didn't close his eyes, he'd completely lose it. He shut them tightly.

"Jake, open your eyes and watch what I'm going to do to you." Carrie's voice was soft, but also erotically commanding.

Carrie removed her hand from his thigh and reached into the opening of his silky shorts, freeing his imprisoned penis through the opening. She wrapped her hand around its length and pulled upward, staring at its smooth taut head. A bead of pearly fluid glistened at the cleft of his opening.

"Be still now, Jake," she uttered. "Don't you dare move. I'm not through exploring yet." She removed her hand from his chest and began easing her own shorts and panties seductively over her hips and stepped out of them. She was now totally naked and ready to make her final moves.

She returned her hand to his chest and toyed with his nipple, the firm pressure telling him without words to remain laying flat. She then grasped and squeezed his fully engorged erection with a milking action. The bead of pearly fluid sitting in the cleft of his opening grew. She watched in fascination as it began to slowly ooze over the edge of the head and run down the under side of his penis. Next she began to do what his imagination was screaming for, but that he didn't think he would be able to stand.

"Oh, my God, no, Carrie. I'll never make it, I swear to you! I'll go right over the edge!" His voice was hoarse and ragged with the supreme effort it was taking to maintain control of himself.

She leaned over him, branding him where her hot nipples touched his skin. She began slowly licking him from the base to the throbbing head of his erection, lapping at his leaking essence with her fiery tongue. She circled the rigid tip of his penis with the tip of her tongue, using the same sensuous, circular motions she was using on his nipple. She closed her lips tightly around the pulsing head and slowly let his length slide deeply into her torrid mouth, until the tip of him touched the back of her throat.   Maintaining suction, she leisurely raised her head back up his length, letting him slide out of her mouth by agonizing degrees. She let her tongue stroke and caress along the sensitive underside of him, all the way to its tip. At the same time, she gently massaging his testicles through the silk of his shorts, rolling each globe gently between her thumb and fingers.

Jake was pleading and crying out for her to come to him. He was delirious from the most exquisite, intoxicating torture he had ever endured. No practiced courtesan could have set him aflame like this angel that was ravishing him now. He slipped his hand between her legs, exploring the flaming flesh of her vulva. Her juices instantly drenched his fingers. Using his other hand, he fondled her breasts and squeezed her budded nipples, feeling the evidence of her readiness. She moaned and started another slow descent over his length, allowing him to again slowly sink deeply into her throat. He increased the tempo of his stroking of her pulsing bundle of nerves; erect and quivering with her own intense need. When he felt his penis touch the back of her throat for the second time, he frantically screamed out her name and she knew it was time. She released him from her mouth and quickly pulled his silk shorts over his hips and down his legs. She swung her leg up over his writhing body and sat astride him, while he frantically reached for her hips. She raised up on her knees and guided him to her opening.

As soon as Carrie could feel him rigidly probing the swollen lips of her vulva, she began slowly lowering herself down his length, controlling her rate of descent by using her strong leg muscles. She instinctively contracted and released the muscles of her passage walls, swallowing him like a snake swallows its captive prey, inch by inch. She thrilled at the sound of his ragged voice, pleadingly begging her to hurry. She lowered her body down, swallowing him deeper and deeper, finally allowing him to bury himself to his hilt. When she felt his length bump tightly against her womb, and her vaginal walls were stretched to their limit by his thickness, she lost all her own carefully measured control.

Jake now felt free to open his eyes, which instantly locked with Carrie's. Hers scorched him with blue fire. He stared, riveted by the erotic scene of her lush breasts swinging above his face as she bucked on top of him while he thrust into her violently with his hips. She leaned forward encouraging him to reach one of her rigid nipples and suck it deeply into his mouth. He held her hips tightly against him, plunging in and out of her furiously. The heady feeling of power she gained heightened her own fiery passions, by realizing that she could drive him to distraction. She claimed his lips and kissed him deeply, sharing with him the flavors of his own male essence mingled with the honeyed taste of her mouth.

Jake swallowed Carrie's scream as he felt her first fevered spasms, signaling the beginning of an explosive orgasm. Buried deeply inside of her, he savored the erotic sensations caused by the contractions of her internal muscles around him. He exploded inside her with a violence he had never before experienced, pulsating and pumping into her body a seemingly endless flow of his own being. Carrie collapsed across his chest, crying tears of passion and release. Jake was aware of his own dampened cheeks and knew he was feeling the same emotions that Carrie was experiencing. He tenderly brushed her hair away from her face and kissed her cheek, murmuring love words to her.

"Carrie, Carrie. Baby, I love you so much. I can't believe what you've done to me! Oh, Carrie, my Darling. You are more incredible than any dream or fantasy that I've ever imagined. God, I love you so much, my Treasure." He kissed her eyelids and her nose and her chin. He caressed her back and stroked her long, golden hair.

"Jake, I don't think I can move. I don't think I even want to move, ever. I want to keep you inside of me like this until we die together. I think maybe we have died together, and gone straight to heaven! Oh, Jake, I love you so!"

They were both spent. They dozed off locked together, then awoke and made love several more times that night. Each time, they fell asleep wrapped tightly in each other's arms until they finally awoke to bright sunshine, streaming through the balcony window.

"Carrie, I want to show you the rest of this part of the ranch today. We'll have another night together here before we need to go to Alpine. It isn't nearly enough, but it will have to hold us until we can make other plans." Jake pulled her more tightly against him and kissed her lovingly.

"I suppose we should get up then, Jake, and get started on the day. Somehow, I have the feeling we slept pretty late, looking at how much sunlight is streaming through the windows."

"I could stay right here in this bed with you, Baby, and not get up at all. But then I couldn't show you all I want to, could I?" He kissed her and rolled out of bed. He walked over to her desk and picked up the phone, pushed one button and spoke to Rosa in the kitchen.

"Rosa, good morning. We'll have our breakfast on the master suite patio in about one-half hour. We need a pot of coffee and some mugs out there right away, though. We'll be down there soon. Thank you so much." He hung up and turned to see Carrie, still lounging across the bed.

"I'm going to go shower in my bathroom while you use yours." He came over and began gathering up his clothes off the floor around the bed. He tossed Carrie's clothes playfully on top of her.

"Get up, you wanton little creature, before I have to paddle your tempting little bottom." He began walking toward her with a lecherous gleam in his eyes.

Carrie leaped off the other side of the bed. Jake made a dive across the bed to grab her, narrowly missing her. "You wouldn't dare, Jake Stockton," she yelled to him and ran giggling into the safety of her bathroom, closing and locking the door.

She stood there laughing to herself, thinking about how free and full of fun and laughter Jake was. She had never experienced such uninhibited joy in any relationship in her life. She never realized that just being alive with another person could complete her, heart and soul.

Carrie finished her long shower, noting that her lady parts were feeling sore from three non-stop nights of lovemaking. She hadn't had sex at all since her break up with Clayton. She thought wryly that the sex she shared with him hadn't been enough to make anything sore.

Her thoughts of making love with Jake sent a shiver through her in spite of the hot water coursing over her skin. Two more nights of splendor with him. She wouldn't miss these next two nights for anything in the world, no matter how sore she might be feeling. She toweled off and sat down at her dressing table. She took another one of her birth control pills. So far, so good. No period yet to interrupt her nights with Jake. It looked like it would conveniently hold off until she was back in New York.

She dressed in clean shorts and a sleeveless knit shirt. She hurried out into the bedroom, and gathered up her dirty clothes and put them in her laundry hamper in the closet. Jake had mentioned yesterday that Carmelita did all the laundry on Wednesdays and for Carrie to put everything she needed washed into her hamper. Carrie thought it would sure be easy to get used to all this service. It was something she hadn't experienced before. She looked at her totally wrecked bed and decided to strip the sheets off and put them in the hamper as well. She was embarrassed by what a mess they had made out of her sheets. She was hoping Carmelita wouldn't notice.

She picked up her camera, put some extra rolls of film in her short's pocket, and slipped on her guaraches. She went out onto the balcony, took some photos of the little patio from above, and a distance view down the valley. She descended to the patio, looking forward to the coffee already sitting on the table. She took some photos of the fountain and the flowers then sat down and poured herself a cup of coffee while she waited for Jake to come down. The table and chairs were mercifully in the shade as the temperature already felt like it was easily in the 90s. She saw Jake through the wrought iron gate, walking toward the patio from around the back of the house.

"Good Morning, my Beauty!" He kissed the top of her pretty head, poured himself a cup of coffee and sat down next to her.

"Well, you look pretty fine yourself, this morning, Jake. I expected to see you coming down the balcony stairs."

"It didn't take me long in the bathroom, so I stopped by the kitchen to talk with Maria about our plans for today. She oversees the whole household so she will make sure that lunch is ready for us whenever we get finished with our tour of the ranch. I also wanted to discuss some possible dinner menus with her. I want your last dinner here with me tonight to be extra special. I want you to enjoy it so much that you'll come back for the food alone!"

"I have to admit that I've found, um, everything I've tasted here to be absolutely delicious." She gave him a lingering, smoky look from under lowered eyelids, as she could see that he hadn't missed the double message in her words. It was Jake's turn to blush furiously.

He shifted in his chair and sucked in a ragged breath as he felt himself instantly growing hard for her. "Carrie, my Sweet, you are asking for trouble, young lady. You'd better watch that sweet mouth of yours or you're going to find yourself flat on your back underneath me right here on this patio." He saw Rosa coming around to the gate with their breakfast tray. He jumped up to open the gate for her, and took the opportunity to readjust the crotch of his shorts after she walked past him.

"Gracias, Rosa." Carrie valiantly tried out her Spanish again. Rosa spoke into a stream of excited Spanish back at her, looking at her with all smiles. Carrie looked helplessly at Jake for assistance.

Jake spoke to Rosa in Spanish telling her that Carrie only knew two words so far, hello and thank you. Rosa reached down and patted Carrie's hand and smiled at her replying in English, "You are welcome, Carrie." She spoke again to Jake in Spanish then left the patio with a satisfied grin.

They both ate as if they hadn't seen food in months. They ate a mountain of buttermilk hotcakes drenched in fresh strawberry syrup, and had bacon and sausage links on the side. There was a pitcher of fresh-squeezed orange juice on the table. They had burned up a lot of calories during their heated night together. They finished by sipping their coffee, used the bathroom off the kitchen, and then headed out on their tour.

Jake took her over to a long, metal horse barn. They went inside and she saw huge fans cooling down the animal pens inside. There were stalls with gorgeous horses and even a few little colts with their mares. It smelled clean - like fresh hay. He led her out the far door at the end and around next to the corral attached to the back. More horses stood in the shade of the building next to a large watering trough full of cool-looking water. He pointed up on the large expanse of roof on the barn.

"This entire roof is covered with solar panels. I designed the system myself. That small building next to the barn holds batteries and inverters, and a large back-up generator. The diesel fuel tank next to the building fuels the generator whenever we're required to use it, which isn't often. We can run this barn and the main house totally off of solar power. And we use the sun to provide all our hot water, besides." He smiled proudly and scanned her face watching for her reaction to his cleverness. He wasn't disappointed.

"I can't believe that! I wondered why I didn't see any power lines when we drove in here yesterday, but I guess I just didn't think about it any further. I figured they must just be underground or came in from another direction." She stepped back and looked at the roof more closely, clearly amazed and impressed.

"You'll notice that each house and building on the property is covered with solar panels on the south side. If there isn't a south-facing roof expanse, you'll see the panels mounted on a large framework sitting beside the structure it provides with electricity. It was costly to put the system in but it makes us completely energy independent. We don't cause any drain on the grid in this part of the country."

Carrie shook her head in disbelief. They walked on and he showed her the windmills he used to harness the wind for pumping water out of the wells and into a large holding tank. "This way, when it isn't windy, we can still have plenty of water from the tanks. The windmills mainly just keep the tanks filled all the time. They shut off automatically when the tanks are full and come back on when the tanks fall below a certain level. We have two windmills and two tanks. We always have one as a back up in case something happens to one of them. We can run the whole place off of either tank. The solar panels here provide the electricity to pump the water from the tanks to the rest of the property." Carrie took photos of everything Jake was showing her. She was totally fascinated.

Next they went over to a small chapel. Jake held the door and Carrie stepped inside. It was heavenly cool and dark and several small votive candles flickered brightly through red glass on the altar. A large, hand-carved crucifix hung above the candles on the back wall. It smelled of incense and holy water. It had wooden pews on both sides of a small aisle and looked like it could seat maybe forty people, twenty to a side. Jake placed his fingers in the little bowl of holy water at the back of the church and crossed himself. Carrie did the same, and they stepped back out into the bright sunlight.

"We have one of priests in Alpine come out here when we need him. We have weddings, baptize all our babies born on the ranch, and bury people from here, as well. Most of the people who work on the ranch were born here. Their families have lived, married, raised families, and died right here for generations. They want to be buried next to this little chapel, close to other family members and life-long friends. Many of my own family members are buried here, too. I'll point out their graves to you some other time."

Carrie could see a small, fenced cemetery with carved headstones adjoining the church. Many of the graves were decorated with colorful paper flowers and crosses. The graves were obviously well tended by the people living on the ranch.

"Jake, this is just lovely. What a peaceful, restful place. It feels so very, how can I explain this, family-ish. I can understand why they'd want to be here instead of in some impersonal graveyard in a distant town somewhere."

Carrie pointed to the little building she had seen when they drove in, the one that looked like a portable classroom. They walked over to it and Carrie could hear children reciting inside. They peeked in a back window so as not to disturb the class session. Carrie saw Maria standing in front of a chalkboard clearly teaching a class of about ten elementary-age students.

"Jake, this looks like a school. I didn't know Maria was also a teacher!" Carrie's eyes sparkled with amazement.

"She is a teacher. She got her Bachelors degree in elementary education from Sul Ross University in Alpine. She teaches all the ranch children through the sixth grade. After that, they go to school in Terlingua. There is a school bus stop right outside the main gate at the highway. Someone drives them out to the bus stop in the morning then meets the bus when it drops them off in the afternoon. We use that large van parked under the carport next to the school. It seats twelve people and they also use it when they want to take field trips. This little classroom has four computers all hooked to the Internet. They also have satellite TV for educational programs, as well.

I want every child on this property to have an education and I guarantee them one if they work hard at their studies. I keep a fund set aside to pay for their college education, if they choose that path. I'll pay for it even if they choose to leave the ranch and work somewhere else. Most of them stay. I also pay for industrial education or trade school if they choose. I see this as my legacy to these people who are like family to me. I can give them the opportunity to make their lives better than the lives of their parents and grandparents." Jake looked serious and committed as he spoke passionately about his philosophy of education.

Carrie just shook her head. She was so utterly amazed by the unfolding complexity of this man she had met out here in the middle of nowhere, and fallen deeply in love with. How would she ever be able to explain him to Diana when she got back to New York? Diana would think she was surely making it all up. Carrie wondered what other surprises she'd find out about Jake.

Bart sidled up to Carrie, nuzzled her hand for attention, wagging his tail. "Bart, where have you been? I haven't seen you since we got here, come to think of it." Carrie knelt down and gave Bart a hug. "You'll have to excuse me, Bart, for being a little distracted since I got here. You've got Jake to blame for that, though." She shot Jake a devilish glance.

"Bart has been spending some time with his own little family, Carrie."

Carrie looked up to see a line of little miniatures of Bart prancing single-file toward them. They waddled and tumbled, nipping at each other's tails and mouths as they followed their daddy dog, Bart, over to where Jake and Carrie were standing. Bart wagged his tail proudly as his brood came over.

"Oh, my God, Jake! They are so cute! There are five of them, too. Where is their mother? Why, Bart, you sly devil. I had no idea of the secret you kept!"

Jake picked up one of the puppies and cuddled it. "I expect she is getting some much-needed rest after we kept Bart away from here for three days. Poor old she-dog. She had to look after this brood all by herself while Bart was off traipsing around the desert with us. We need lots of dogs around the place. They keep away some of the wildlife that can really make a mess of things, like armadillos, Javelinas, coyotes, and more. Unfortunately, a lot of the puppies like these don't survive to adulthood. There were originally seven in this litter, now we're down to only five."

Carrie looked at Jake questioningly, clearly distressed. "What happens to them, Jake?"

"Coyotes get them, mainly. Coyotes will slink around just waiting for a puppy to wander off from the group. They'll quickly snatch it up and take off with it. If an adult dog doesn't keep them chased away, they'll seize a chance to get what they can. Sometimes an eagle will swoop in and carry one off, but more often, it's coyotes."

Carrie shuddered. "That's just horrible, Jake. I can't stand to even think about it. Poor little puppies."

Carrie scooped up one of the puppies from under her feet, brought it protectively close to her and kissed it. She held it up in front of her and looked into its clear eyes and at its tiny pink tongue reaching out trying to lick her face. She marveled at how soft and clean it was and how good it smelled from the hot sun on its fur. She instinctively cuddled it close to her breast.

"Jake these guys are just too cute." Jake loved watching her so genuinely excited over the little puppies. "Boy! Are these chick-magnets, or what? I mean, how could I ever say no to a guy with a yard full of puppies?"

"Jake gave her a dead-serious look. "I'm counting on you not saying no to me, Carrie. I don't know what I'd do if you did, say no, that is." He looked so vulnerable, standing there like a little boy, shuffling his boots in the dirt, one hand stuck in his back pocket and a puppy cuddled against his chest with the other.

Her heart melted. "Jake, I love you. I don't know what else to say right now." She put the little puppy down and it jumped up on her legs, whimpering and begging to be picked up again. "Oh, brother, am I ever a goner," she laughed down to the tiny dog.

They walked back toward the house and Bart herded his unruly litter back toward one of the little outbuildings. Carrie and Jake laughed at their hilarious antics on their way in for lunch.

"We'll eat lunch, then we'll just hang out in the cool house during the heat of the afternoon. You can read in the library with me while I get some paperwork done, if you'd like. Maybe we could take a little afternoon nap," he added with a sly wink.

She laughed and looped her arm casually through his as they continued walking back to the main house. They walked around to the back of the house toward the kitchen door. Jake showed Carrie the large vegetable garden used by the main ranch compound. It was two acres enclosed by the adobe walls she had seen surrounding the gardens in the little villages in Mexico. It was off the kitchen on the other side of the wall from the main patio.

"We can grow all the vegetables we eat here on the ranch. If you look off to the right of the garden, you'll see a lot of dark green trees. That is our orchard. We grow our own fruit, as well. We have oranges, lemons, two kinds of limes, grapefruit, avocados, apples, peaches, pears, pecans, almonds, and others that I can't even remember right now. We also have a few date palms, as well."

"There's a windmill on the other side of the orchard that supplies the water for our garden and the trees. We've installed drip irrigation for the orchard and garden, as well as all the landscaping around the houses. It operates on timers so that the water comes on after dark when there is less loss of moisture through evaporation.   Even though we have plenty of water available from our wells, we still don't waste a drop of it.   In this part of the country, water is the most precious resource there is. As you've seen first hand over the past few days, lack of water can mean death pretty rapidly.

"Jake, you just amaze me to no end. I had no idea you could do all these different things. This place is a true oasis in the desert in every sense of the word! You've carved out a good healthy living out here for so many people.   You've built a real community with its own functioning economy.   It looks like you are pretty much self-sufficient, aren't you?"

"Carrie, I don't just see myself as a landed gentry guy with an inflated sense of noblesse oblige. I believe that I have been very blessed and I feel a real responsibility to assist the other people around me. It is something I genuinely want to do. I provide health care for all my employees and I even make sure all the animals on the property have vaccinations and veterinary care.   Those cute little puppies we saw a few minutes ago already have their puppy shots. One of my ranch hands is an ex-veterinary technician and he's in charge of making sure everything that roams around this place stays healthy and doesn't pose a danger to anyone by carrying disease."

"Carrie, I try to do what I believe in the right thing for the people and the land. I'm not a rabid environmentalist, but it's easy for me to see that caring for the land ultimately benefits every person, plant, and creature living here."

"Let's go inside. It's too hot to eat on the patio. We'll eat at the little nook in the kitchen. It's comfortable there and then we'll settle into the library for the afternoon. How does that sound to you, my dear?"

"That sounds like a good plan for the day. I'll enjoy looking at all the interesting things you have around your library as well as your collection of books."

They ate a light lunch of turkey sandwiches and bowls of icy cold Gaspacho soup, made from crisp, fresh vegetables from the garden. They spent the rest of the afternoon in the library. Carrie chose a book from one of the shelves and stretched out on one of the leather sofas while Jake did paperwork at his desk. He glanced up later and saw that she had fallen fast asleep, her book open across her stomach.

Chapter Ten

Jake and Carrie passed a lazy afternoon together in the cool library. While Carrie, slept, Jake caught up on paperwork. He left the library and his sleeping beauty for a short while to consult with Carlos about ranch matters. They sat out on the patio so as not to disturb Carrie's sleep.

Carlos was Jake's closest, most trusted friend, and the brother Jake never had. They had grown up together and even went away to the same college, though Carlos was two years older than Jake. Carlos also pursued a degree in agriculture, while another pretty rancher's daughter, Maria, got her teaching degree. After college, Carlos and Maria returned to the ranch and married in the little church Jake had shown Carrie that day. Carlos and Maria started their family right away.

When Jake's parents turned the ranch over to him, taking a lifetime income as a comfortable retirement, Jake set up a trust for Carlos and Maria to guarantee their future and retirement. It was enough to independently ensure Carlos and Maria's future, as well as that of their children. Jake and Carlos worked more as a team than just an employer and an employee. Jake loved Carlos and Maria as dearly as he loved his own two parents.

"You are a different man this week, Jake. I have not seen you this happy since Rachel died. I have grieved for you, my friend, watching you be too lonely for so long. It isn't right that a man should be without a woman. I couldn't breathe without my Maria."

"I know, Carlos. I have to find a way to make Carrie want to stay here with me. Like you, I feel I won't be able to breathe without her. I know she needs to return to New York to finish this project she's doing. But I am so afraid for her to go. What if she decides to stay there? I believe she loves me, but I wish so much I could be sure. I have to know she'll always be in my life."

"I'm sure you two will work it out, Jake. I can see that by the way she looks at you that she's in love. You two seem destined for each other. Maria and I are praying to the Blessed Virgin for you every morning in the church. The little candles on the altar are burning for you and Carrie. The Blessed Virgin won't let you down, Jake. You must have faith."

Carrie woke up and saw that Jake wasn't at his desk. She wondered how long she had been asleep. She felt wonderfully rested and refreshed. She found herself sleepy in the afternoons lately, with the all-night lovemaking keeping her awake most of the night. She wasn't complaining, though. She put her book back on the shelf and went looking for Jake.

Jake was coming in from the patio as Carrie was leaving the library.

"Hey, sleepyhead! How was your nap?" Jake closed the patio door and kissed her lightly.

"Fantastic! I feel so rested. How long did I sleep? I have the feeling that the afternoon is almost gone."

"You slept a good two hours. I'm glad you had the chance. I want you wide awake and frisky later, my shameless little vixen." He whispered the last part of that sentence in a husky voice as he pulled her into a full embrace. He kissed her again, only this time not at all lightly like before.

"You're pretty shameless, yourself, you know, Jake? But I'm finding I adore a shameless man." She wriggled her lithe body against his, brushing herself across the front of his pants, feeling his growing bulge.

"Hey, I don't want you adoring just any shameless man. Only me.

And that's an order. And I'll swear off any shameless women except you. Deal?"

"You've got yourself a deal, Jake." She smiled up into his deep green eyes and kissed him gently. She could see her own tender emotions mirrored in his loving eyes.

"Are you ready for happy hour, Señorita? I sure am. Let's sit out on the patio and watch the sunset over the garden walls. It's beginning to cool off out there. You wouldn't be willing to go up and put on your pretty village clothes for me tonight, would you? He pulled her close and continued speaking close to her ear. "I'd love to think that you didn't have anything on underneath, either. I want to look at you all evening knowing you are naked and accessible to me under that beautiful gypsy-like outfit."

"I suppose that could be arranged, Señor." She stood on her tiptoes and whispered into his ear. "But only if you put on your village pants with nothing underneath. I want to look at you all evening and know that what is underneath is nothing but your skin." Carrie blew a hot stream of breath across the outside of his ear.

"Now that is a deal if I ever heard one! I'll meet you back on the patio in ten minutes. I need to check with Rosa in the kitchen regarding our dinner. Then I'll go upstairs and change, too."

Carrie went up to her room. The bed had been freshly made up. She went into the closet to get her clothes and noticed that the dirty clothes she had placed in the hamper that morning were all clean and neatly folded inside her open suitcase. She decided to take a shower since she felt sticky from sleeping so long on the leather sofa. She undid her hair and took off her clothes and folded them into her suitcase. They'd be leaving for Alpine right after lunch tomorrow, so there was no point in putting them in the laundry hamper. She took a quick shower and washed her hair.

She dried off and put on her colorful Mexican clothes, and as Jake had asked her, she left off her bra and panties. She sat down at the make-up area and brushed out her hair, deciding to leave it down around her shoulders the way she knew Jake liked it best. She rubbed a little Jasmine lotion on her dry skin and dabbed a little between her breasts and on the pulse spots along her neck. She knew her own body heat would continue to release its fragrance. She looked at herself in the mirror and retied the ribbon at the opening at the front of her peasant blouse, allowing more of her cleavage to show. She was amazed at how Jake had brought out an instinctive sensuality in her that she never realized was there.

She never thought about herself as being particularly prudish about sex. Just terribly inexperienced. No one had ever excited the raw, nerve-tingling passion she discovered was inside her when she was with Jake. He was a playful, imaginative lover with a warm and loving nature. He made her want to give herself completely, without inhibition. It was purely contagious, though, since he gave of himself so completely. She could already feel herself growing wet just thinking about him making love to her. How was she ever going to be able to go back to New York? But she believed in her heart that it was completely necessary for both of them to find out if what they shared was real enough to last when they were three-thousand miles apart.

Her hair was already mostly dry in the desert air, by the time she skipped down the stairs and out to the patio. She felt energized and lighter than air. Jake was already on the patio, still damp from his own shower. He also had on his San Vicente village clothes. He stood up when he saw her coming out the patio doors and whistled and made the same clicking sounds with his tongue as the men in the village did when their Señoritas danced for them. Carrie laughed and twirled for him and he caught a tempting glimpse of her thighs as her dress swirled up around her legs. She plopped herself down in one of the patio chairs and slung a shapely leg up over the arm of the chair. Jake held his breath noticing that she had artfully assumed a pose that shielded his full view of her naked crotch by only the thin cotton of her skirt.

His eyes darkened to the deep jade color that Carrie knew signaled his intense arousal. She was enjoying the obvious potent effect she was having on him. She noticed a pitcher of Margueritas on their table, in place of the pitcher of Sangria they had last night. Jake had already poured some for both of them. She picked up her glass and sipped from it, maintaining heated eye contact with him from under her hooded lashes.

"My wicked little temptress, you're heating the patio up out here." Jake got up and flipped a switch under a weatherproof electrical box. A gentle spray of water began misting out through small black plastic tubes running along the edge of the roof of the main house. It wasn't enough to reach the ground, but evaporated into the dry air above the patio like steam.

"What is that for, Jake?" Carrie watched the misters spread their gentle spray.

"It is more evaporative cooling. The fine mist of water causes the temperature of the air down here to drop. As the mist of water evaporates, it carries away the heat in the air along with the water. It's the same principal as those big old boxes you often see on the tops of homes called swamp coolers."

"Oh. Speaking of water, I am wondering why your water tastes and feels so much better than the water in town? The water at the motel tasted pretty awful and it made my hair feel stiff after washing it. When I shower and wash my hair here, I don't even need to use a conditioner and it's still soft and easy to brush out."

"Did you notice that large tank at the far end of the back of the house off the kitchen? It's as tall as the second story roof? Next to that tank is a small shed and inside that shed is a large reverse osmosis water system.   The well water circulates through five different kinds of filters before it gets pumped into the holding tank. All of the household water even the showers, toilets, dishwasher, and washing machines use the filtered water from that tank.   That way, there is none of that mineral build-up that stains sinks, toilets, and showers so badly, and turns your clothes yellow.   All the drinking, cooking, and household water is completely pure. Every impurity is removed from the water by my system, including chemical contamination. The water that comes out of the ground in deserts usually contains high levels of impurities like arsenic. I want all that stuff out of the water we use. There's no need for a separate water softener."

"Again, Jake, I'm so impressed by your ingenuity. I hardly know what to say. It seems that I am always learning something new about you every time I turn around."

"I wish I knew more about your work, Carrie. In fact, I want to know everything about you. I want to know about your past and who's been important in your life and who's important in your life now. So many things I wonder about."

"Well, I guess it just gives you something to look forward to, Jake." Carrie's reply was bright but didn't offer any answers to his many questions.

She changed the subject. "What time do you think we should leave tomorrow to get to up Alpine before too late? I like your idea of returning my rented jeep tomorrow and not having to do it Friday morning before my flight."

"I think we'll leave right after lunch. That will get us to Alpine by four o'clock and we can return your jeep first thing. Then we'll check into the Corner House and get settled for the evening. I can't stand the thought that tomorrow will be our last day together and tomorrow night our last night. I makes me feel so panicked, Carrie." Jake scooted his chair closer to hers so he could touch her hand.

"Jake, lets not think about it tonight. I'm struggling with the idea of leaving, myself. Maybe when I'm gone, you'll feel differently. I have to know for sure that what we're feeling isn't just some kind of temporary insanity thing." She gently squeezed his hand and smiled so tenderly at him his heart melted.

"So tell me, Jake, my amazing man. What are we having for dinner tonight? This Margherita is going straight to my head and we probably ought to eat pretty soon, don't you think?"

"I just want to sit here and look at you a little longer first. I want to memorize every feature of you. I want to imprint the image of you so deeply on my brain that I can call it up in a flash and see you sitting here with me any time I want to." He picked up his drink and sipped at it, slowly letting his appreciative gaze roam over her.

They ended up spending another hour, talking together and laughing at each other's teasing innuendoes like long time lovers do. Jake finally knew he'd better tell Rosa to bring their dinners before he couldn't stand it any longer and hauled Carrie upstairs to the bedroom. He excused himself and went to the kitchen to give Rosa the word. He noted that the patio had cooled down sufficiently and he switched off the misting system.

Rosa served them a full Mexican dinner of tortilla soup, Chiles Rellenos, Enchiladas de Jocoque, ranch beans, and fresh tomato and guacamole salad. They finished with a dessert of sugar and cinnamon Mexican Sopaipillas with honey. They sipped strong coffee with cream Mexican style, made with dark piloncillo sugar, cloves, nutmeg, cinnamon and cardamom. When they were finished, they sat back from the table and groaned.

"Jake, I'm so stuffed I can hardly move! I can't keep eating like this or I'll end up as big as your house here." Carrie grimaced at the thought.

"Well, for myself, I plan to exercise away all these calories during the night, Carrie. You are welcome to join me, if you'd like." He gave her a leering look, and mischief sparkled in his eyes.

"Well, I guess we'd better get started then, don't you think, Mr. Stockton?" Carrie stared back at him with a half smile and stood up to make her retreat for the patio door. When Carrie turned her back, Jake picked up the squeeze bottle of honey from the table and took it with them without Carrie noticing. Boy, did he have a surprise for her tonight. He could hardly wait.

As they went inside, they met Rosa coming from the kitchen to clear the dishes from the patio. "Buenes noches, Señor y Señorita."

"Good night to you, Rosa." Carrie replied to Rosa assuming she had said good night in Spanish to them. She had understood the señor and señorita part.

As she and Jake went up the stairs, Carrie asked Jake a question. "Are we alone in the house at night, Jake?"

He guessed what she was thinking and wanted to reassure her of their privacy. "We are completely alone, I guarantee you. All the household staff have their own homes on the place. They leave after the kitchen is cleaned from dinner, and they don't return until five or six in the morning. So you can feel free to cry out or scream away while I'm pleasuring you without any fear of embarrassment. And I can promise you that you'll be doing just that tonight, my sweet."

Carrie shivered at the salacious promise contained in his words. They entered her room and Jake closed the door behind them. He led her over to the bed and pulled the frilly spread and top sheet completely off onto the floor over the footboard. "I like to have a clean workbench. It's a guy thing, I guess." He turned and began caressing her as he pulled her into his embraced. He kissed her lips gently at first, then began a deep plundering of her sweet mouth. Her arms wrapped around his back and she slipped her hands up under his shirt to make contact with his heated skin. He slipped a hand around and stroked her breast through her cotton blouse. He felt her instantly harden at his touch, and she moaned into his mouth.

"I think I'm still hungry for more dessert, Carrie." He began slowly pulling on the bow that held the front of her blouse together. As it untied, he separated the front revealing her full breasts and taut pink nipples. He pushed it the rest of the way off of her shoulders, letting it hang around her waist. He reached out and cupped both her breasts in his hands, running his thumbs over their erect little buds. Carrie swayed toward him and moaned deeply, her eyes closed against the burning power of his touch. He released her breasts and hooked his thumbs into the elastic waistband of her skirt and slowly eased it down over her hips and legs. Crouching at her feet, he steadied her as she stepped out of her clothing. He pushed them under the bed and looked up at her naked body standing next to the bed.

Her eyes were closed and he could see that she was shivering from the passion he was igniting in her. He could tell she was waiting for what he might do next. He stood and gently eased her back onto the bed on her back.

"Keep your eyes closed, Baby. I have a surprise for you that I think you are going to like. We're going to share a little more dessert but I'm not going to be a gentleman. I'm going to eat mine first. You'll have to wait, but I don't think you'll mind waiting all that much."

The suspense of what was coming next was sending jolts of electricity shooting through her body. Every nerve was alive and tingling; waiting for a touch, or a kiss, or a caress. She had no idea of what he had in mind, but she was sure it was going to be something extraordinary.

Jake reached for the plastic squeeze bottle of honey he had hidden from Carrie. He suspended it over her and squeezed it, allowing a large drop to fall on one erect nipple. Carrie jerked when she felt the cool drop of honey touch her sensitive nipple. She could smell the rich, floral fragrance of clover and knew instantly what it was. She felt it oozing out over her areola as her hot nipple warmed it and caused it to run.

Jake quickly shed his own clothing. "Carrie, I still have such a craving for something sweet. The sopaipillas just weren't enough for me." He leaned down and Carrie felt him lave her with his fiery tongue then draw her into his mouth sucking off all the sticky honey. She writhed on the bed, her hands twisted into the sheet at her sides. He stood and let another generous drop of honey fall onto her other nipple.

"You are just too sweet - my own little private dessert bar." He leisurely lapped the sweet syrup off her breast, starting around the outer edges of her pink areola and working his way out to the erect tip. He again suckled on her until the stickiness was gone from her hot skin. Next he kissed her deeply, forcing her to part her lips and accept his sticky sweet tongue deep into her mouth. She writhed and moaned pleadingly under him, sucking at his tongue frantically.

"One more taste, and then you can have your turn." He reached down to her legs and eased them widely apart. He separated the swollen lips of her vulva with his fingers exposing her erect, pulsating nerve bundle. He let a large drop of honey fall from the bottle onto her quivering, pink pearl.

"Jake, Jake, no, My God! You're killing me!" She writhed and twisted the sheet tighter in her fists, paralyzed by the anticipation of what she knew was coming next.

Jake set the honey bottle on the nightstand a climbed between her splayed legs. He leaned forward and let the just tip of his tongue reach out and lick the end of her honey-coated pearl. He pushed two fingers inside her soaking entrance then sucked her rigid clitoris into his mouth, letting his tongue stroke her, as he massaged her internal walls with his fingers. Carrie cried out with a piercing scream and thrust her hips up to meet his mouth while she reached out and tangled her fingers into his hair, pushing his head toward the center of her torment as if she was afraid he'd stop.

He felt her climax first begin with violent contractions deep in her vagina followed by the small pulsing thrusts of her clitoris, mirroring the pumping actions of the male penis. She continued thrusting her hips upward for several more seconds, crying out his name over and over. He continued his suction of her, pushing his fingers in and out of her until he felt her muscles ease their spasms. Keeping his fingers tightly up inside her, he released her clitoris and, lay down across the top of her. He found her moaning mouth and kissed her deeply, again thrusting his tongue deeply in her mouth sharing her own honeyed taste with her.

He covered her face and her eyes with tender kisses and spoke soft love-speak to her. She was weeping softly; overcome with the passion he had released in her. He slowly removed his fingers from her and lovingly cradled her in his arms, still raining kisses down on her flushed face. She gradually settled down and hiccuped a few times as she ceased sobbing. He rolled off of her and pulled her close to him, with both of them resting facing each other on their sides.

"Jake, your sensuous imagination is beyond my wildest comprehension. What ever possessed you to think of doing that? I didn't think I was going to live through that, and I'm not kidding. I was on fire." She laughed and shook her head.

"You fire up my imagination, Sweetheart. I just thought how much sweeter the honey would taste on you than the sopaipillas we had at dinner. The rest just followed. Did you mind waiting while I had my dessert first?" Jake had a fiery light in his eyes when he asked her this question, and she could feel his hard erection pushing against her belly.

"You are a very patient man, and I'll let you eat first any time you have a dessert like that in mind. But now I think it's my turn to enjoy a little honey-coated Jake, don't you?" She reached down and took him in her hand and massaged his length. "I think your little friend here is hungry for something sweet, don't you?"

Jake moaned as Carrie rolled off the bed and reached for the honey bottle. Jake lay their motionless with tormenting anticipation. It had been all he could do to keep his control when he pleasured Carrie earlier. But he knew she'd want to take her turn at their love play and he wasn't going to deprive her of that, nor himself, either, for that matter.

Jake's erection lay stiffly on top of his belly. Carrie took it in her hand and squeezed him in her grip. She worked her hand up and down him as he pulsed and swelled to even greater proportions. Carrie watched him grow with fascination. She ran her thumb back and forth across the engorged, velvety head and watched his creamy fluid start to ooze out his cleft.

"He looks like he's smiling at me, Jake. Don't you think so?" Jake opened his eyes and saw Carrie's hand tightly gripping his penis, aiming it's fluid dampened tip toward his face so he could see it's smiling cleft. He saw her smiling at him lustfully, her lush breasts hanging within reach with their rosy, peaked nipples betraying her own arousal. Her wild hair framed her face and hung down almost to her breasts. He had to immediately shut his eyes against the erotic scene.

She held his penis up straight with her hand and squeezed some of the honey out, letting it drip onto the end of his throbbing head. He could feel the coolness of it as it hit the overly sensitive tip and began running down the sides. He dug his fists into the sheet at his sides to keep from grabbing Carrie and immediately plunging into her. But he wasn't going to miss what he knew she'd do next. She would perform the most exquisite form of torture a woman can do to her man. Carrie set the bottle down and climbed onto the bed between Jake's legs, still holding him straight up.

"I sure wish I could have a photo of you like this for when I get too lonely for you in New York." Jake writhed and moaned at her licentious suggestion.

Jake replied through gritted teeth. "If I thought it would guarantee you'd come back to me, I'd almost let you do it."

Carrie leaned down and began laving him with her muscular tongue. She stroked up the sides to the tip and then paid particular attention to licking the honey off the end and out of his cleft. Jake was pushing up toward her with his hips, whispering her name over and over, and encouraging her on. She took the end of him between her lips and suckled on it, while continuing to lave the sensitive underside with her tongue. As she increased her suction, she began her slow swallowing descent.

"Carrie, Carrie, if you don't let go of me this minute, you're going to get a mouthful, I mean it!" His voice rose in intensity as he cried out his warning to her.

She refused to release him and grabbed his hips with both of her hands to keep him from pulling himself out of her eager mouth. She kept sucking and drawing him deeper into her mouth, letting her teeth lightly scrape tantalizingly down his length. He arched his back and thrust his hips frantically deeper into her sublimely ravishing mouth. He yelled out her name and grabbed for her hair and felt himself explode, pumping down into her hot throat. Carrie swallowed and swallowed each spurt, continuing to suck him hard, as if she were drinking in ambrosia from a god. Jake writhed and cried out on the bed, trying to pull Carrie up to him. She continued to suckle him, releasing him from her mouth slowly by degrees, allowing him time to regain his heartbeat and breathing before she freed him completely.

She moved her body alongside him and kissed him deeply, brushing her tight nipples against his body, causing him to instantly begin hardening for her again. He rolled her onto her back and mounted her, driving his reinvigorated rod deep inside her. She thrust her hips up to meet each of his downward strokes. He increased the tempo of their rhythm and fondled her breasts, allowing the friction of his thumbs across her nipples to drive her on. He could taste his cum in her honeyed mouth as she increased the franticness of her thrusts. His arousal reached a fevered pitch.

Carrie screamed into his plundering mouth then he felt the beginning of his own spasms pumping into her. He threw back his head, sucked in a breath and thrust deep into her with all his might. Carrie writhed and clutched him tightly against her as she felt the contractions of her vaginal walls, clinching and unclenching rhythmically around him. Jake collapsed across her body, still deeply imbedded inside her.

Their breathing was ragged and it was a while before either of them could speak. They were beyond exhaustion from the intensity of their play and lovemaking.

"Carrie, I hardly know what to say. I was going to make this a night that you'd never forget and you turned the tables on me. The ecstasy you gave me was something a man only imagines in his wildest dreams! Only the reality of it happening is far beyond the most incredible dream."

"Oh, Jake. The pleasure you give me makes me want to give back to you all the most exquisite pleasure I possibly can. I'm new to this erotic love play and I seem to be following some instinct that I never knew was in me. I didn't realize that lovers could want to do things that I'd never have believed anyone would want to do. I really like it and you won't hear me ever complaining. I just hope I please you half as much as you please me."

"You just keep doing whatever pops into that beautiful mind of yours and I can guarantee you that I'll be more than pleased."

Jake pulled her close against him and buried his face into her hair and inhaled the scent of her deeply. They lay wrapped around each other until they both fell asleep. Utterly sated and exhausted, they slept clear through the rest of the night until morning.

Jake and Carrie slept until eight o'clock. They kissed and cuddled for a while, just feeling the need to be close and loving. They both showered and dressed for the day. Carrie gathered her pretty village clothes off of the floor, shook them out, folded them, and packed them into her suitcase. She emptied the water out of the Camelback in her daypack and packed it as well. She placed her hiking boots in her straw bag and added that to her suitcase, deciding to wear her guaraches on the plane.

She took her last birth control pill and thanked God her period was still holding off. She just didn't feel like it was going to start today. She had only tonight left with Jake, and then she didn't care when it started after that. She almost dropped the empty plastic container into the trash, then thought better of it. There was no need advertising to whoever cleaned her room that she took birth control pills. That was her private business. She stuck the empty container in the bottom of her suitcase, planning to throw it away when she got back to New York the next day.

She took one last look around to make sure she had everything. She closed her suitcase and carried it over near her bedroom door. She looked around the bright, sunny, yellow bedroom and took some quick photos for her own private memories. In some strange unexplainable way, this place felt like it was her home. She puzzled at this new and unsettling feeling. She couldn't allow herself to think thoughts like that. She quickly picked up her suitcase and carried downstairs, setting it next to the front door. She went into the kitchen to have some coffee and wait for Jake at the little nook where they had eaten breakfast the day before.

Jake finished dressing and hung up the phone after telling Carlos he'd be going with Carrie to Alpine overnight. Carlos was in complete charge when Jake was gone from the ranch. He told Carlos to have someone bring his truck and Carrie's Jeep around to the front door after lunch.

Jake went down the staircase and stopped dead when he saw Carrie's suitcase sitting next to the front door. His heart clinched painfully in his chest and he felt like he couldn't breathe. He seriously didn't know how he was going to live without her. He had to pray that after she was gone, she would realize that their love would be as strong as ever, even when they were separated. He knew he had to have the patience to give her the space she needed to be sure of his love for her.

Jake found her in the kitchen sipping coffee and trying to talk to Rosa in slow deliberate English. Rosa seemed to understand her and responded in halting broken English. They were both smiling broadly and apparently enjoying their success at communicating. Jake was so pleased to see how Carrie just fit in with everyone who knew her.

Jake sat down across from Carrie and poured himself some coffee. He knew he needed to stay bright and optimistic and not sink under the terrible weight of knowing Carrie would be gone in only twenty-four hours. He smiled broadly at her, while Rosa brought them homemade waffles and Spanish omelets. The omelets were covered with fresh salsa. They both devoured their breakfast, eating like starving people who hadn't seen food in a week.

"Jake, after that dinner last night, I didn't think I'd ever be hungry again. Now I've cleaned my plate at breakfast, less than twelve hours after eating that monster dinner! I don't know what's gotten into me."

"I told you that you'd burn the dinner calories up during the night." He gave her a sly wink and she blushed a rosy pink.

"Jake, you're outrageous. I can't believe what you get me to participate in with you. It makes me crazy just remembering." She lowered her lashes and Jake reached for her hand and squeezed it.

"You make me want to do wild and crazy things with you. I want to laugh and shout and play, and be completely uninhibited with you."

Carrie sucked in her breath and pulled her hand out of Jake's. "I want to take some pictures around this part of the ranch while I still have the morning light. If I don't get going on the pictures, I'm afraid I'll end up back upstairs with you. You're starting to make me feel all crazy for you again."

Jake smiled a self-satisfied, happy smile at her. "OK, Carrie. Do you want me to go with you, or would you rather wander around on your own?"

"I think I'll go on my own. You'll just distract me from my professional judgement," she teased. Carrie rose and thanked Rosa for the delicious breakfast and went outside through the kitchen door. She spent the next hour walking around taking shots of all the things Jake had shown her the day before. She wanted a photographic record of everything so she wouldn't forget a single detail. She thought to herself that the most significant things she saw and experienced would have to remain burned into her memory, as there were no photos of those things.

When she was finished taking the pictures she wanted she walked back to the house. Bart had followed her around part of the time and she pet his head and ruffled his ears. She entered the house through the back door of the great room off the main patio. Jake was working at his desk in the library.

"I suppose I was gone a lot longer than an hour. It's nearly noon already." She seemed quite surprised when she saw how her solitary thoughts had led her through the morning.

"That's OK, Honey. It's time for lunch. How about we just have some more Gaspacho soup, and then we'll have a nice dinner together tonight when we're at the Corner House.

"That's sounds great to me, Jake. I'm still feeling full from breakfast."

So the two of them ate together with little conversation, both silently dwelling on how little time they had left before she needed to leave. It was clearly weighing heavily on both of their minds. After lunch, Jake loaded Carrie's suitcase into his truck.

"You drive the Jeep and I'll follow you in the truck, Carrie. We can go straight to the rental car office at the airport. Then we'll go over to the Corner House and check in. How does that sound to you?"

Carrie wanted to scream that it sounded awful to her and that she never wanted to leave this place, ever. She felt her eyes start filling up with tears and she searched desperately for something to distract her attention before she completely broke down and made a complete fool of herself. Bart then wandered up to her. God Bless his timing! She knelt down and wrapped her arms around his neck and buried her face in his warm fur.

"Good bye, Bart. You're the very best dog I've ever known, and I love you." Bart licked her face a wagged his tail as she hugged him, struggling to get control of her emotions.

Jake felt his own eyes fill watching Carrie and Bart. Bart walked over to Jake and whined next to the door of the truck. "No, Bart. You can't go with me this time. They won't want you in the Corner House. You'll have to stay here and help Carlos look out after the place." Jake ruffled his neck fur and rubbed his sides. Bart seemed to understand everything Jake was saying to him.

Carrie took the opportunity to wipe her eyes while Jake wasn't looking. She jumped into her Jeep and started it up. She turned the air conditioning on high to try to cool it down quickly. Jake got into his truck. Carrie pulled around the drive and headed back out to the main road with Jake following behind her just beyond the dust cloud she was kicking up.

Returning Carrie's Jeep to the rental office went smoothly. They drove over to the Corner House and checked into the Tree House Room for the night. Jake reserved a quiet table for their dinner in the restaurant later on. Carrie lay down on top of the bedspread to close her eyes for a few minutes. It was still too hot outside to go for a walk before dinner. She fell asleep quickly. Jake took off his boots and lay down next to her, being careful not to wake her. She looked so peaceful and angelic lying there fast asleep. Her features were relaxed in sleep, something Jake hadn't seen in her face all day. He could only imagine that her tension mirrored his own. Tomorrow morning she would leave, and Jake was already feeling like he was suffocating.

After their nap, Jake and Carrie left the little Bed and Breakfast and strolled around the downtown area of Alpine. Jake showed Carrie around the little bookstore where he had bought her Alaska book. Carrie selected a few books about the Big Bend area to take back to New York with her tomorrow. She still had a little extra room in her suitcase. They left the bookstore just before six o'clock and walked back to the hotel. They dropped Carrie's books off in their room and went downstairs for dinner.

They sat at their table looking over their menus, neither one of them particularly hungry. Carrie had a big knot in her stomach where her food was supposed to go. She didn't think she had room for anything but the huge knot - it filled her so completely. She finally decided on a chicken Caesar salad and some iced tea. Jake ordered a small dinner steak with a baked potato, a salad and iced tea. Neither of them felt like having anything alcoholic to drink. That would make it too much like a celebration and neither of them felt like celebrating.

After ordering, the waiter brought their tea. They sat quietly, holding hands across the table and saying very little. It was a striking contrast to their playfulness and levity over the past few days. They both had known tomorrow was coming, but had consciously chosen to ignore it as long as possible. They instead lived moment by glorious moment to the fullest during the time they had left together. Their dinners arrived and they picked at their food, neither of them eating very much. Jake paid the bill and they went back to their room. They watched television, hoping it would distract them from their gloomy thoughts. It didn't work. They decided to go to bed and just hold each other.

"Carrie, I want you to promise me that you'll truly consider coming back here to me. I know you need some time, and I'll respect that, but God, Carrie! I want you here with me so badly it hurts. I really believe you love me, too. I pray that you'll realize our love is real as quickly as possible. I truly don't think I can live without you, Sweetheart."

"I know, Jake. It's a big decision. I don't know that I can live without you, either, but we both need to find that out for sure."

They made love several times during the night. Not the wild, passion-filled joining of the previous nights, but the quiet intimate sharing of their bodies and souls. They held each other closely and Carrie softly cried.

Their alarm woke them at seven. They showered together and dressed, exchanging few words. Carrie closed up her suitcase for the last time and they went downstairs for breakfast. Neither one of them felt like eating. They had coffee and some bagels. Jake went upstairs to get Carrie's suitcase and Carrie went to the front desk to check out. They climbed into Jake's truck for the trip out to the airport, both of their bodies feeling like they were moving under water in slow motion.

Carrie checked her suitcase and camera equipment through to New York. Her agency carried extra insurance on all her equipment. She kept all her undeveloped film with her in her purse. She wouldn't let her precious rolls of film out of her immediate possession. It made her purse bulky, but she had done this many times before. She and Jake sat at her gate, waiting for the plane to land that would spirit her away from him. He held her hand tightly in his as they sat staring out at the empty tarmac, watching the waves of heat shimmering off of the hot pavement in the morning sun.

"Carrie, I don't even have your phone number or email address in New York." Jake's voice held a note of helplessness.

Carrie dug into her purse and came up with one of her business cards. She hastily scribbled her home phone number on the back and gave it to Jake, just as her jet landed and pulled up to the gate. A few people got off and it was time for Carrie to board. Her luggage was already being placed in the cargo hold. At small airports like Alpine, Texas, the exchanges of passengers and luggage happens quickly.

They both stood and stared at each other for a few seconds, as if memorizing every detail. Carrie looked into Jake's eyes then quickly look away when she saw them swimming with unshed tears, threatening to spill over down his face. He pulled her into his arms and she felt like she was going to shatter into a million tiny splinters. She tried in vain to stifle a ragged sob and pushed away from him, feeling like if she didn't do so immediately, she'd never get on her flight. She reached up and gently kissed his lips one more time then turned and rushed over to the ticket agent at the gate, handing him her boarding pass.

Jake hurried over to the large window and watched Carrie walk quickly out to her plane, the strong desert breeze whipping at the loose strands of her hair. She turned one last time before going up the stairs and saw Jake at the window, the palms of his hands pressed against the glass as if he were going to collapse without the support. His face was tortured as he tried valiantly to smile, but his smile came out looking more like a grimace.

Carrie turned away and ran up the stairs. She knew she had to find her seat before she collapsed with her own agony. Diana had booked her a window seat in first class. The plane was pretty much empty, especially up front in the expensive seats. Mercifully, no one was sitting next to her. She slid into her seat, fastened her seatbelt and completely fell apart, dissolving into racking sobs. A stewardess came over and asked her if she was all right or needed anything. She handed Carrie a small box of Kleenex and a pillow, and Carrie sobbed that she'd be OK. The woman smiled sympathetically, touched Carrie's shoulder, and told her she'd bring her something to drink once they were at cruising altitude. Carrie acknowledged her with a nod and choked out a one-word "thanks."

The jet swung away from the gate heading out to the end of the runway. Carrie tried to see Jake but her tears and their distance from the small terminal building made it nearly impossible. As her jet sped down the runway on its take-off roll, she saw the small figure of Jake, still glued to the window of the terminal in exactly the same spot. Carrie buried her face into the small pillow and cried her heart out.

Jake felt helplessly paralyzed watching Carrie's plane taxi out to the runway and take off, carrying her away from him. He could feel hot tears coursing down his face, but he was beyond caring if anyone around him noticed. His heart felt like it had turned to thick clay and was barely beating. The last time he had felt such intense grief was when Rachel and the baby had died twelve years ago. The only thing that was saving him now from completely losing his mind, was that he was hanging on to the hope that Carrie would come back to him. He stood at the window until her plane completely disappeared from view. He was vaguely aware that most of the other people who were seeing passengers off were already gone.

He turned away from the window and walked rapidly out of the terminal, seeking the privacy of his truck. God, but he wished he had brought Bart along with them. He knew it was crazy, but he could hardly face the drive back to the ranch alone. Bart would be some comfort. As soon as he got into the truck, he was hit with Carrie's lingering scent in the heated cab. He turned the air conditioner on full blast, put his head down on the top of the steering wheel and sobbed like a baby.

Chapter Eleven

It was after midnight when Carrie let herself into her empty apartment. She thought about her tiring flight as one long blur. She had slept off and on with her head on one of the little airline pillows leaning next to the window, avoiding the usual polite chitchat with a seat mate. Most of the others in first class were business people absorbed in their own work anyway. She couldn't summon the will to even care if she appeared rude.

Her apartment was cold inside. She had turned the thermostat down when she left the week before to not waste heat on an empty apartment. She couldn't avoid thinking about the contrast between the cold early spring in New York and the glorious warmth of the early spring in Texas. Jake's world was full of color and sunny heat and she had returned to her world of cold and cloudy monochrome shades of gray. She shivered and turned the thermostat up to seventy, feeling spent.

Carrie left her camera equipment just inside her door. She slid her heavy suitcase into her bedroom, too exhausted to lift it. She'd unpack it later. She stripped off her travel clothes and pulled a nightgown out of her dresser drawer. She got into her bed, pulled her down comforter up around her neck, hoping her shivering would stop. Sleep mercifully claimed her, then betrayed her by handing her over to Morpheus, who tortured her all night with dreams of Jake.

Her alarm woke her at eight. She stumbled out of bed toward her shower. She knew she didn't have much time as she needed to be at her office by ten. The people in the photo department needed a couple hours to develop all her film and get the proof sheets to her and Diana by noon. Then she and Diana needed time to evaluate and sift through what Carrie had and allow time for the photo people to print 8x10s of the pictures they liked best before the magazine people arrived at three. As any good professional photographer knew, you took ten shots for every one you ended up keeping, so she knew they'd have hundreds to evaluate. She also knew that she had taken many for her own personal memories. She didn't know how she'd sit there with Diana and look at pictures of Jake, Bart, the little springhouse, San Vicente, and everything else she had photographed without falling apart all over again.

At least her apartment had warmed up during the night. She looked at herself in her bathroom mirror and groaned out loud. Her eyes were swollen and red, puffy to the point of barely looking like they were open. They were sunken into her face with dark circles underneath. Her skin looked raw from too much wiping away tears from her face and eyes with Kleenex. She felt slightly nauseated and remembered that she had eaten nothing after her bagel at breakfast yesterday morning with Jake at the Corner House. The kind stewardess on the plane out of Alpine had brought her some ginger ale right before the plane took off.

She got into her shower and stood there letting the hot water wash over her head and body. She was hoping the heat and steam would take away some of the puffiness around her eyes and make her look less like a refugee from some third-world country. Thank God it was Saturday, and the office would be mostly empty, but she still needed to face Diana and the magazine people. She knew Diana would take one look at her and unleash a barrage of concerned questions. What was it Diana had asked her on the phone when Carrie had called from the store at the park? She thought she recalled Diana asking her if aliens had kidnapped her. Maybe she could tell Diana that's what had happened to her, but she could only hope not to have to get into a discussion about Jake right away.

Carrie dressed and went into her kitchen and looked in her refrigerator, hoping there was something she could grab quickly. It was mostly bare. She took out a quart of milk and a carton of yogurt. She knew she needed to eat something, even though she still felt nauseous and had no appetite. She started pouring the milk over a bowl of granola and realized too late that it had gone sour. The smell of the soured milk caused her stomach to rise toward her throat. She ran to the bathroom just in time to heave into her toilet. There was little in her stomach to come up and she suffered several more dry heaves before she was able to splash cold water over her face at the bathroom sink. God! She had to get control of herself. This overwhelming despair caused by leaving Jake was actually making her physically ill!

Carrie went back to her kitchen, held her breath and ran the spoiled milk and granola down her garbage disposal. She grabbed a spoon out of the drawer and went into her living room away from the sour smell and ate the yogurt. She needed to get out into the cold air fast. She put on her shoes and coat and picked up her purse to leave. She then glanced at her answering machine and saw that the message light was blinking. It was clearly full of messages. She hadn't even thought about checking them before. She hesitated only a moment before deciding that anything there could wait until she got back home later that evening. She closed the door, locked it, and took the elevator to the lobby and out into a cold, gray street.

Carrie walked the block to the subway station and arrived at her office at 10:15. She picked up her phone and called the photo department. Someone immediately came up to collect her film so they could get started with the developing and printing the proof sheets. Carrie heard Diana's voice speaking to Sandy in the hall. Diana must have had Sandy come in so she'd have her secretary to help them throughout the day. Carrie steeled herself for what she knew was coming when Diana saw her.

Diana hurried into Carrie's office. "You don't know how glad I am that you're back. We've got to be ready for…" Diana stopped mid-sentence and stared at Carrie in disbelief. "My God, Girl! What in the world has happened to you? You look like a train wreck! You've sounded so strange when I've talked to you on the phone the last couple of times. What the hell happened to you down there?"

Carrie looked at Diana and immediately broke down in tears. Diana closed the door to give them some privacy and went over to Carrie and took her into her arms. Carrie sobbed on her shoulder like a little girl. Diana opened Carrie's desk drawer and plucked a Kleenex out of a box.

"Carrie, it's going to be all right, Honey. Sit down and tell me what's happened to you. I knew something had happened, I could just feel it over the phone. Please tell me. We've got some time before the photo people get the proofs up to us." Diana picked up Carrie's phone and buzzed Sandy.

"Sandy, can you get us a pot of coffee in here and a couple mugs? I need it right away, too, please." She hung up and moved her chair closer to Carrie's. Sandy knocked and Diana went to the door and took the insulated carafe of coffee and mugs from her without having Sandy come into Carrie's office. She gave Sandy a loaded look and inclined her head in Carrie's direction indicating that she needed some privacy at the moment. Sandy smiled and winked indicating that she understood.

Diana poured them both some coffee. "OK, Carrie. Out with it. I want to know everything that's going on."

Carrie took a sip of her coffee and was thankful that her earlier nausea seemed to have passed. "Diana, it's impossible to explain everything that happened in the little time we have right now. To sum it up simply, I think I'm in love. No, I don't think I'm in love. I know I'm in love." She was grateful to see that Diana wasn't going off the deep end with her revelation, which encouraged Carrie to continue.

"It's Jake. It's such a long story, Diana. Jake and I shared an incredibly intense adventure together over several days. It was one of those life-altering situations that compresses time and forces people to get to know each other really deeply in a short period of time. Like I explained it to Jake when it was happening, it's like a staged encounter group thing, only this was happening to us for real."

Diana saw the intensity in Carrie's face as she spoke about Jake. She had to ask Carrie the next question. "How does Jake feel, Carrie? Do you think he's in love with you, too?"

"I believe he thinks he is, but I told him we needed time apart to be sure it was real between us, and not something that was happening because of the magic spell of the desert spring. I was worried that the incredible intensity of our feelings might just be the result of the desert being so powerful." Carrie hiccuped back a sob, threatening to lose her composure all over again.

"And it looks to me like you already know that what you are feeling is real. I can see that plainly, Carrie. You're a mess! Only real love will do that to a person. If it wasn't real, you could have walked away from him, cried a few tears on the plane, and then moved on. Clearly something profound has happened to your heart. I can see it written all over you."

"Now I guess I'll just have to wait and see how Jake will feel now that I'm gone. He's managed to stay single a long time and maybe that's so because affairs with him don't last. How can I know that he won't find he doesn't really love me when I'm not right there conveniently in front of him every minute?" Carrie found it almost impossible to believe what she was offering to Diana as possibilities regarding Jake's apparent love for her. But she believed she was in way too deep to be objective. After her disastrous relationship with Clayton, she wasn't sure she could trust her own judgement.

"Diana, I have to quit thinking about Jake and get ready for our clients this afternoon. The proofs should be up soon and we need to plan what we're going to present. I can tell you more details about what happened out there in the desert later. It's going to take a while to tell the whole story. I want to wait until I have the pictures in front of me as I'm going to need photographic proof to get you to believe a lot of what I'm going to tell you." Carrie gave Diana a wry laugh and dried her eyes, trying desperately to let her pragmatic professionalism take control of her.   She and Diana switched to talking about who would be coming from the magazine later that afternoon.

Jake barely recalled the long drive back to the ranch as he stepped through the front door of the hacienda. The drive back home had passed in a hazy fog of sensations of profound loss. The feelings sometimes threatened to completely overwhelm him, when he realized that Carrie was really gone. The house was silent as a tomb and he could hear the sound of his own footsteps on the tile floor, mocking him with their echoing through the empty hall. He went to the kitchen knowing he needed to try to eat something.

Rosa was working in the kitchen.   She looked at him with concerned shock, clearly worried about what he knew she read in his face. She spoke to him in Spanish asking him if she could get him something to eat. He asked for a simple sandwich and some tea. He scooted into the little nook to eat, his body language indicating to Rosa that he wished to be alone. She left the kitchen until he was finished eating.

Jake sat staring at his lunch wondering how he was ever going to get it down. His appetite was non-existent but he knew he had to eat something. He had a ranch to run. At least he could distract his thoughts during the day with business concerns, but how would he ever get through the nights? He took a bite of his sandwich and heard a scratching at the kitchen door. He got up and opened it to find Bart looking at him quizzically.

"Bart, am I glad to see you, Boy! Jake pulled Bart against his legs and rubbed down his sides.   Come on in, Bart, and keep me company."

Bart walked into the kitchen and clearly began looking around for Carrie. He disappeared into the rest of the house, searching every room. After what turned out to be a fruitless search for Carrie, Bart came back over to Jake and stared up at him and whined.   Bart's questioning eyes pierced Jake's heart like a knife.

"Carrie's not here, Bart. She had to go back to New York. I can tell you miss her. So do I, Bart, even worse than I ever imagined." He spoke to Bart as if he could understand his words. Bart could sense Jake's feelings of despair, as dogs can do so well with their masters. Bart made a whining noise as he settled himself on the floor next to Jake.

Jake spent the rest of the day in the library, trying to distract himself from thoughts of Carrie with ranch work. It wasn't working. Thoughts of her assailed his consciousness nonstop. The image of her stoically hiking down the hot difficult trail to the river, never complaining and instead finding wonder in the scenery along the way. He saw her bright smile, the way she took to Bart and Bart to her, her pretty blond hair and the way she looked in the gypsy clothes Carmen had given her for the fiesta. He could hear her laughter at the wonder of each of her new discoveries. The most painful of all were the images of her laying under him in the night, naked with her hair streaming out across the pillow, staring into his eyes with passion and love. These images tortured his spirit the most.

He had to make contact with her. He had told her he'd give them the space she believed they needed to sort out their feelings. It was a promise he couldn't totally keep. He had to keep letting her know that he loved her, even after she was gone. He needed to let her know he was sure. He got her business card out of his wallet and turned to his computer, switching programs to his email. He typed in her email address. cturner@mediaphoto.org. He typed out a short message.

"Carrie, my love. I want you to know that you fill my thoughts continuously. I don't know how I will get through tonight without you, not to mention the rest of my days and nights. As I write this, you are on the plane back to New York. I just had to let you know I am thinking of you constantly and missing you desperately with all my heart and soul, my dearest love. I love you, Carrie. Jake   PS. Bart misses you, too. It's easy to tell."

Jake pushed send and sat back wondering if he should call her number and leave a message on her answering machine. No. He couldn't trust his own voice right now. He thought he'd lose it when he heard her voice on her machine. He'd wait until she replied to his email, taking a clue from her answer about whether he should call her so soon.

He suddenly realized that it was getting dark. He had completely lost track of time. Rosa buzzed him on the phone from the kitchen to ask him when he wanted his dinner. He told her to bring it to him out on the patio in an hour. Jake wasn't a drinking man, but he went over to the liquor cabinet and got out a bottle of 100 proof Knob Creek and a whiskey glass. He headed for the patio door while Bart shadowed him as if he knew he should stay as close to Jake as possible. They went outside and Jake sat down in one of the chairs at the patio table. He poured himself several ounces of the amber liquor that he prayed would dull his senses enough to get through this first night without Carrie.

The liquor didn't help. That first night without her was pure hell. He felt like he was going through an acute phase of withdrawal only he knew it would never get better. He tossed and turned and when sleep finally came, it was full of vivid dreams of Carrie. He'd reach out to frantically pull her close to him in his frenzied sleep, only to find himself clutching empty sheets. He even let Bart sleep on the foot of his bed, something he hardly ever did. Bart would hear Jake crying out in his sleep and put a comforting nose against Jake's fevered skin.

Jake got up and went into the adjoining room he had slept in with Carrie. He saw that her bed was freshly made up. He went into the large closet of her room and found their sheets in the laundry hamper waiting to be washed next Wednesday. He pulled out a sheet and buried his face in it, inhaling the fragrance of her scent - and their scent. He childishly carried it back to his room, wrapped himself in it, and laid back down on his bed, trying again to sleep. He finally found some rest by breathing in her fragrance and pretending she was still with him.   The next morning, he guiltily folded the sheet and put it under his pillow, making up his own bed so no one would see and remove his last trace of Carrie to the laundry hamper.

He woke the next morning feeling more exhausted than when he went to bed the night before.   He ate little for breakfast and Maria and Rosa were clearly worried about him.   He told them he was fine but they both knew it was a lie.   Later, Maria stopped at the little church to pray for Jake and Carrie with a fervor she hadn't had before.

Back in New York, the photo department brought up the proof sheets.   Carrie's raw emotions were rubbed raw all over again when she looked at all the pictures she had taken over the past week. Diana was stunned at what Carrie had captured on film, both as a professional outdoor photographer, and as a woman clearly in love. They marked the photos they wanted to offer to the magazine people with red ink and sent them back to photo to be printed as 8x10s as quickly as possible.   Carrie told the photo people to print all the rest as 5x7, double copies.   She had promised some to Jake and she'd follow through with her promise.

Diana had Sandy order deli sandwiches to be delivered, and she and Carrie talked about business while they waited for their lunches to arrive.   Diana could tell instinctively that she better keep Carrie focused on the project at hand or she'd lose her to her overpowering emotions just when she needed her the most.   They ate quickly together while they sorted through the 8x10s that the photo people were bringing up to them as fast as they could get them printed.   By two-thirty that afternoon, they were ready for their meeting.

Sandy buzzed Carrie's office to tell Diana the magazine people had arrived.   Diana went out to greet them and take them to the big conference room, where Carrie had spread the photos out on the huge conference table.   This made it easier for everyone to look them over.   She entered the conference room and made the introductions.

"Carrie, this is David Morgan, Nathalie Erics, and Bridget Scott from Backcountry Adventure Travel Magazine." She gestured to Carrie and continued. "Meet our own famous Carrie Turner." Diana beamed proudly.

Nathalie Erics spoke first. "It's so nice to finally meet you, Miss Turner. We've admired your work for years and we are incredibly honored to have you doing the photography for our issue on Big Bend."

"You have quite a well-deserved reputation with your wilderness photography. I've seen your publications on Alaska and Glacier National Park. We believed you'd be able to get exactly what we wanted for our readers." David Morgan spoke as he began looking greedily over at the photos spread out across the conference table.

Bridget Scott remembered to be polite and asked Carrie, "Is it all right if we just look at these and choose some we think would work with our article? We'd like to work with you over the next couple of days on how you think they could best be presented. We have a copy of the draft of the article, and we'd like for you to take a look at it and see if there are any details you would add or change after having been there." Bridget pulled the draft article out of her briefcase and handed a copy to both Diana and Carrie

"I'd be happy to do so. I'd like for you all to call me Carrie, since we'll be working closely together. I'd be much more comfortable with that, myself." Carrie smiled at these people who seemed more genuine and friendlier than what she had expected.

"I think if you read this draft tonight, then we can all start on the same page tomorrow. It would be nice if we could work tomorrow afternoon and maybe Monday, as well. That's probably all the time we'll need to plan the issue. How does that sound to you two?" Bridget's colleagues added their agreement, obviously riveted by Carrie's dramatic photos of the Big Bend area.

David and Nathalie were talking excitedly selecting this photo, and that one, exclaiming over the beauty Carrie's camera and artistic eye had captured. As soon as they had chosen a few, they picked up others, finding it almost impossible to choose from the gorgeous selection. Bridget began adding her own ideas about which ones they should use.

Diana and Carrie exchanged proud and satisfied glances as they watched the obvious excitement and pleasure their clients exhibited regarding Carrie's spectacular work.

"Why don't you three take these photos back to your hotel and spend some more time looking over them tonight? We usually don't let client's take photos out of this office, but I know the reputation of your magazine and I'm willing to allow it if it's all right with Carrie. Then we can meet back here at one tomorrow and spend the afternoon going over the layout. Carrie and I will have time to read your draft article tonight and be prepared to make any comments tomorrow."

Carrie added her agreement. "Yes, please take them with you so you can have a chance to discuss them privately. If Diana says she trusts you with them, then it's OK with me."

Bridget gathered up the photos and put them carefully in her briefcase. "Well then, we'll just excuse ourselves until tomorrow at one. It was so nice to meet you and we'll look forward to working with you tomorrow."

Diana ushered their clients out of the office. She and Carrie collapsed into the chairs in the conference room, let out a collective sigh, and exchanged looks of both satisfaction and relief.

"Carrie, I'm taking you home with me for dinner. I know you don't have anything in your refrigerator after being gone for a while. You never do. We will be much more comfortable talking in the privacy of my apartment than in some public restaurant somewhere." Diana's voice held a note of authority that Carrie couldn't argue with.

"You don't have to ask me twice. You're right. There's nothing in my refrigerator. I'll get my purse and the envelope of my copies of my photos and we'll go. I've decided to tell you everything, Diana. Let's get to it before I lose my ability to talk about it at all."

They took a cab to Diana's and Carrie told Diana the whole story of everything that had happened to her over the past week. She told her about the instant attraction between her and Jake, the truck breaking down, their desperate hike down to the village, and Bart. She told her about the little spring house and the scary drug runners in the night. She described San Vicente and the Stockton Ranch and most of all, Jake. She showed Diana all her personal photos and spoke with such love for this man that Diana wept like a child. Everything spilled out of Carrie over the course of the next several hours. Diana had ordered pizza delivered as she was unwilling to give up time away from Carrie's fascinating story to bother with cooking.

"Carrie, I can't believe this! That is the most romantic adventure anyone could ever imagine. You should write a book about it! I swear, it would make a killer of a movie! I can see by looking at these pictures of Jake that he loves you." Diana pulled out several and lined them up on her dining room table. "I want you to look at these closely. Pretend you are an objective observer seeing them for the first time. Can you tell me that Jake isn't a man in love with the person taking these pictures? You can't, can you? Its impossible because it shines through his eyes in every single one of these pictures."

Carrie tried to see the pictures through Diana's eyes. "I have to agree he does look like a man in love. But how can I be sure he'll still be in love after I'm gone a week? That's what eats away at me. I need to be sure." Her eyes began filling up again.

"Look, Babe. I think you'll have your answer before very long. This guy doesn't look to me like someone who doesn't know what he wants or how to get it. And it looks to me like he's made up his mind he wants you and he is sure of it."

"You know, Carrie, if you decide you want to go back to Jake, you can work as easily from the Stockton Ranch as anywhere else. You don't have to choose, Carrie. You are lucky in that respect. Your kind of career allows you the freedom to operate from any place on this planet. You know I'd miss you like the devil, but you could come to New York when you needed to, and I might just hie my ass right down to Texas to take a look at this unbelievable place for myself!"

"Oh, Diana, I love you." Carrie hugged her tightly. "You make it sound so simple and maybe I'm making it seem too hard. But I have to know he really wants me and not just the magical dream that we shared together. I need to be sure the love is real and forever."

Diana bundled Carrie into a cab and sent her home for the night. They had a busy afternoon planned and she wanted her to get some sleep. She didn't think Carrie had gotten much the past few nights.

Carrie sat down on her couch and pushed the play button on her answering machine. The first few messages were from telemarketers. Ugh. She hated them. Then there was a familiar voice asking if they could get together at his club for a drink, leaving his number for her to call back when she returned. Clayton! He had a lot of nerve calling her after six months like nothing had ever happened. He was hopeless. After Jake, she wondered how she had ever been willing to settle for a man and a relationship that was missing so much. She supposed it was because she had no idea what she was missing until she had loved Jake. When she reached the end of her messages, she pushed the erase button. She made a mental note to let her answering machine screen all her calls, as she had no wish to even speak to Clayton Jordan ever again. Disappointment seized her that there were no calls from Jake.

Carrie turned on her computer to download her email. She had several messages from clients and friends then she saw one from jstockton@ranchlink.com. Her heart stopped beating. She opened his email and read it over and over again. Tears filled her eyes as she typed out her reply.

"Dearest Jake, I miss you terribly, too. I'm very busy with work as I knew I'd be, but it doesn't ease the pain. I love you. Carrie   PS. Hug Bart for me."

Carrie hit the send key and fell across her bed, weeping her heart out. The next week was filled with working on the Outdoor Adventure Travel Magazine project. Carrie worked hard at trying to concentrate on what she was supposed to be doing. She and Jake exchanged emails everyday and Jake never failed to tell her over and over how much he loved her and missed her. He told her to be prepared for him to call her on the upcoming Saturday night, as he couldn't wait any longer to hear her lovely voice. Carrie didn't know if she could stand it.

By Thursday, she was beginning to be consumed by nausea every day, especially during the mornings. She'd sometimes have to hurry from her office to the bathroom to vomit. Friday morning, after throwing up twice already, Diana came into her office and found her pale, sweaty and shaking. She closed Carrie's door and pulled up a chair to her desk.

"OK, Carrie. Out with it. I wasn't born yesterday and it's clear to any woman alive that you're pregnant." Diana always was one to speak exactly what was on her mind.

Carrie looked at her, completely stunned. "It's not possible! I finished all my birth control pills."

"Oh, yeah? Well it sounds to me like you must have missed at least two unless you're going to tell me you had them with you in your daypack when you guys got stuck in the middle of freaking nowhere!" Carrie's naiveté never failed to amaze Diana.

"But I took them as soon as I got back to the motel," Carrie wailed. "I only had three left, and I took them the next three days in a row, without fail! It was the end of my cycle and I had taken most of them already. I thought I'd have gotten my period by now. It always comes like clockwork as soon as I take the last pill in the case." Carrie wept into her Kleenex.

Diana's voice softened. "Look, Carrie. Maybe you're late because you've been so upset and under so much stress. But I'm truly worried. You are puking sick, just like a pregnancy. You're weepy beyond words. You've missed your period. I think we need to find out fast what's going on."

Carrie stared at her, dabbing at her eyes like a little girl. "How can I find out this early? I'm sure I'll start my period this weekend sometime."

"We're not waiting, Carrie. You're coming home with me and we'll stop into the drugstore in my building and buy a home pregnancy test. We do it tonight. You need to know as soon as possible if you're carrying Jake's child."

"But isn't it too early for something like that to be able to tell? I'm so damn stupid about these things, Diana. It's never been something I ever had to worry about. I've always been so careful." She started crying again. "You've scared me to death. I won't be able to think about a thing the rest of the day!"

"Look, Carrie, I'll finish up some things and we'll leave for lunch and take the rest of the afternoon off. It's Friday and we're about finished for the week, anyway. Sandy can handle anything that comes up and she can always call me at home or on my cell phone."

Carrie blew her nose and wiped her eyes. She felt weak and shaky. "OK. Whatever you say, Diana. God! I don't know what I'd do without you. I'm such an idiot sometimes. I can't believe how that shoot in Big Bend has utterly changed my life. I'm just not the same person at all anymore."

Diana got up and left Carrie's office, clearly worried. If Carrie thought her life wasn't the same now, just wait until she got the results of that pregnancy test! Diana, grimaced to herself. She had seen lots of pregnant women in her life, and she'd stake everything she owned on her hunch that Carrie was carrying Jake's child. "Lordy, Lordy. What in the world was Carrie going to do about that?"

When they arrived at Diana's apartment later that afternoon, after stopping at the drugstore, Carrie looked pale and exhausted. She had barely touched her lunch, afraid her heaving stomach would throw it back up again. As soon as they got inside, Diana dug out a paper cup and sent Carrie into the bathroom to collect a urine sample. Diana opened the pregnancy test and read the directions. It was simple enough and indicated it could tell ninety-nine percent for sure if you were pregnant within one day of missing a period. Carrie had missed hers by more than a week.

Carrie came out of the bathroom carrying her cup of pee. She set it down in the bottom of the kitchen sink and Diana used the plastic eyedropper in the kit to drop two drops on the little window of the plastic indicator stick. She set her kitchen timer for exactly ten minutes. They both stood there, still as stones, listening to the clicking noises of Diana's kitchen timer, each lost in their own private thoughts. The timer rang and they both looked in the little window of the indicator. There was a dark blue plus sign showing.

Carrie walked over to Diana' sofa and collapsed onto it. She was stunned speechless. Diana sat down across from her on the edge of a chair, watching Carrie intently, as if she half expected her to get up and jump off the balcony of Diana's eightieth floor apartment. Carrie put her hand across her belly in an instinctively protective move as old as time. Diana watched a slow, easy smile spread across her face.

"I'm carrying Jake's baby, Diana. Do you realize that? Jake's baby is growing right here inside me! It's the most profound feeling I could have ever imagined."

Diana let out a slow sigh of relief. She was truly afraid Carrie was going to flip out on her when she realized she was truly pregnant. She could see now that whatever happened in the future, it looked like Carrie was going to be able to handle it. Women discovered unplanned pregnancies everyday and dealt with them, each in her own way. Somehow, Diana wasn't totally surprised at Carrie's reaction, as she knew Carrie wasn't the kind of woman who could ever have an abortion. Some could, but not Carrie.

"Are you giving some thought as to when you are going to tell Jake? I'm sure he would want to know right away. He just seems like that kind of guy after all you've told me about him."

"I don't know. I have to think this through carefully, Diana, now more than ever. I don't want Jake to marry me just because I'm pregnant. I can raise this baby myself, you know. I have means of my own. I don't want to marry Jake if he's only doing it because of the baby. Besides, what if he doesn't even want the baby?"

"You're kidding yourself, Carrie! After everything you've told me about the kind of man Jake is, I would guess he'd be shouting and weeping with joy over the news. It's clear to me he loves you fiercely, and it should be clear to you, too, Carrie, if you'd quit being so damn stubborn! Just look at that picture you took of him cuddling that puppy and tell me that's a man who wouldn't want the baby he created with the love of his life! You'd better tell him, and soon, Girl. He has a right to know about his child!"

Carrie looked at Diana intently as she spoke to her, knowing in her heart that Diana was right. "Jake is calling me tomorrow night. I just can't tell him then. I'm still absorbing the shock of this myself. I'll wait one more week and then I'll tell him."

"I'm not going to let you put it off, Carrie. That sweet man has a right to know about this child. I'm not going to stand by and watch you let this situation go on for too long. I love you like my own child. Hey, this kind of makes me almost a grandmother, don't you think?" They both laughed heartily for the first time in days.

Carrie spent Saturday morning in bed, too nauseated to think about getting up. She finally crawled out at lunchtime, and ate some cereal. She began to feel a little better. She decided to finally unpack her suitcase, which had been sitting on her bedroom floor unopened all week. She opened it, and was immediately hit by the smell of Jake and the desert on her clothing. She pulled her San Vicente dress from the top and inhaled its aroma. It smelled like Jasmine and Jake and her, all mixed together. She wept into the fabric with an aching loneliness that completely overwhelmed her. She removed the books she had purchased at the little bookstore in Alpine the night before she left. She placed them on the coffee table in the living room to look at them later. She finished unloading everything from her suitcase and closed it up and put it in the back of her closet.

She cleaned her apartment, stepped down the street to the grocery store and came back to wait for Jake's call. She was so nervous, she could hardly stand it. She thought about what she would say to him over and over again. Whenever she thought about being pregnant with Jake's baby, she felt a wash of euphoria and terror all mixed together rush over her. She loved him so very much and she could only hope that he loved her the same way. After fixing herself a light supper of scrambled eggs, juice and milk, she sat on the sofa looking at her Big Bend books and photos over and over again, while she waited for Jake's call.

Jake had thought of little all day except his call to Carrie that night. He couldn't believe how time crawled when she was gone and passed like lightening when they were together. This past week had been agony. He had lost weight and was cranky and out of sorts with everyone. It wasn't like him at all, but everybody seemed to understand and treat him gingerly, mostly just trying to stay out of his way. He felt guilty and remorseful about his behavior, but at the same time, felt powerless to do anything about it.

He had tried to stay busy at the ranch. But everything he tried to do to take his mind off of thoughts of Carrie, only seemed to remind him of her more. He couldn't stand to look into her empty bedroom when he walked past her room, so he kept the door closed. It knifed him in the heart when he'd see the bed where they had shared such intimacy, love, and closeness. He still childishly kept her sheet in bed with him, having hidden it in his dresser drawer on laundry day. He was sure Consuela must have wondered where the heck it was when she did the wash, but he didn't care. Just as long as he could keep her scent close to him at night for a little while longer. Sometimes, he thought he was completely losing his mind.

Jake watched the clock obsessively. He'd call her at eight o'clock her time, which would be seven o'clock in Texas. He could stand it no longer. At a quarter of seven, he sat down at his desk in the library and dialed her home number. Carrie answered almost immediately, which pleased him enormously to know she had been waiting for his call.

"Hello?" She tried to speak confidently, but heard her voice crack with her nervousness.

"Carrie, my Carrie! Oh, God, Honey! I've missed you like crazy all week. How are you, my precious?"

"I'm doing OK, Jake.   I've missed you a lot, too."   She unconsciously reached down and placed her hand over her belly and their baby.

"Carrie, you sound so distant. I feel like I'm talking to you on the moon. Tell me what your magazine people thought of your photos. Did you get some made for me? How did they turn out?"

"It went really well, Jake.   They loved the photos and they are going to include more than they originally planned.   I made some changes and additions to their article about Big Bend so they decided to expand the issue. They had asked me if I'd add to the draft article, so I did. I'll see that you get a copy of the magazine when it comes out."

"But Carrie, isn't that the June issue? Are you telling me we won't see each other until June?   Carrie, what the hell is going on? I can't live without you here, I mean it!   I've been going stark raving mad here this week without you. I love you, Carrie! How can I make you see that? Just say the word."

What Carrie was thinking was that through all Jake's pleading with her, he had never mentioned the M word; marriage. She wanted a settled life with a home and a real family. She wanted to raise her children with their father in a committed, married relationship, not just shacked up with someone. As much as she loved him, she wasn't going to settle for just living with him.

"Jake, I'm sure we'll see each other before June. We can keep writing to each other and talking over the phone and see how things develop with time."

"Carrie, you sound strange and disconnected from me. It's killing me, Honey. You sound like something's not right."

"I've just been depressed lately, Jake. A lot happened to me the past couple weeks and coming back here has been such culture shock. I'll be fine though. Next time we talk, I'll bet you'll notice a difference." Carrie tried to consciously brighten her tone of voice.

Jake saw through her ruse and became more convinced that there was something that Carrie wasn't telling him. He made the decision right then to call Diana at Carrie's office Monday morning. He knew Diana was Carrie's best friend and professional mentor. Carrie had told him that Diana was like a mother to her. Surely Diana would know very well what was going on with Carrie, and if she was half the woman he sized her up to be, she'd tell him what was going on. He'd convince Diana how much he loved and wanted Carrie in his life forever.

"All right, Carrie. I'll let it go for now and maybe you'll be in better spirits next time we talk. I'll call you back next week, meanwhile I'll keep sending emails. I love you, Carrie, more than you can ever imagine, Baby."

"I love you, too, Jake. Good bye." Carrie hung up and fell across the sofa and cried and cried.

The next day, Diana called her at lunchtime. "Did Jake call you last night? Did you tell him about the baby?"

"He called, Diana, and I didn't tell him about the baby yet. I just couldn't."

"Well, why the hell not?"

"Because, in all his talk of wanting and needing me, he's never mentioned marriage. I'm not going to just go out there and live with him and raise bastard children. I value myself too much for that, Diana. As much as I love him, and I believe he really loves me, it appears that he isn't willing to make that total commitment."

"I see what you mean, Carrie. Sometimes men are idiots, though, and they just assume that a woman knows they are talking about marriage, so they don't bother to come right out and ask them, proper-like."

"Well, he's going to have to ask me "proper-like" as you put it, or I'm not going out there. I want to know that he's willing to make a lifetime commitment to me because for me, it's all or nothing. I won't be any man's whore. Maybe that sounds ridiculously old-fashioned these days, but its who I am. And I don't want him marrying me just because I'm pregnant, either. If he did that, he'd eventually end up feeling like I trapped him and he may grow to hate me for it. I couldn't stand that."

"OK, Carrie. I see your point. Just relax, Honey. Things are bound to work themselves out. It sounds like you two can't go on like this, both loving each other so much and needing to be together. I'll see you tomorrow at work. And Carrie, you don't need to come in early. I know that's your worst time of day. There's nothing scheduled that can't wait until you get in after lunch. OK?"

"I may take you up on that offer, Diana. At least for a while. This terrible morning sickness can't go on for too much longer, can it? Thanks for being there for me."

Carrie stayed in bed Sunday morning. She didn't have the energy to get up. She felt drained and exhausted. She heated up a can of soup for lunch. She drug herself into work for another afternoon meeting with the Outdoor Adventure Travel people. She slept Sunday night off and on, feeling like she had been drugged. She felt paralyzed by the leaden lethargy that had settled into her body and soul.

She woke up Monday morning with the nausea still there to greet her. She forced herself to get up to try to go in to work. She ate a little cereal, immediately threw it up, gave up and went back to bed. She'd try again after lunch. Her afternoons seemed to be her best time of day. She made it back into work for what should be the last meeting with the magazine people. Fortunately, they finished up completely on Monday afternoon.

Jake got up early Monday morning. He knew it was an hour later in New York so at eight o'clock he went into the library and closed the door. He sat at his desk and dialed Carrie's office phone number printed on the front of her business card. He prayed he'd get her secretary, as he didn't want Carrie to know he was calling. He needed to talk to Diana privately. He could feel with every fiber of his being that there was something Carrie wasn't telling him. It was high time that he found out what was really going on.

"Mediaphoto Incorporated, good morning, how may I direct your call?" Sandy's voice greeted him with the strong New York accent that always sounded so strange to Jake.

"May I speak with a woman named Diana, please Mamm?" Jake's slow Texas drawl immediately got Sandy's attention. She suspected it was Carrie's handsome cowboy.

"One moment please, I'll see if she's in her office." Sandy put Jake on hold and buzzed Diana on her line.

"Diana, there's a man on the phone asking to speak to you. He has a strong Texas accent and I'd bet my life it's that guy, Jake Stockton, calling from Texas. Do you want me to put him through to you?"

"Yes, of course! He's just the man I want to talk to right now! Don't scare him off by asking for his name first. He probably doesn't want Carrie to know he's calling and might hang up. Just put the call through and I'll handle it if it's not Jake." Diana's pulse quickened. She might be meddling, but someone needed to meddle a little here. There was a whole lot worth meddling over at stake in this relationship.

"Sir, I'll put your call through now." Sandy pushed the button on her phone that switched Jake's call to Diana's line.

Jake's heart was hammering in his chest and he could hear his pulse roaring in his ears. His palms were sweaty as he waited for his call to be transferred and for Diana to answer. Possible reactions from her ran through his thoughts. Would she refuse to tell him anything? Would she cut him off at the knees? What had Carrie told her about him? Would he be able to enlist her support? He took a deep breath as he told himself he was about to find out as she just picked up her phone.

"This is Diana. Who is this?" Diana deliberately kept her voice in a neutral, professional tone until she found out for sure who was calling.

"My name is Jake Stockton, Ma'am. I'm a friend of Carrie Turner's down in Texas. She doesn't know I'm calling you, but I'd like to talk to you about her. I know you're her best friend and her boss and all, and I'm hoping you can help me figure out what is going on with Carrie. I'm really worried about her." He made himself stop running on until he assessed what Diana was going to say next. He wanted to see if she would be receptive to listening to him any further.

"Jake. I'm so happy that you've called. In fact, I was thinking of calling you myself, as I'd like to talk to you about Carrie, as well. She'd be upset with me for meddling, but since you called me first, I guess I can tell her it wasn't my doing." She gave Jake a conspiratorial little laugh that completely put him at ease. "But I want you to go first, Jake. I want to hear exactly what you're thinking before I say anything regarding Carrie. I love her like my own daughter and I won't do anything to cause that girl more pain. You need to know that up front."

"Ma'am, I want you to know my clear intentions regarding Carrie." Jake began.

"Wait just a minute, Jake. You can cut out that Ma'am crap and call me Diana because I'm going to call you Jake. Got that? You can continue now that we have that straight."

"OK, Diana. Like I was starting to tell you, I love Carrie with all my heart and soul. She's become my very life and I can't live without her. Since she left, I can't eat or sleep, or think straight. She told me she needed some time to be sure what we had was real and would last. I can tell you it's real for me, and gets more real all the time, even though she's gone. I have the strongest feeling something isn't right with her. You're the only person that I know who would truly know what's going on with Carrie. I'm so worried about her but I don't want to pressure her."

"You know, Jake, I'm going to be perfectly frank with you. OK? Carrie's told me everything about what happened down there between you two. I've seen pictures of you and you look to me like the kind of man who shoots straight, as I'm sure they say down in Texas. I want to tell you something about Carrie Turner. She's a pretty straight shooter herself, in spite of being a New York career woman. She isn't looking for a man to shack up with, to put it bluntly. She deserves more."

"My God! I'm not looking for someone to 'shack up' with, as you put it, either! I want to marry that girl and share the rest of my life with her! I want to make her mine forever. I've told her she can keep doing her wonderful photography. I really want her to. She has so much talent. I don't want to make her a prisoner here, but I want her with me every minute she can give me. She can go to New York or anywhere else she needs to go anytime she wants to. Her career is important to who she is. I know and accept that. I'm not some backward clod, you know, just because I'm from Texas."   Jake sounded indignant that Diana would think he was some Neanderthal in regards to women.

"Wait a minute, Jake. Have you actually asked Carrie to marry you? Have you said the magic words or just assumed that she'd know what you had in mind?"

"Well, of course I assumed she knew exactly what I had in mind! After all we shared? I've told her a thousand times how much I need and want her in my life forever. What else would that mean? Of course it means marriage!"   Jake seemed dumbfounded that his intentions might be so misread or unclear.

It suddenly struck him dumb that maybe Carrie had misinterpreted his intentions, as well. "Are you trying to tell me that Carrie doesn't think I'm talking about marriage? Are you saying that's the only thing keeping us apart right now? My God! How could I have been such an idiot? I want you to transfer me to her office as soon as we're through talking here and I'm going to ask her to marry me. No! Wait a minute! I'm going to get on a plane to New York today if I have to hijack one, and ask her to marry me in person. I'll get down on my knees! I'll get her the biggest diamond ring I can find in that city of yours! Tiffany's is the best jewelry store in the country, I think. First thing tomorrow morning, I'll come right there to her office and surprise her." Jake was breathless in his elation, rattling his plans to Diana a mile a minute.

"Hold on a minute, Jake. There's something else you need to know about Carrie. I was waiting until I found out for myself what your intentions were before I told you. Carrie's not here."

"Oh, my God, no! Where is she? Something hasn't happened to her, has it? How come she's not there?" Jake voiced had risen in pitch with his obvious panic. He was getting frantic.

"Jake! Hold on a minute and listen to me. Carrie is at home this morning because she's been sick. Actually, she's been sick every morning since she got back. Carrie's pregnant, Jake. Congratulations, my man, because you're going to be a father1"

"Yikes! Tell me you aren't kidding me? I can't believe this! Do you have any idea how happy that this news makes me? A baby! Carrie and I made a baby! Oh, Diana, thank you so much! I'll be there tomorrow. Oh, my God! We're going to have a baby, Diana!"

"Slow down a minute, Jake. Don't show up here at the office in the morning. Go to Carrie's apartment. She doesn't come in here until noon. I won't say a word to her about our conversation and I'll make sure she stays home tomorrow morning, for sure. In fact, I'll tell her to take the whole day off. I'll tell her we're having the place fumigated or something."

"OK, I understand. I've got to go right now, though. I've got to get to Alpine for that eleven-thirty morning flight that Carrie took last week. If I leave now, I'll just be able to make it. I'm sure looking forward to meeting you, Diana. I can't thank you enough for what you've done."

"You'd better take good care of my little girl, Jake, or I'll be down to Texas in a New York minute to set you straight! Understand?" Diana's voice held notes of teasing and seriousness at the same time.

"Don't you worry for a minute, Ma'am - I mean, Diana. I've got to go. Bye."

Jake hung up and immediately dialed the airline and booked himself onto the eleven-thirty flight from Alpine. There were empty seats in first class, but he would have been willing to ride underneath with the baggage if he had to. He flew up the stairs to pack a suitcase while Maria and Rosa stood dumbfounded in the hall. They watched him fly down the stairs with his suitcase not five minutes later.

"I'll be back when I get back. I'm going to New York to get Carrie! Get the place ready for her to move in, and I'll call you as soon as I know when we'll be back!" He stopped at the door, put down his suitcase, ran over and hugged and kissed Maria and Rosa, picking each of them up and swinging them around in a big circle. He tore out the front door and jumped into his truck, and sped off toward the highway in a cloud of dust.

Maria and Rosa both stood there laughing, wiping at the tears running down their faces. They were both so happy for Jake. The hacienda would again ring with life and laughter when Jake brought his beautiful Señorita Carrie home to stay.

Chapter Twelve

Jake finally arrived in New York late Monday night. He found a hotel room close to Carrie's apartment. He looked up the address for Tiffany's in the yellow pages and noticed in their ad that they opened at nine in the morning. He figured to be there the minute that they opened. He paced back and forth across his hotel room floor, channel surfing on the TV, too wired to sleep. He propped up the pillows on his bed, lay back and continued changing channels with the remote control, trying desperately to find something that would relax him enough to begin feeling sleepy. He finally dozed off, sitting up against the pillows, fully dressed, with the remote still in his hand.

The front desk gave him a wake-up call at six, as he had requested when he checked in. He jumped when his bedside phone rang, startled out of a fitful sleep. He took off his rumpled clothes and climbed into the hot shower. He was excited beyond words. He dressed in a long-sleeve cotton dress shirt, long slacks and even added a sporty tie. He slid on a pair of handmade, full-quill ostrich western boots, his one concession to being a Texas rancher. He had packed a warm leather coat knowing it was still cold up north in the early spring.

Jake ate a quick breakfast in the hotel restaurant, fortifying himself with hot coffee after his run of lack of sleep lately. He took a cab to Tiffany's, arriving just after they opened. He asked to be shown diamond engagement rings. The clerk looked him up and down with a barely concealed sneer, taking in the boots and leather coat, and instantly sizing Jake up as a rube. He reluctantly led him over to one of the lighted glass case displaying engagement rings.

Jake scanned the case then stood up tall and looked the haughty man straight in the eyes. He let his slow Texas drawl slide down over the snobby clerk like cold molasses.

"I've always heard that Tiffany's was supposed to be the best jewelry store in New York. I guess I'm kind of disappointed in your selection. I'm afraid I should have looked for something in Dallas where they sell real diamond rings, not toys."

The clerk visibly flinched at Jake's negative reaction to Tiffany's jewelry, exactly as Jake had expected he would. He wasn't the rube this man had mistaken him for.

"We do have others in our private collection. I must warn you that they are quite a bit more expensive than these." He stood watching for Jake's reaction to his warning concerning the prices he should expect.

"Well, I certainly hope they are, Mister, as I find the ones here tacky and tasteless. I'm looking for something that is worthy of the quality of my ladylove. I'm more interested in quality and beauty than the price."

The clerk led Jake into a back room containing more lighted displays. Jake looked carefully over everything then selected a stunning five-karat, blue-white, pear-shaped solitaire, with two baguettes framing it on a pure gold band. After making his selection, Jake made out a cashier's check from his Texas bank.

"I'd like that ring wrapped up in one of those pretty little velvet boxes. Do you know what kind I'm talking about?"

"Exactly sir! I'll show you exactly how it will be presented." The clerk was all smiles and politeness all of a sudden. He showed Jake a green velvet box with Tiffany spelled out in gold lettering on the inside of the top. This little velvet box fit inside another small box that also had Tiffany spelled out in the same gold lettering across the top. He handed Jake his receipt and asked him if he'd like a bag.

"No thank you. I'll just put it in my inside jacket pocket. Thank you for your time." Jake nodded to the little man and left the jewelry store.

He hailed a cab and asked to be taken to a florist. He went in and described exactly what he wanted and told them he wanted to wait for it to be made up. He wished to deliver it personally. He ordered a large bouquet of white roses, at least four dozen, with little pink and blue ribbons tied throughout. He wanted white sprigs of Jasmine and some frilly greenery to fill in the empty spots. He told them he wanted the bouquet to stand about three feet tall and be a good two feet across. The clerk warned him that something that size with those kinds of flowers would cost around five-hundred dollars. Jake took out his wallet and laid five, one hundred-dollar bills on the counter.

"This will take at least a half-hour to put together, sir. If you'd like to wait in the coffee shop next door, you'd be more comfortable. We'll come get you when it's ready."

"All right. That'll be fine, Ma'am. I'll take your advice and wait in there for you." Jake left the florist and slid into an empty booth next to the front window of the coffee shop.

He watched the New Yorkers hurrying along past the window of the coffeehouse. He sipped his espresso and noted that no one here seemed to smile very much. Down in Texas, people walked down the streets with their heads up and smiled and nodded to other people. Here, they rushed past, with their heads down and never made eye contact with anyone. He decided he liked Texas a lot better. He was so excited and nervous he could hardly stand it. It was already eleven thirty, but he was too nervous to eat any lunch. As soon as the florist came and got him, his next stop would be Carrie's apartment.

Carrie had stayed in bed all Monday morning, hoping she could avoid throwing up if she didn't move around much. She was able to finish up with the magazine people on Monday afternoon. Diana told her not to come in at all on Tuesday because they were fumigating the offices in the building that day. Carrie had never heard of such a thing, but Diana assured her it was a routine maintenance thing and that no one else was coming in either. Carrie didn't argue and was glad she'd have another day to try to ditch this puking feeling.

She decided to try to get up about eleven on Tuesday morning. She got into the shower and felt well enough to stay out of bed. For the first time, she didn't throw up the first thing. She dressed in a pair of sweat pants and a T-shirt and heated up some soup. She noticed her breasts felt swollen and tender today, probably from the pregnancy. When she looked in the mirror, she saw that the dark circles that had been under her eyes all week were beginning to fade.

She had just finished washing up her soup bowl and spoon when her apartment buzzer rang. She went to the door and pushed the intercom button. It was the doorman telling her that she had a floral delivery. He asked her if he could send the guy from the florist up. Carrie sighed and told him to send him up. She hoped they weren't from Clayton because if they were, she was going to refuse to accept them and have the deliveryman take them back to the florist. Clayton had called her two more times lately and left messages on her answering machine wanting to see her. She kept erasing his calls hoping he'd think she was gone on a lengthy shoot and quit calling.

Her doorbell rang. Carrie peaked through the little viewer in her door and saw nothing but flowers. She pulled open the door, intending to immediately ask who the flowers were from, and saw Jake standing there, grinning at her around the side of the enormous bouquet. She froze in her tracks, completely speechless.

"Is it OK if I bring these inside Miss Turner? They're pretty heavy." Jake's eyes sparkled with love and mischief, like she always remembered them when she thought of him.

"Jake! What are you doing in New York? Why didn't you tell me you were coming? Come in. Of course, come in." Carrie stepped aside so Jake could maneuver the enormous bouquet through the door and into her apartment. She shut the door behind him and stood staring in shock. He walked over and set the bouquet next to her TV in her living room. It filled the whole wall.

Carrie stared at the flowers in disbelief. She walked over to them and noticed all the little pink and blue bows. This couldn't be just a coincidence. Who would order flowers made up with pink and blue bows? It looked like an arrangement you'd send to a new mother in a hospital. She turned and stared at Jake questioningly.

He walked over to Carrie and took her by the hand. He silently pulled her along over to her sofa and made her sit down. He took off his coat, surreptitiously slipping the little jewelry box out of the pocket. He threw the coat across the back of a chair, then came over and stood in front of her.

"Carrie, I'm going to do this the right way this time, the way I should have done it before you ever left Texas." He got down on his knees in front of her and pulled the little box from behind his back, offering it to her.

"Carrie, will you marry me? I love you more than life itself. I want you to be my wife and the mother of my children. I want us to be together for the rest of our lives. I want to grow old with you by my side, and if God is gracious, I want to us to die peacefully in each other's arms after a long and happy life." His eyes brimmed with tears as he looked straight into her eyes, waiting for her reply.

"Oh, Jake. I love you so much. Yes, I'll marry you. Of course, I'll marry you!" Carrie pulled his head closer and kissed him gently. Jake pulled her into his arms and wept into her hair.

"Oh, Carrie, my beloved Carrie. I've missed you so much. I can't live without you, Sweetheart. This past week was the worst week of my entire life. I was utterly miserable. God! I'm so happy right now!" He sobbed, drawing deep breaths as he tried to compose himself. He slipped up onto the seat of the sofa and wrapped her tightly in his arms.

"Jake, let me go a minute. I want to open my present from you." Carrie looked like a little girl at Christmas as she opened the first box and removed the velvet box from within. She sat back on the sofa and slowly opened the hinged lid of the velvet box.   Her eyes widened in shock and surprise.

"I hope you like it, Carrie. If not we can take it back and you can choose something different. I thought it would go perfectly with a plain gold band. I'd like for both of us to have matching gold bands."

"Jake, I've never seen such a beautiful ring in my life! I wouldn't exchange it for anything. You picked this out special for me and I'll cherish it forever. It is magnificent!" Carrie removed it from the little box.

"Let me, Carrie." Jake took the ring from her and slid it onto the third finger of her left hand. "Carrie, I give you this ring as a pledge of my love for you and as my full commitment to our marriage." The ring was a perfect fit. Jake had guessed her size correctly.

"Now about those flowers, Jake? Tell me how you came to choose that particular arrangement. It is a very curious color combination." She eyed him suspiciously, with a gleam in her eye.

"They are to celebrate our engagement, Carrie, and our baby. I know about our baby, Carrie. I can't find the words to express my joy and pride. I feel like the luckiest, happiest man in the whole world, right now, my precious love!" Jake placed his hand lovingly on her belly where their child grew, nestled inside Carrie.

"Diana? Of course, it was Diana. I suspected she'd end up doing something like this. That crazy woman."

"I called her first, Carrie. And she didn't tell me about the baby until I told her how much I loved you and wanted to marry you. It was only after she was convinced of my worthiness and the sincerity, that she told me about our baby. I think she knew exactly what I'd do next, because she gave me your address and told me she would make up some cock and bull story about the office being fumigated so you'd be sure to be at home when I arrived on your doorstep today."

"Carrie, I want you to come home to the ranch with me. We can be married in our little church on the ranch. Diana already told me she'd come down to give you away. You can wear a pretty white dress and all the friends we've enjoyed around there can be present to help us celebrate. If you want to get married someplace else, that's OK, too."

"I would love to be married at the ranch, Jake. I fell in love with that little church! It's the perfect place to begin our married life together. Do you think Jose and Carmen can come from San Vicente for our wedding? I'd love for them to be there, too. In fact, I want the whole village to be there!" Carrie's whole demeanor had changed since she and Jake were back together, this time for good. She was bubbling over with and happiness, talking excitedly about possible wedding plans.

They spent the afternoon planing and talking about their future together. Jake glanced at his watch and saw that it was nearly five o'clock in the evening.

"Carrie, I think we should call Diana and tell her the good news. She'll be going crazy waiting to hear. After all, she did have a hand in helping us both get through our insanity phases, don't you agree?" Jake handed Carrie her cordless phone.

Carrie speed dialed Diana's private line into her office. "Diana, it's me, Carrie. Guess what! Jake's here with me, and we're engaged!"

Jake could hear Diana screaming through the phone. Carrie promised to bring Jake to the office to meet her the next afternoon. "If the fumigators are gone, that is. For Pete's sake, Diana! To think I fell for that! We've never heard of fumigators coming into our building before. I should have been suspicious that you were up to something right then." Carrie laughed and told Diana they'd see her tomorrow. "And thanks, Diana. You've been the dearest friend I ever could have had."

Jake cooked dinner that night. He made something totally bland for Carrie's queasy stomach. He cooked plain baked chicken breast, some mashed potatoes and steamed carrots. He was so sweet and tender towards her and told her again and again how excited he was about their baby. Carrie could tell he really meant it, too, which filled her with joy.

While Jake cooked, Carrie sat watching him lovingly from the sofa. "Jake, tell me more about you. I know there's more to your personal history than you've told me so far. I think I should know everything about you, if we're going to be husband and wife. Don't you?" Carrie was thinking to herself that she needed to tell Jake about Clayton some day. It's a subject she wished to finally put to rest, but it could wait. It wasn't anything all that interesting or important.

"Later, Carrie, after dinner. We'll settle onto your sofa and I'll tell you the whole story of Jake Stockton. I won't leave anything out, I promise." Jake was trying to act nonchalant about his promise to tell her everything, but he was a nervous wreck inside.

He still had to clear the hurdle of having Carrie think he was a monster, for what he considered was his fault in Rachel's death. And the baby's. He'd die if Carrie decided she couldn't trust him to make sure nothing would happen to her and their baby she carried. He'd just have to trust Carrie to understand. There was no other choice. This wasn't something a man should keep from his wife.

They ate dinner together at Carrie's little kitchen table. Jake washed up the dishes and left them to dry on their own in the drain basket. He brewed them a pot of herbal tea, and they both retired to the sofa.

"Carrie, I'd like for you to promise me you'll listen to my entire story. I've never told this story to anyone before. People down in my area all know it but it's faded into the background because it happened so long ago now."

Carrie sat with all her attention focused on Jake. She could tell he was about to tell her something profound. She steeled herself to remain impassive and listen to his whole story as he had asked her to do before she made any comments. She nodded at him, encouraging him to continue while she sipped at her tea. The steam from it swirled off of the hot surface, curling into the air in front of her face.

"Carrie, I was married once, twelve years ago. I was only eighteen. I was in love with a girl in my high school named Rachel."

He saw Carrie's eyes widen in shock, but she kept her promise and listened to him without saying anything.

"You know how kids do crazy things. We eloped one night right after we graduated from high school. Rachel got pregnant right away."

Carrie shifted nervously on the sofa and set down her tea. This wasn't what she had expected to hear. She tried to keep her face a blank mask until she could let him finish. She was wondering where in the world Jake's child was? He or she would be almost twelve years old by now.

"My parents were terribly disappointed in me but they tried to make the best of it. Rachel and I lived in one of the small employee houses on the main property. I worked on the ranch for my dad in order to support us. My parents wanted me to go to college, and I did too, and we decided I'd go on to college after Rachel had the baby."

Jake's gaze wandered off, staring into space as he continued with his story, as if he were seeing it like a movie.

"Rachel's baby was due in the spring. We often get a lot of violent thunderstorms in the desert in the spring. A really big thunderstorm came through late one afternoon. Those storms can drop several inches of rain in a short period of time. The rain can't soak into the desert fast enough when it falls that fast. It runs off those steep mountains creating devastating flash floods in the low areas. Sometimes it takes days to clear and repair the roads when they wash out during a storm."

"Rachel went into labor fast and furious. It was two months too early. There was no way we could get her to the hospital in Alpine. All the roads were washed out. She gave birth in our little house. Some of the women tried to help her, but nothing went right. I was crazy with fear. What does a nineteen-year-old kid know about having babies? My parents were worried sick, but there was nothing anyone could do. My dad called Alpine and hired a helicopter to bring a doctor out to the ranch. Rachel was bleeding heavily. No one could get the bleeding to stop."

"There was something wrong with the baby, too. She was much too small, and was struggling to breathe. She only weighed two pounds. Rachel bled to death before the doctor could get there. After I realized that Rachel was really dead, I wrapped my little girl in a blanket and sat down and rocked her telling her over and over again that I loved her and begged her to live. She stopped breathing while I held her. The helicopter arrived with the doctor but it was too late. I just kept rocking and rocking my baby until my parents and the doctor finally convinced me to give them my dead baby girl."

"For years I blamed myself for what happened. I thought there must have been something I could have done differently to prevent them from dying. My parents and everyone else tried to tell me it wasn't my fault. The doctor explained to me what happened and told me there was nothing anyone could have done. He said that even in a hospital, they lose mothers with Rachel's kind of problem. Her uterus had ruptured and she bled to death within minutes, actually. The baby was too small. Now they can save babies that small, but only in big hospitals with lots of special equipment."

"So that next fall, I went away to college. I was bitter and carried a chip on my shoulder for years and years. I felt sorry for myself and blamed myself for what happened. I never let anyone get close to me. Rachel's family moved away from Texas. They couldn't stand the painful memories of living there. I haven't spoken to them in over six years. Gradually, with time and maturity, I can see that what happened wasn't my fault. But I still feel guilty, like there must have been something that I could have done to make a difference, even though I know in my head that there wasn't."

"Carrie, I've been so afraid to tell you. I've been worried that you'd think I was some kind of monster who allowed my wife and baby to die. I had to tell you, though, and take the risk. I love you too much to keep a secret like this from you. I'm sure you would eventually hear it from someone else around there someday. Then what would you have thought of me for keeping something like that from you?"

Carrie was weeping silently against the cushions on the couch. Jake was afraid to even touch her, not knowing what she was thinking about him. Then she lifted her head and looked at him, and the pain and love and sympathy he saw in her eyes was palpable. Jake felt his own eyes spill over from the grief and sadness of his confession, and from the relief he felt from finally telling Carrie what had happened.

"Oh, Jake. That's the saddest story I've ever heard. How you must have suffered all these years thinking that such an awful thing was your fault! I'm so very sorry for you." Carrie pulled him into her embrace and kissed his hair and rocked him against her.

"Jake, I don't think you're a monster. There was nothing you could have done. It sounds like there was nothing anyone could have done, even if you had gotten her to the hospital right away. Sometimes terrible, tragic things happen to people, even innocent people like Rachel and your little baby girl. All we can do is go on and try to celebrate their lost lives by living the time we have on this earth to the fullest."

They sat holding each other for a long time; sharing closeness and understanding that went beyond words. They spoke to each other with touches and caresses, and gentle kisses, each reassuring the other that they would be there for each other through anything that might happen to them in the future. Jake shared his fear for Carrie and their baby in light of his past tragic experience, and Carrie reassured him that everything would be just fine this time. The statistics were totally on their side.

They finally fell into Carrie's bed, making love gently and tenderly, Jake was worried about hurting Carrie in her pregnancy so they took it slow and easy until Carrie saw a doctor made sure that everything was proceeding normally.

The next day, Jake made airline arrangements for both of them. He next called the office of Dr. Portia Wright, the best OB-GYN in Alpine, scheduling an appointment for Carrie for the same afternoon that they'd be arriving back in Alpine. He wanted her to see Dr. Wright as soon as possible, to make sure everything was going well with Carrie and the baby before they went back to the ranch for their wedding.

They decided together that Carrie would keep her apartment in New York for when she needed to be there for her work. Jake told her he'd come back with her when she needed to come back, and they could enjoy a little big city life together. Carrie took Jake to her office and introduced him to Diana and Sandy. Diana promised to be down for their wedding in Texas, as soon as they settled on the exact date.

Jake and Carrie flew to Texas the next day. Carrie's appointment with Dr. Wright reassured both of them. She confirmed a perfectly normal pregnancy and told Jake and Carrie that their baby was due the middle of February. They decided to marry on May fifteenth. They sent out limited invitations to the wedding because the church was so small. They would invite the others to a big bar-b-q on the ranch at a later date. They chose to have a quiet honeymoon on the ranch in their own comfortable hacienda.

May fifteenth dawned clear and bright as one could always count on in the Texas desert spring. Diana had arrived the day before and was staying in one of the guesthouses. She needed to leave right after the wedding to return to New York. She came over to the big house to help Carrie dress for her wedding day. The women on the ranch had hand-made Carrie a gorgeous, white lace wedding gown in the traditional Spanish styling of old Mexico. She would wear a tiara and a veil of flowing white Spanish lace. Diana wept when she saw Carrie dressed and ready to go out to the little church. She was absolutely lovely and looked like an angel. Happiness radiated from her pretty face. Her pregnancy had filled out her breasts and figure beguilingly.

Arm in arm, Diana and Carrie went down the long staircase of the hacienda. Diana ran to the kitchen and got Carrie's bridal bouquet out of the refrigerator. Diana had given Carrie a string of perfect white pearls as a wedding gift. It was something Carrie's mother would have done had she been alive and Carrie had them on under her dress.   She borrowed a tiny white Bible from Maria, which she carried beneath her bouquet. Her touch of blue was in the ribbon of the lace garter she wore under her dress. Now they were ready. They walked out the front door and over to the little church.

The guests they had invited were already seated. They had arrived throughout the morning. Lit candles and white flowers adorned the little church, thanks to Rosa and Maria. Carrie could see the priest standing in front of the altar. Jake had set up a music system for their wedding music since the little church had no organ. Jake and his best man, Carlos, walked in from a side door in the church and now stood with the priest waiting for Carrie. Diana, dressed in a white linen suit, walked up the center aisle and stood on the opposite side from Jake. The wedding march began playing and everyone rose to their feet and turned to watch Carrie walk down the aisle. A little girl from the ranch had earlier scattered white rose petals in the aisle.

Carrie took a deep breath and began a slow walk down the aisle of the little church, smiling warmly at the standing guests as she went past each one. Everyone gasped when they saw how gorgeous she looked in her white Spanish lace wedding dress. Some of the women cried and dabbed their eyes with Kleenex. She spotted Pearl and gave her a sly little wink.

Then her eyes locked with Jake's. He was staring at her with a mixture of love, pride, and awe on his face. He was thinking that he had never seen Carrie look so radiantly happy before, and that was saying a lot. He was trying with all his might to keep from breaking down into tears, he was so overcome with happiness. Carrie saw Jake's eyes shining with tears of emotion, and she felt nearly overcome by her own feelings of pure elation. As she neared the altar, Jake reached out his hand for hers, and tucked it under his arm as they both faced the priest.

After the ceremony, they walked back down the aisle to the cheers and laughter of their guests. A photographer from Alpine took photos, and they later exited the little church in a hail of rice. Everyone went up to the hacienda in a joyous procession, where tables had been set up in the decorated great room.   They cut their wedding cake and their guests congratulated them and wished them well.   Jake surprised Carrie with the small Mariachi band from the Starlight Theater restaurant, where they shared their first dinner together.   He had also arranged for Manuel and Carmen to be there for their wedding.   Jake and Carrie both promised them they'd be down to San Vicente soon for a fiesta with the whole village.

By late afternoon, all their guests had left and the house was mostly put back to normal.   Rosa served them a simple wedding dinner on the main patio.   They ate in candlelight still wearing their wedding clothes, and had more of their delicious wedding cake for dessert.   After dinner, Rosa told Jake she would clean up in the morning, leaving them alone in the privacy of the hacienda on their wedding night.

Jake stood and offered Carrie his hand.   "Well, Mrs. Stockton, shall we retire to our rooms for the night?"   A shiver shot through her at his touch and the heat she could hear in his voice.

"Yes, I think that would be fine, Mr. Stockton."   She stood and he led her across the darkened great room to the staircase.

They climbed the stairs in silence, each thinking their own private thoughts, looking forward to the ecstasy of the night ahead.   When they reached the door to Carrie's room, Jake stopped and picked her up in his arms, and carried her inside.   Carrie gasped in surprise when she saw their flower petal strewn bed.   There were candles burning around the room, bathing it in an ethereal glow of flickering light.

Jake kicked the door closed with his foot and deposited Carrie next to the bed.   He stepped back and looked at her with heat in his eyes.

"Now, Mrs. Stockton, I'm going to enjoy the pleasure of removing my new wife's beautiful wedding dress."

Carrie was paralyzed by the husky need in Jake's voice.   They hadn't made love for several nights before their wedding.   Jake reached out and carefully removed the tiara and veil from her hair. He draped it over a chair.   Next, he turned her and began to unbutton the row of tiny pearl buttons down the back of her dress.

When he finished, he turned her to face him and eased the dress off her shoulders and down to the floor. He gasped when he saw her swollen breasts spilling out of the top of her corset. She wore thigh length white silk stockings held up by lacy garters threaded with blue ribbons.

He tossed her wedding dress over the chair holding her veil. She looked like a goddess, ripe and swollen with his child. He began removing his own clothes. He knew he wasn't going to last long tonight. When he was stripped naked before her, he spoke. "Woman, look at your husband. My body is now yours, as yours is forever mine."

Jake knelt down and began removing her garters and rolling her silk stockings down each of her legs in turn. He kissed his way down her legs as he went. Carrie moaned and swayed above him. He stood and reached out easing first one breast over the edge of her corset, then the other. Her nipples were standing in tight little peaks, her aureolas a darker shade of rose with her pregnancy. He gently rolled their swollen buds between his fingers and thumbs.

A shock went through Carrie. Her nipples were supersensitive since she had been pregnant and Jake's touch sent a deep coursing of need surging through her womb. Dr. Wright had told her she would experience heightened sexual pleasure from all the changes happening to her body, which was wonderful news to Jake. He looked forward to satisfying all her increased appetites and found himself hoping that she would be insatiable.

Jake was enjoying the visually arousing way she looked, standing there with her lush breasts hanging over the top of her lace edged corset. He decided to leave the corset on her for a while as seeing her in it drove him wild He eased her back across the bed and when he scooted her back from the edge, he saw that she didn't have any panties on underneath the provocative corset. The erotic idea of her wearing no panties under her wedding dress drove him wild. He parted her legs and thrust his fiery tongue deep inside her, while fondling her exposed breasts.

Carrie let out a scream at the touch of his tongue on her. She found that all her lady parts were even more sensitive than her breast. She could feel her clitoris stiffly throbbing with each torturous pass of his hot tongue across it. Jake continued teasing at her swollen tight nipples while he stroked her with his tongue, bringing her to heights she never thought were possible. Suddenly, she stiffened and screamed out his name thrusting her hips frantically upward to meet each stroke of his tongue.

Jake threw himself forward and plunged deeply inside of her, thrusting his own pulsing maleness deep inside his woman. He immediately came and came, filling her to overflowing with his essence.

"Oh, Carrie, my wife, my beautiful bride! I'll never get tired of calling you my wife, my darling. I wanted you so. I can't believe you're really mine!" He kissed her again and again.

"Jake, I love you so much. I'll never get tired of calling you my husband, either. Now we're together forever and soon there will be our baby to share our love."

They kissed and cuddled and Jake explored Carrie's changing body with reverence and awe. They slept and woke and made love and slept some more, both finally content to have found love in the spring in the desert.

Epilog

During the spring and summer, Jake showed Carrie around the rest of the twenty thousand acres of the main ranch. They also took some overnight trips to the other properties further west. Jake showed her the oil and gas wells and they watched some wildcatters at work on new drillings. They camped out these nights, making love and sleeping under the stars as they first had done in the little spring house on the long trail to the river.

Carrie was quickly learning Spanish and was able to communicate better with many of the people in their lives. As Carrie began to shake that first awful nausea of her early pregnancy, they became more adventuresome in their wanderings. They did some hiking in Big Bend in the early mornings and the late evenings when it wasn't too hot. They made a trip back to San Vicente for a village-wide fiesta celebration of their marriage. This time, they drove to the river landing across from Boquillas del Carmen and Manuel picked them up in his boat. They filled Manuel's boat with gifts for all the villagers. They stayed with Manuel and Carmen in the little guest room where they had spent their second night together making love, many months ago.

During Carrie's September doctor's appointment in Alpine, she complained about feeling like she was getting bigger than a barn so quickly. The doctor listened to her expanding belly with her stethoscope very carefully. She then moved her stethoscope to the other side of her tummy and listened some again. She asked her nurse to hand her a Doppler stethoscope, which produced an amplified, audible sound of a baby's heartbeat.

"You don't think there's anything wrong, do you Dr. Wright?" Jake was nervously concerned about Dr. Wright's extensive listening and her request to her nurse for this new device. "There isn't something wrong with the baby's heart, is there?"

Carrie lay on the examining table with her bare belly sticking up. "Hey, Dr. Wright. You're scaring us. What do you think is wrong?" Carrie's eyes reflected Jake's own fears and she was beginning to feel real terror that something might be wrong with their baby.

"Relax, you two. I don't think there is a thing wrong here. But I want you to listen to the heartbeats for yourselves." Dr Wright squeezed some clear slippery gel on Carrie's bare belly and placed the Doppler against her right side, pressing it deeply into her belly, searching for the baby's heartbeat. The sound of a rapid heartbeat along with some whooshing noises echoed loudly from the device.

Jake and Carrie smiled at each other as they heard the first sounds of their baby's heartbeats. Jake took Carrie's hand and squeezed it tightly; both lost in each other's eyes.

"I'm going to use my watch to count the heartbeats for one minute, so just lay there quietly while I count." Dr. Wright stared at her watch, mentally tallying the rapid beats. They sounded like the heart beats of a little bird, very rapid and faint, almost drowned out by the whooshing noises.

When it was clear she had finished counting, Carrie asked her a question. "What are those whooshing sounds we hear?"

"Those are the sounds of your blood pumping to the placenta. You're hearing the whooshing of it as it courses through your uterine arteries. If you counted the whooshing pulses, they would be the same rate as your own heartbeat, which is much slower than the developing fetus's tiny heart. I counted one-hundred fifty-eight beats per minute for the baby. Your heart rate is about seventy-two beats per minute. Now I'm going to move the Doppler to the other side of your belly, a little lower down, and count again."   Dr. Wright spread some more slippery gel on the left side of Carrie's belly and positioned the Doppler over an area where the heartbeat was the loudest. The whooshing sounds were also audible on this side. Dr. Wright again stared at her watch for another full minute, and a slow smile spread across her face.

"I counted one-hundred sixty-five beats this time."   She spoke excitedly while she exchanged knowing glances with her nurse.

Jake immediately had another question. "Why is the heartbeat so different from the right to the left side? Wouldn't it be beating at the same rate no matter which direction you were listening from?"

Dr. Wright continued her explanation.   "You'd expect it to be beating at the same rate if you were hearing the same heart. What we're hearing today is two little hearts. Congratulations, folks, in my professional opinion, you're having twins."

"Twins?"   Carrie and Jake both asked in high-pitched unison, obviously stunned.

"Yes, twins. I'm going to schedule you for an ultrasound today. I usually do one at this stage of pregnancy routinely, and I definitely want to confirm what we're dealing with here. I'm sure we can do it this morning, since I know how far you have to drive for these appointments. I'll have you go over to the ultrasound department right now, then you can come back to my office and we'll go over the results together."

Carrie and Jake walked hand in hand to the ultrasound like they were floating on air. They talked excitedly, hardly believing how lucky they were.

"Jake, how are we ever going to be able to manage with twins? Holy smoke! I don't know anything about babies. What will we do with twins?" Carrie's eyes shown with excitement, as well as more than a little trepidation.

"We've got Rosa and Maria, and you're forgetting that I'm going to be there most of the time. Carlos will just have to run the ranch mostly by himself for a while. He's done it before. I can't wait,

Carrie!   There will be one for each of us, and I'll be the most involved father you ever saw, I promise."

After the ultrasound, they met back in Dr. Wright's office. She showed them the ultrasound images and explained them in detail. She pointed out to Jake and Carrie that there were two perfectly formed fetuses. She asked them if they wished to know the sexes of their babies. Jake and Carrie looked at each other questioningly, then answered that they might as well find out right now. Dr. Wright then pointed out the details that clearly showed the baby on the left was a little boy and the baby on the right was a little girl.

"Would you like to take these ultrasound images with you to show your families friends and put in your baby's books? You are welcome to them, as I'll have the originals in your medical record.

"Thank you so much! We'd love to have them. This is the most exciting thing that has ever happened to us, isn't it Carrie?" Jake was already reaching for the first pictures of their babies.

"Yes, thank you so much, Dr. Wright. I don't know when I've ever gotten such exciting news. Scary, too, though. What happens next?" Carrie was thinking that this would probably change a lot of her prenatal care as time went along.

"I'll want too check you more often, Carrie. Then when you get close to your due date, we'll evaluate whether you can deliver vaginally or need a C-section. That will depend on the size and positioning of the babies and how you are doing medically. We can make that decision at the proper time. I'd prefer to have you deliver then vaginally, if possible. You can make your next appointment out at the front desk and if you have any questions or concerns before I see you again, you can call me or email me. All that information is on my card. Also, I want you to sign up for the childbirth classes for when you're in your seventh month."

"We'll definitely do that," Jake added. "I want to be Carrie's coach and be with her in the delivery room when our babies are born. We've already decided that she will breast feed the babies, too."

"Jake's right about that. I want to give my babies the best start possible, and I know mother's milk is the very best for them. Thank you so much and we'll see you again in a few weeks, Dr. Wright."

Jake and Carrie spent the next few months fixing up the room across the hall as a nursery and making all the preparations for the arrival of their babies. They talked about names that each of them liked. Everyone they knew shared their excitement and good fortune to be expecting twins. Maria and Rosa and all the other women on the ranch eagerly volunteered to help out with the babies. Even Bart seemed excited and hung around Carrie protectively, as if he knew she was pregnant.

Jake laughed when Carrie mentioned this to him one afternoon when Bart was shadowing her every move. "Well, he's had enough of his own, so I guess he's learned to tell when babies are coming."

One clear, cold night in the middle of January, Carrie shook Jake awake at three o'clock in the morning. "Jake, I'm having contractions. They've been getting stronger and stronger. I think we should leave for the hospital in Alpine."

Jake shot out of bed, dressed, and grabbed Carrie's suitcase, ready to go in a flash. "Oh, my God, Carrie, I'm so nervous I can hardly stand it." Jake called Dr. Wright's after hours phone number and said they were leaving for the hospital.

"It's OK, Jake. Dr. Wright said everything was perfectly fine just the other day. She expected the babies would come soon. Stop worrying. I'm going to need you to help me through this. Don't fall apart on me now."

They arrived at the hospital at five. Carrie was settled into her birthing suite and Dr. Wright arrived and checked her. Her contractions were hard and long, coming less than one minute apart.

Dr. Wright checked her internally. "Well, Carrie, my dear. You are almost fully dilated and the babies are in good positions. I expect you to deliver within the next hour or two. It looks like you were cut out for this line of work."

Carrie and Jake worked through each contraction as a team. Soon Carrie began feeling an overwhelming urge to push, and everything began happening at once. Dr Wright came back in, gowned and gloved and two nurses wheeled in two baby warmers and stood by, ready to receive the infants. Jake and Carrie's Pediatrician arrived, waiting to check the babies as soon as they were born.

Carrie was panting and breathing between contractions. With each contraction, Jake propped her forward and counted out pushing seconds. Soon, a tiny black head emerged between her legs. Dr. Wright held the little head and as Carrie pushed with all her might during her next contraction, Dr. Wright eased the tiny head out. She suctioned the little mouth and nose, and with Carrie's next contraction, she worked the baby's shoulders out. A perfect little boy slipped from Carrie's body.

Jake and Carrie were crying tears of happiness and Carrie was still pushing her way through contractions as the next baby slipped into her birth canal. Jake held her up and forward as she pushed their little girl into the waiting world. She collapsed back on her pillow, exhausted from the powerful effort of delivering two babies. Jake held her and kissed her tenderly, both of them still teary-eyed with emotion. Then Jake walked over to the two little warmers as the pediatrician finished checking both babies.

"They're perfect, Jake. Congratulations, my man. The boy weighs five pounds ten ounces and the little girl here weighs five pounds eight ounces. Those are good weights for twins. They're pinked up and breathing just fine and their Apgar scores are both tens. You have a fine set of twins here."

Identification bracelets were attached to both babies. The nurses dried off the babies and wrapped them in pink and blue receiving blankets. They carried the twins over to Carrie, as Dr. Wright finished up delivering the placentas and doing a little stitching of some small tears in Carrie's perineum. They handed her the tiny babies, settling one under each of her arms. Jake and Carrie kissed their babies and each other, and exclaimed over each of their baby's tiny little features and fingers. They argued about which one looked the most like the other and finally agreed that they looked like both of them. The nurses helped Carrie put each baby to her breasts for their first meal.

Two days later, Jake proudly drove Carrie and little Morgan Turner Stockton and Adrien Marie Stockton to their home on their ranch next to Big Bend.